Sweet Holy Honey

Angel DeVille

Published by Angel DeVille, 2024.

SWEET HOLY HONEY

First edition. September 4, 2024.

ISBN: 979-8224640867

Written by Angel DeVille.

Table of Contents

Prologue

Alicia

I know Shaunice doesn't like Maurice, but he's been there for me since I started my music career. I don't think he would steer me wrong, he has been making moves as my manager by getting me gigs day after day. I haven't seen any money come through, Maurice said that he's been putting it back into the budget to get me back and forth to the venues as well as for him to promote me and my music. He said he needs a budget to meet with people in order to get contracts signed. I have no knowledge of how it works in the music industry therefore I have to depend on Maurice.

"Girl, I'm tryna tell you, I don't trust Maurice. There is something that just ain't right about him." Shaunice said, looking at Maurice standing across the room at the venue for tonight. He was talking to a few guys from the CFE Group.

"I know how you feel about him. You've told me *plenty* of times." I agreed with her. She never ceases to tell me how she feels about him.

"Then when are you going to listen? I'm telling you, he's doing something behind your back."

"Maurice has been with me this long and he gave me opportunities that I didn't make on my own,"

"Just because you didn't make the moves, doesn't mean you couldn't. Besides, I think you can do so much better without him as a manager."

"But Maurice said *this* was the one. He's over there talking to the owners of CFE! What if he makes a deal?"

"I believe it when I see it. He ain't nothing but a fake, ass buster." Shaunice did not hesitate to express her hatred for Maurice, even in his face.

Maurice was laughing and shaking hands with the guys as they glanced our way. I got excited because he was really coming through this time. Things were actually taking a turn for the better. Maurice and the owners of CFE walked over to us as we sat at the bar.

"Here she is, my beautiful Princess, Alicia," Maurice voiced as he approached. "Alicia, this is Marcus Harper and Franklin Studdard of...,"

"Chicago's Finest Entertainment," I interrupted as I turned towards them. "I am beyond honored to meet you. Maurice said that he knew you two." I looked at them. They looked at each other and shook their heads.

"Uh yeah, well it's nice to meet you, Alicia. You have some pipes girl, we want you to come by the studio so we can see how you sound."

"Are you serious?" I stammered.

"See girl, I told you, you stay with me, I'll take you places." Maurice bragged.

"Ta ha! Yeah right. You didn't even know them. You're ass probably got on their last damn nerves and they agreed to meet Alicia just to get you to leave them alone." Shaunice snapped and pivoted to one side, folded her arms across her chest and smirked.

I knew she was gonna call him out on his shit. She always does. I know it comes from a good place, but sometimes she goes in for the kill. And tonight was not the time or place.

"Damn Shaunice, you ain't gotta be all loud and shit," He turned towards her frowning.

"Look," Franklin stepped up, stopping those two idiots from going head to head.

"We were already planning to meet up with Alicia before your manager came over to us," He uttered.

"He ain't no damn manager. He's just a wannabe. You need to talk directly to Alicia, if you serious and not that stupid, ass nigga." Shaunice interrupted and was not letting up this time. She knew this was a serious deal and she wasn't about to let Maurice get any type of credit for this one. She really didn't trust him.

"Damn Shaunice, why don't you take your ass somewhere?" He huffed rolling his eyes. Marcus and Franklin witnessed this banter between the two of them and I just shook my head.

"Why don't you? I'm looking out for my girl, which is better than what I can say for you!" Shaunice stepped directly up to Maurice.

"Ah shit, she's a little firecracker!" Marcus said, covering his mouth. "Hey, I don't know about the dude here, but you should hire her as your manager, I'm just saying."

"What?" Maurice felt defeated as he turned and looked at Marcus.

"See! You ain't shit!"

"I'm sorry about them. As you can see, they don't like each other." I apologized to save face. They were getting on my last nerves embarrassing me.

"It's all good. But come to the studio tomorrow around 2 pm. That works for you?" Franklin said, handing me a business card with the studio logo and the address.

"Yes, thank you! Oh my goodness." I couldn't believe it, I had an audition with CFE!

"You're welcome. It was nice to meet y'all." They waved at us and left.

"Ha! She got her shit down without yo' stupid ass!" Shaunice said, walking over to me. I was floating on cloud nine.

"Fuck you Shaunice!" Maurice came over to me and tried to take the card from my hands.

"What the fuck Maurice?!" I snatched it back and gave him a look that could kill.

"Told you, she don't need yo' ass,"

"Chill Shaunice, I got this." I said looking at Maurice.

"Bitch!" Maurice blurted.

"I got your bitch Maurice!" Shaunice yelled. "

"Would y'all stop for one damn minute!" I yelled. "Shit! I'm tired of y'all asses."

"Let's bounce baby," Maurice looked at me.

"Not tonight Maurice," He looked upset. He looked at Shaunice, who was quietly laughing and sticking her tongue out. "Shaunice is coming over tonight."

"She can come over any other night, I'm coming tonight." He said confidently.

"Not tonight you ain't," I answered.

"Why the fuck not?"

"Because I don't want to deal with your shit tonight Maurice. I'm tired, okay?" He looked at me and then at Shaunice. His phone buzzed in his pocket. He pulled it, looked at it and smiled.

"Nevermind. I got shit to do." Maurice uttered. "I'll holla." He kissed me quickly on the cheek and left.

"See that's the type of shit I'm talking about, Alicia. You know he just left because he fucking with someone,"

"C'mon Shaunice, he just got me this gig?"

"*YOU* got yourself that gig, not him. I love you girl, but you dense as fuck sometimes. I know the dick ain't that good. Did he fuck you clueless?" Shaunice asked.

She was right. I didn't want to admit it. I had had an inkling for a while now, about Maurice fucking around on me. I knew I was in denial but he has been in my corner, pushing me to reach my goal of becoming a singer. The dick was good too, to be honest. But I knew he wasn't faithful to me - I get it. I have a cute face and an amazing voice, but my body type doesn't match the types of girls I know he's hooking up with.

"I know girl, you're right." I finally agreed. "I need to let him go, but it's hard." Maurice and I have been together for almost a year.

"Fuck him," She blurted out quickly. "You just focus on your singing. *Mr. Right-For-You* will come along before you know it." She sounded so confident, it made me want to believe it.

"I know, it's just hard." I asked.

"Then we have to find you a distraction."

Chapter 1 - CFE Studios

Alicia

I was excited and nervous at the same about having gotten the opportunity to audition for Marcus and Franklin of CFE. I wanted Shaunice there, but I know she's gonna have an issue with Maurice being there as well. But I don't care, they are gonna have to learn how to deal with each other.

"Girl, I can't wait to go to the studio tomorrow. You coming with me right?" I asked as we walked through the door to my apartment.

"Girl, you know I am. I can't let you go over there and me not see you blow them away? I want to see history in the making." Shaunice took her shoes off and walked over to the couch and plopped down in the middle.

"I don't think I could do it without you there." Shaunice was my best friend. We had been through a lot.

She's always been my support system; the one who had been in my corner since day one. She has urged me to show my talent when we were in school. It was a talent show and she told me to sing my heart out and I did; I won first place. Shaunice and I both bonded a lot because we were both only children so we looked at each other as sisters since we didn't have any siblings.

"I'm hungry Alicia, what you got to eat?" Shaunice flipped through the channels, landing on America's Got Talent.

"Nothing, I was planning on going shopping tomorrow." I responded looking in my fridge at the emptiness it revealed.

"Well GrubHub it is." She said picking up her phone, opening the delivery app. "What do you have a taste for?"

"How about some Panda Express?"

"Oooo, I ain't had that in a minute. Yes!" Shaunice scrolled through her app while I went to the room to change into my lounge jumpsuit. "You like the same stuff, right?"

"Yeah," I yelled from my bedroom. "Lo Mein noodles, no rice."

I went back to the kitchen and grabbed the bottle of Sweet Red wine from the door of the fridge, grabbed two wine glasses and returned to the living room.

"That's what I'm talking about," Shaunice stood up and grabbed her bag. "Let me go and change my clothes so I can get comfortable too."

"We're drinking this tonight to celebrate."

"Yes Ma'am!" She yelled as she closed the bathroom door. Shaunice returned with her navy blue onesie and furry slippers. "I'm ready now."

I poured her a glass of wine and handed it to her. "Are you gonna be alright with Maurice there?"

She rolled her eyes before she took a sip of wine, "I guess. Only for you girl, I'll behave. But if he gets out of pocket, like he did some shit, I can't promise anything."

"Thank you. I appreciate that." I took a sip of wine and allowed the cool liquid to swish around my mouth before swallowing. It was refreshing and well deserved.

"But you need to see him for what he is, Alicia. You deserve so much better. I just get a bad vibe from him."

"You've been saying that ever since I got with him." I replied.

"Yeah, that's because I think he's with you for the wrong reasons."

"Girl, I ain't nothing he can bank off of?" I swished the wine around in the glass.

"He knows you are about to blow up and he is trying to get in on the scene using your talent." Shaunice quipped. I looked at her and she pursed her lips up to the side and raised one eyebrow.

"I know you keep telling me that," I responded. I know she means well, but Maurice has been trying to help get me noticed. I had to give him that. "But he's been hitting the streets trying to get me booked to sing places."

"Yeah, but you need to watch him. I just don't think he's in it for the right reasons. I don't think he's in it for you, you feel me?" She asked.

"I feel you." I just agreed to satisfy her, otherwise she would keep going on and on.

"Good. So we gotta pick your outfit for tomorrow."

"Girl, this is an audition not a fashion show." I rolled my eyes at her.

"True, but you still need to look cuter than you already are." We giggled and gave each other a high five. She was right, I needed to make an impression. Marcus and Franklin already heard my voice, but I want to present a type of look for my career.

Shaunice and I went through my closet and had a damn fashion show by the time the food arrived. We finished at least half the bottle of wine by the time it showed up; we had to stop drinking otherwise we wouldn't have had any to go along with dinner. We laughed and ate, having a great time together like always. I was glad to have someone like Shaunice on this journey with me, she will definitely keep me grounded.

Shaunice

I was so excited for my girl, Alicia. To be honest, I think I was more excited than she was and I wasn't the one that was singing at all. Alicia had the opportunity of a lifetime and I was so happy and proud to experience it with her. Alicia and I arrived at CFE studios around 1:00 pm, we didn't want to be on *'cpt'* this time because this was way too important to arrive late; first impressions are everything.

"Hey lil mamas, how you doing?" Marcus said as we walked through the door.

"Good!" We both sang as we closed the door.

"We'll, I'm glad y'all made it. Franklin will be here short-ly, so make yourselves comfy." He motioned to the couches and chairs in the sitting area.

We sat down and I examined the place. It looked like a loft in an industrial building. It had been converted nicely in-to a recording studio, equipped with all the high-end equip-ment needed to record a song or two. The rest of the place looked like a studio apartment with the sleeping area above the recording booth.

"Y'all serious up in here. Y'all sleep here too?" I asked, being nosey. I ask a lot of questions. My Granny used to say, you won't know anything until you ask. Anything you want to learn about, ask questions.

Marcus looked up at the loft and laughed. "This is where I started out. I used to stay here night after night trying to get the right sound and record the right melody. I couldn't give it up, so I turned it into the headquarters."

"Nice. This is a bit of history." I was amazed and proud of my black people who are focused on creating a positive influence to give generations to come, like mine. I felt at that moment, I wanted to have a purpose for leaving a positive history for others to see and learn about.

"Wasn't there someone else with y'all?" He asked, walking over to the sound board.

Maurice's ass hadn't shown up and Alicia had been trying to get in touch with him since we got up this morning. Knowing him, he's probably laid up with some bitch, but Alicia won't believe me. She is too in love with this gutter nigga and it pisses me off that she doesn't see it because she's blinded by his dick.

I just know it's not that got-damn good, she's just self-conscious about her weight. She's cute, thick and curvy in all the right places. Alicia is a caramel drop with dimples as deep as oceans, with eyes that sparkle when she smiles. Alicia has an awesome personality and she loves everyone equally and hard; she's genuine and I feel that Maurice is taking advantage of her.

I looked at her frantically checking her phone to see if he responded to her numerous text messages and unanswered phone calls. She looked stressed and disappointed; this is another reason I couldn't stand that motherfucker, he works when he wants to work.

"I'm here, I'm her manager now." I said looking at her. She looked at me and gave me a soft smile.

"This is Shaunice Weathersby. My best friend. She needs to be informed on everything." Alicia said, introducing me confidently.

"Well alright Ms. Firecracker," Marcus joked. We chuckled. "Nice to meet you." He held out his fist and we bumped.

Suddenly the door flew open and rush air blew across the room; in walked Franklin followed by two pregnant women walking into the studio. They looked overheated as they stopped at the door embracing the cool air within the studio.

"Wooo Chile," One woman said as she fanned herself. "It's getting hot-hot outside."

"Yes and we're both pregnant." The other woman said as she walked over to the couch nearest the soundboard.

"Hey Alicia and Shaunice, y'all can come over here so we can talk." Marcus called us and we looked at each other. This was it, Alicia was really on her way to becoming a singer. We smiled at each other and raised up off the couch at the same time.

"This is my significant other, Monica Brown. The mother of my child to come, my soulmate and also a partner in this company." Franklin said, holding Monica's hand and rubbing her belly. He looked like a proud daddy to be.

"You made those girls uncomfortable, introducing me like that. Hi y'all, I'm Monica. Don't worry about that fool." She smiled and waved her hand. "I'm sorry but I'm not getting up for a minute so, it's nice to meet you."

"Hello, Nice to meet you." Alicia and I said in unison, blending perfectly. Eyebrows raised and Monica looked at the other woman.

"This is Alicia Givens and Shaunice Weathersby." Marcus said, walking over to the other woman. "And ladies this is my fiance, Siedah. She is also a partner in CFE."

"Hi Siedah." Alicia said. I waved and nodded.

"Which one is the singer? Sounds to me like we might have two." She said and my eyebrows raised.

"Nah, I can't hold a note. That's Alicia, she's the songstress. Her voice is amazing and original; it's hypnotic." I boosted Alicia all the way. It wasn't about me, it was about her.

"Well, she is one hell of a manager, Alicia, because she just made me interested by just describing you." Siedah said.

"I know right," Monica said looking at me. "Shaunice is it?"

"Yes Ma'am?"

"You may have a career in entertainment as an agent if you keep focused on your artists, like you did Alicia, and not how much you can make off of them."

I beamed. I didn't know what she saw, but she saw something in me.

"Thank you." I replied.

"Ok, Alicia, let's get you in the booth." Franklin said as he sat down next to Marcus at the soundboard.

Alicia walked into the booth and placed the headset on her head. I sat down in a chair that sat perpendicular from Siedah and Monica.

"How long have y'all known each other?" Monica asked, nodding towards Alicia.

"Since elementary school."

"Oh ok, so y'all have known each other for a long time?" Monica wanted to get some information on seeing if they could depend on Alicia to do what she needed to do or if she would be a waste of time and money.

"Yeah, she's my best friend." I smiled.

"There it is. That makes sense." Siedah chimed in. "You gotta go to bat for your girl. I love that. She needs someone in her corner."

"In more ways than one," I slipped out. I covered my mouth but Siedah and Monica had already heard it. "I'm sorry. It's just.."

"It's just what, Honey?" Siedah asked.

"Her man is a bitch ass nigga and I can't stand him." I blurted. Monica and Siedah chuckled and looked at each other.

"Honest. I like her." Monica nodded her head.

And speaking of the devil, the door opened and in walked Maurice, talking to someone over video loud as hell. Everyone's attention turned directly towards him as he walked in. I had to play nice because Alicia asked me to do so.

But let me catch him alone, all bets are off.

Chapter 2 - I'm Grown Now

Alicia

Maurice burst into the studio and I was instantly embarrassed. He was late and he was supposed to be representing me. Then he flashed that smile as he came over to me apologizing about oversleeping and I overlooked it.

"I'm sorry baby for real," Maurice came over to me, kissing me on the cheek. "My alarm didn't go off and I didn't charge my phone or my watch." He said.

"*How convenient.*" Shaunice said from the couch on the side. I shot her a look and she raised her eyebrow and twisted her lips. Maurice ignored her.

"Don't worry about her, I'll deal with her later. I'm sorry for real. Go show them what I already know about you." He kissed my cheek again. "Go blow them away." He flashed that smile that melted my heart as he gazed into my eyes.

I could see how proud he was to be with me and I felt the confidence build within myself. He saw hope in me when I didn't and I appreciated that.

"Thank you Maurice, I needed that. We'll talk later, okay?" I asked.

"Promise." He planted a kiss on my lips and I went off to the booth.

Once inside, I felt my nerves creeping up across my shoulders, down my arms and spine at the same time. My breathing altered and I felt as if I was going to panic. This was real and this was happening. The excitement was overwhelming. I had to keep it together and grabbed the headset and placed it over my ears. It drowned out the white noise already in the booth now it was just a matter of dealing with the noise inside my head.

I looked over and saw Maurice talking forcibly towards

Shaunice and her pointing back at him as if she was yelling. I zoned in trying to read her lips but she was talking too fast; however I did get a chance to catch *you a fucking liar* as she rolled her neck and made sure he understood every single word.

I looked at the both of them acting like straight asses in front of the entire management of CFE. I leaned against the window and Shaunice looked my way. I was panicking and doubt was settling in quickly. Imposter syndrome was knocking at the door as I started thinking about removing my headset.

Shaunice saw my face and paid no attention to Maurice or anyone else, just me. She knew I needed her and she heard my screams before I opened my mouth. I closed my eyes trying to control my anxiety and the voices in my head screaming, *they weren't going to like how I sound*. The imposter was banging at the door loud as I started to count in my head trying to drown it out and then I heard Shaunice, loud and clear.

"Watch out world, I'm grown now." She sang directly into my headset; her voice cracking a bit, but soft and sweet. She was singing directly to me, our favorite song from Chloe and Halle from the *'Grown-ish'* television show. I smiled and opened my eyes to see Shaunice bending down at the microphone outside the booth. "It's about to go down." She smiled and tilted her head. I nodded and joined her.

"My heart beatin' so loud," I sang and added a few personal ripples that made Siedah and Monica sit up at the edge of the couch. Franklin walked over to Marcus. "Mama, look, I'm grown now." We sang together and our voices blended together perfectly. She was my rock and she knew how to bring me back. "I'm Grown!" I ad-libbed at the end. And we finished.

"Girl, you betta stop playing with me!" Monica said from the background, standing up fanning herself.

"Are you okay, now?" Shaunice asked.

"Yeah girl, I'm good. Thank you."

"You know I got you." She said and she left the microphone. She looked back and I mouthed *'I love you boo'* and she held up the Korean finger heart with both hands. I chuckled along with her as she sat down. We had a love for K-dramas and she knew I would know exactly what she meant.

"That was tight. I might have to get Ms. Firecracker in the booth too. Don't think I didn't hear that, Lil' Mama." Marcus said as he spoke on the microphone. Shaunice smiled hard and waved him off.

"Okay Alicia, you ready?" Franklin said through the headset.

"Yeah, just a little nerves, that's all." I said looking at Shaunice. Maurice was scrolling through his phone, not paying attention to me at all. I stared at him as he was swiping right and left on his phone. I couldn't see his screen clearly from the distance but I had an inkling of what he may be doing. I blocked it out and I was not going to let him ruin this chance for me.

"Don't be nervous Lil' Mama. Just do what you gotta do to get in the zone." He said and I nodded. I closed my eyes and zoned out. I was alone in the studio and the music started playing.

I opened my eyes and sang out my first line flawlessly and fluidly. Siedah stood up as I looked at her and she was bouncing along with Monica; both of them were rocking to the song that *I* was singing. I've been told I sound similar to Alex Isley with a little hint of Malia, which I consider an honor as both women sing remarkably better than me. But to be considered similar to them, made me feel wonderful about myself.

I really felt the song and added a few dips and trains ending in a soft mezzo-soprano. I was happy about that song as I really got into it. I saw Franklin and Marcus give each other a high-five and a bro hug. I looked over at Shaunice, Siedah and Monica and they were standing up, mouths open, clapping and pointing at the booth. Marcus turned on the outside microphone and I heard them screaming for joy.

"We got it, Lil' Mama. Come on out so we can talk." He said. I smiled and removed my headset. I looked around and saw Maurice still on his phone near the door of the studio. He was focused on something or someone but I didn't care to be wondering what he was doing. I planned to talk to him later when he comes over.

Siedah

This girl that Marcus found could blow. She was raw, original, organic and honest. She just finished singing her heart out in the booth. Alicia had a unique sound, something that we were looking for. We've been doing well. The guys brought in a lot of young talent which was great because they had stamina which meant staying power. We signed a few new, untouched and fresh young singers with a lot of potential; some with a bit of drama but we are used to the drama and we definitely know how to handle it.

I was finally able to give up my editing job at the publishing company and I started my story that I had thought about so long ago before I met Marcus. I decided to write about our love story. It's called, 'That's Why I Love You'. It gives everyone an insight on how we met and ended up with each other, enjoying every minute of life - together.

Marcus is happy that we are expecting Marcus Jr. or MJ for short. I can just imagine the both of them dressing like twins; MJ will be Marcus' mini me for real. I was happy I wasn't doing this pregnancy alone, Monica was pregnant right along with me. It's nice that Marcus and his best friend Franklin get to be there for each other when it comes to fatherhood. Monica was having a boy as well and I could tell they will be best friends when they come out. I didn't expect all of this when I met Marcus and to be honest, I hardly remember life without Marcus and now we were about to have another baby and one of our artist's, Taye, just got a song added to a motion picture which was produced by MGM

Studios. We have truly been blessed.

"Alicia," I waved her over when she came out of the booth. "Come over here girl, we gotta talk to you."

I watched her walk over to where Monica and I were sitting with her best friend, Shaunice. She looked over at her boyfriend and he was busy on the phone, not really present for something that is important and is supposed to be representing his talent. Shaunice walked over and stood in the view of Maurice; Alicia looked at Shaunice and smiled. She turned towards me and sat down. Shaunice sat on a chair next to her.

"Hey y'all" She smiled and looked a bit nervous.

"You sang that shit, girl." I nodded looking directly at her. She looked at Shaunice and they held hands trying to contain their excitement.

"Thank you."

"Marcus and I would like to have you come aboard CFE, how does that sound?" I asked.

Alicia looked behind her looking at Maurice, who was now taking pictures near the CFE logo on the wall. Shaunice noticed that I was looking at him and jumped in like a real friend should.

"What are the terms?" She asked. I raised my eyebrows and bumped Monica. Alicia looked at Shaunice and nodded.

"She's my manager and my best friend. I trust her with everything. You can tell her everything I need to do and she will make sure it's done."

"Well a'ight."

"Shit, I would have hired her from the start because that lil' nigga over there has been on that damn phone since she went into the booth. What manager does that?" Monica chimed in.

"That motherfucker over there." Shaunice quipped and we all turned and looked at Maurice, who was still taking selfies. He stopped and looked in our direction.

"What?" He asked, holding his cell phone against his chest. That was a typical move of someone who was trying to keep a secret.

"Nothing fool." Shaunice yelled and rolled her eyes. "You see what I'm saying?" She said to Alicia who looked disappointed, but her friend was there to support her all the way, 100%.

"Okay, this is a simple contract to start you off in the Company. We will have you on our roster as an artist, but we need to get your voice toned first, you have a beautiful voice and you have control but we want you to be able to maintain it because we plan to stretch your voice and challenge you. And we need to find your image; you're a new artist and not many people know you, therefore we want you to work on a few singles, get your image just right by enhancing you in every angle so that you love everything we love about you." I said a fucking mouthful.

"Damn girl, I was wondering how long you were planning to talk. Shit, don't say anything else, I gotta pee." Monica said getting off the couch.

"Shit and here I was holding mine, I'm going too." I followed behind her.

When we returned, Maurice was in a heated discussion with Alicia. Alicia had left the sitting area and confronted Maurice about him being on the phone. Monica and I slowly walked over to the couch while listening to everything that went on.

"What the fuck Maurice?" Alicia yelled.

"What you mean what the fuck? I ain't do nothing!" He responded ,waving his arms.

"Exactly, you ain't doing anything but standing over here talking to some bitch!"

"I ain't talking to no bitch. Now you sound like Shaunice!" He pointed in her direction.

"Do something!" Shaunice yelled trying to egg him on.

"Maurice, You've been over here on the phone since I went into the booth."

"I'm making moves baby, you know this." He tried to persuade her.

"Taking pictures and selfies is making moves?"

"Yes! It's best to keep your profiles updated as much as possible." He literally was in the relationship for him I thought. I had had enough, she needed to wake the fuck up and see this nigga for who he was.

"Alicia, can you come over this way, please?" I called her over to where we were sitting previously..

Alicia stopped talking to Maurice and walked back over to her original seat.

"You really need to get rid of his stupid ass motherfuck-er." Shaunice said receiving no reply from Alicia.

"You need to listen to your girl, she knows her business. And right now, you are her business. That is what a manager does, at least a good one." Monica stated.

"Give it some thought because he could become a hazard to your career. Are you willing to give it all up for him? Is he worth it?" I asked.

Alicia looked at me and then at Monica; I could see the wheels turning in her head. She turned around and looked at Maurice taking yet another selfie. She finally turned to Shaunice; she nodded and turned toward us slowly.

"He's not, but I'm stuck on him." She responded with so few words yet the understanding was loud and clear.

"Then you have a decision to make. Are you doing this for you or for him?" I asked. She looked at me, then at Shaunice and then back at me.

"For me, always."

Chapter 3 - Making Manager

Alicia

Maurice and I finally made it back to my place after the studio, Shaunice said she would catch up with me later. I knew she was upset because Maurice was over. I get it, I had to make a decision which had my career hanging in the balance. I know he's not the best for me but he's been with me for a while and I care that he has gone out his way to try to get me noticed.

Maurice had me sing anywhere someone would let me, and I know it wasn't much, but it was something; it was a whole helluva lot more than what everyone else was complaining about and wasn't doing for me. Everyone was quick to tell me what was wrong with what he's doing, but they ain't coming to me with places I can perform and showcase my talent or radio interviews to do to get my name out there. I had to stick with someone who was in my corner; even though he would lose his damn mind sometimes, I always got him straight.

"Hey baby," Maurice said, coming back from the bathroom tossing a wet towel for me to wipe myself clean. "You felt so good, baby. You know how to really ride a nigga dick good as fuck."

I smiled as he handed me the towel. He leaned down and kissed me, his tongue quickly probed my mouth. I swung my legs around to the side of the bed where Maurice stood naked in front of me. He looked fine as fuck, and this nigga was mine. He was loving all this fluff and I was loving all of that caramel wafer that stood before me. His lollipop was still throbbing in front of me; I gazed at him and watched him lick his lips.

Just as I was about to stand up to wipe off, Maurice's phone rang and he instantly answered it. I rolled my eyes and wiped myself clean. Any chances of going for another round in the bed was out of the question.

"Wassup my nigga," Maurice spoke on the phone. "Nah, I ain't doing shit. What up? What's going on?" He said walking out the room pulling his shirt over his head. I could hear him laugh while he faded away in the background.

I wanted to go again and maybe cuddle a bit, but Maurice was on the same shit again which made me feel just like some ass to him. I know I got that *good-good* but lately he's just been hittin' and quittin'. Especially when his phone rings, he seems to never miss a call, but ironically he missed my calls today.

I started getting upset because, it was important for me and he showed up late as fuck. I was so glad Shaunice was there because I would have lost it. She has been my rock since forever, and honestly I think she would be a better manager than Maurice.

"Hey Baby, I'm about to bounce. Something came up and I gotta go check it out." Maurice said as he gathered his shoes and socks from the floor.

"Wait, I thought you were staying the night?"

"Aww Baby, I was but then my boy, Carlos, called me and told me about this place that has a stage and I wanted to check it out."

"Is it some place I can sing?"

"I don't know. That's why I gotta find out." He put on his shoes and grabbed his wallet and keys.

"But why you gotta go now? It's damn near midnight, Maurice?" I was getting heated. I knew he was on some bullshit, but this is ridiculous.

"Well baby, I want to check out the crowd and see how packed it can get. I'm doing this for you Alicia, you know that." He said, kissing me on my forehead. "I'll holla at you tomorrow."

Maurice left so quickly, I didn't even get a chance to see him out the door. He said he was doing it for me, but at the moment, it didn't feel like he was. Maurice was doing this for Maurice.

Shaunice

I decided to hit up a new spot and see if I could do this manager shit for Alicia. She needed someone in her corner, because Maurice is on his own shit and not really worried about Alicia at all. At first I thought he was good for her, he was smooth, attentive and he looked like he was really into her. I was like she finally hit the jackpot with him. Until his true colors started showing his ass and I haven't trusted him since.

I was able to meet up with the owner of the club, it just so happens to have been a friend of my cousin who owned the place. So it was nice to have a hook up at least, that would give me some place to start. I met my cousin, Aria, there who introduced me to the owner, Dallas Tucker. He was a fine, ass white boy who grew up with my cousin; they went to the same high school together. Aria had been gushing on and on about him back in the day, but I didn't know they had found each other again.

Aria was the cousin on the side of the family that lived in the suburbs away from the 'hood'. She was able to attend school with other ethnicities so she made connections with people who had money or at least more money than my family did. Her family was lucky to get out of the hood, her father, my uncle, landed a nice ass job working at the O'hare airport so they moved out to Naperville. Aria never forgot about her roots though, she never changed because her address did. She always kept it real; I guess that's why so many people resonated to her, like Dallas.

Dallas looked like your typical white boy, blue eyes and blond hair but he had swagger. His father married a black woman after he divorced Dallas' mother. She added some flavor to his life and Dallas has been *'Down with Brown'* ever since. They made a cute couple together, I could tell they really were into each other so much, it made me smile.

I turned my head and my smile faded. Maurice was there with his buddy, Calvin. Calvin was a bad influence all by himself, but with Maurice, it was like they were double trouble. They were hanging at the bar, talking and laughing with two chicks. I figured as much; this is the shit I wanna tell Alicia about. I quickly pulled my phone out and snapped a few pictures. In the last picture, Maurice looked my way. He did not look happy and I really didn't give a flying fuck.

I saw Maurice excuse himself and started walking my way. I was standing in the VIP area so I just knew he had a lot of questions going through his big, ass head. He was trying to figure out how I got here because his fake ass got all the connections. And then, he's tryna figure out if I'm gonna show Alicia the proof of his ass being the dick that he is. On his way, weaving through the crowd, he got caught by another chick who stopped him.

He looked at me like he wanted to get away, while trying to see if his new 'boo thang' saw him speaking to the other one on the floor. He thought he was slick, thinking Alicia wouldn't find out about his ass. I just needed some damn proof so she could finally drop his ass. About 10 minutes later Maurice had made his way over to the ropes of the VIP area.

"That's my girl right there," Maurice was pointing to me from the ropes trying to convince security that he got some pull. "Yo , Shaunice! A little help?" He yelled at me.

The security looked at me and I turned around to see who he was talking to. I looked back and the two, hefty built men were shaking their heads in disagreement of Maurice's request.

"Yo, Shaunice! That's how it is?"

"Don't act like you know me, fool!"

"How you get up in there?"

"Don't worry about it. I got *real* connections." Fake ass nigga. I couldn't stand him.

"You ain't gonna hook a brotha up?" He asked, still standing at the rope between the two security guards.

"Now you know, I ain't gonna do that one, fa you. What happened to your connections?"

Maurice was fuming that he didn't bother me because I saw him for what he was. A raggedy ass nigga that aint got shit to offer anybody but a headache that Ibuprofen couldn't cure.

"Fuck you Shaunice." He snapped.

"Fuck you Maurice! Take your raggedy ass back over to them bitches you and nasty ass Calvin got over there."

"I see how it is,"

"It's how it's always been." I replied looking at him directly in his eyes.

"A'ight.I just know Alicia betta not see those pictures."

He threatened me.

"Are you threatening me Maurice?" I settled back on my back foot and folded my arms in front of me. "I just know you ain't that stupid."

"You heard me Shaunice." He said looking back at me. He was dead ass serious, getting mad at me because he got caught up fucking around on my girl.

"Yeah, I heard you. Now you listen to me," I said leaning in between the two guards still standing at the rope entrance. "Your bitch-ass don't scare me and you don't fucking threaten me either. You betta watch your back nigga, you don't know who you fucking with, ya heard me?!" I said, bugging my eyes, making sure he understood what I was saying.

"Yeah, a'ight." He said looking at me and then at both of the fucking guards. He didn't know I knew them too, but that was beside the point. He needed to get shit straight. He finally walked off and back over to Calvin the two chicks.

"Thanks y'all," I said to the guards patting them on their backs simultaneously.

"Shit, I was making sure you wasn't gonna jump on dat nigga." The one on the left laughed.

"Does Auntie know you down here clowning on niggas like that?" My cousin Bobby said laughing. His brother just shook his head looking at me.

"Naw, she don't and don't go telling her either." I said pointing my fingers at both of them. Bobby and Charlie were Aria's twin brothers. "Love y'all".

"Love you too Shaunice." They waved as I walked back over to my seat. Maurice was watching me just as I sent the pictures over to Alicia.

Moments later Alicia sent a text message saying knew something was up.

[Alicia] That motherfucker just left here talking about he was going out to check out the club for me.

[Shaunice] Well he's checking the club out along with the females too.

[Alicia] I had a feeling it was Calvin he was talking to.

[Shaunice] Calvin's nasty ass.

[Alicia] He's always with Calvin doing some stupid shit.

[Shaunice] He is gonna fuck around and give you some sexual disease.

[Alicia] I'm done with the lies.

[Shaunice] Good. Now you have me as your manager and I'll do whatever I can do to get you to blow up.

[Alicia] Thank you girl, I should've listened to you when you were tryna tell me before.

[Shaunice] It's all good. I know it's hard, but you'll find someone better.

[Alicia] True.

[Shaunice] In the meantime, you got a show to do on Friday. I got you a spot at the club.

[Alicia] What! Are you serious?

[Shaunice] Yes boo! I'll call you tomorrow with all the details. Love you.

[Alicia] Love you back.

Chapter 4 - It's My Time

Alicia

Shaunice sent me the picture that took my breath away. Honestly, I had been in denial for a while, it's just seeing the proof right in front of me was the evidence enough it was time for me to leave Maurice alone. It hurt because we had just had sex and he left to go and be with his boy, Calvin and some other female.

I didn't want to talk to him because I knew if he had the opportunity to 'explain' then I would fall right back in with him, and I was *tired of being tired* of dealing with him. The next day Shaunice and I went to the studio to sign the contract and inform them of an upcoming show that she had lined up for me at her cousin's club.

"Aww shit, that's nice. Didn't that place just open up? How did you get a show so quickly?" Monica asked.

Monica and Siedah were the only ones in the studio as Franklin and Marcus had other business to tend to with their other artists. We were going over the contract and scheduling some studio time to record a few songs for the show.

"It's my cousin's club. Her and her guy just opened it up. I asked if she could do a small show and they were thrilled. They've known Alicia could blow for a minute."

"Nice, I like the connections you got, girl." Monica responded.

"Right. That's the making of a manager right there." Siedah said, looking at me. I looked at Shaunice and agreed. She was the perfect manager for me.

"You're right. That's why from this moment forward, Shaunice will be my manager." I announced.

"Good call." Monica voiced. "But what about dude?"

"Yeah, did you tell him yet?"

I looked at Shaunice and just stared. I was so mad I didn't even know how to voice it calmly. I looked away, trying not to get emotional.

"Not yet. I just found out some news last night and I'm trying to figure out the best way to deal with it and him."

"What news?" Siedah asked, honestly curious. I looked at Shaunice and I shook her head.

"I was at the club last night and I peeped Maurice with other women." She said holding up the pictures she had taken.

"Oh wow," Monica blurted. "Well there's only one way to do that, which is quickly."

"Yeah, I know. I haven't talked to him because I know how he's gonna get. And I don't want to deal with all that. So I figured I would just ghost him."

"And you think that will work?" They said in unison, looking at me skeptically.

"Probably not. But I don't know what else to do. I don't want to talk to him. At all." I voiced.

"What my friend here is failing to explain is that she is *dickmatized*' and he has a way of getting her to do exactly what he wants her to do." Shaunice jumped in. The both of them raised their eyebrows and looked at me.

"Unfortunately, this is true." I admitted.

"Well you need to figure out how to tell him because he is going to figure something is up if you ain't responding to him."

"He ain't even contacted her since last night." Shaunice chimed in.

"Does he know you sent the picture?" Siedah asked.

"Yup and he had the nerve to threaten me."

"Threaten?" Both Monica and Siedah quipped. "We take threats very seriously."

"So do I." Shaunice said, opening her handbag to reveal a nice .22 caliber glock. "I have a license to carry a concealed weapon."

"Well Damn, she ready if shit should pop off!" Monica blurted out.

"But it's not gonna happen because you need to say something the first chance you get." Siedah stated.

"I know. I'll figure something out."

"You can do it here if you feel comfortable enough." Siedah offered.

"Yeah, that way he won't act an ass and he'll know we all know that he is no longer managing you and the relationship is over." Shaunice chimed in.

"True." I nodded in agreement. Now it was just a waiting game for Maurice to contact me.

He knows I know about what he'd done because I sent the picture to him after I got it from Shaunice, along with the caption : *Really though?'*.

"So we're good, you'll set it up for you to come here when everyone is here. Alright?" Siedah said just as Marcus,

Franklin and another guy burst through the door.

"Hey y'all, I was hoping y'all would be here." Franklin said as he stepped in the doorway.

"We're always here, Franklin." Monica whined.

"Woman, I'm talking about Alicia and Shaunice."

"Is that Suave Rob behind you?" Siedah sat forward looking at the guy walking behind them.

"Yes it is. He's coming over to CFE." Marcus smiled proudly and patted him on the back.

"From TS Entertainment?" Monica chimed in.

"Yes Ma'am." Suave Rob spoke confidently. His voice sounded like butter to my ears.

"Wow, you know Tavion is hating you right now, don't you?" Siedah said as Marcus came over and rubbed on her belly. He leaned down and kissed her forehead and then kissed her belly. She smiled at him; he was happy she was having his baby. I wanted love like that.

"Yeah, but fuck him. He should have known we were gonna do this shit betta than him anyway." Marcus removed his messenger bag and laid it on the table.

"Shit, he decided to leave us anyway so that's on him." Franklin said, sitting down next to Monica. He lifted her feet to his lap, removed her sandals and massaged her feet.

Now that was love. I wanted what they had from their men, the caring and nurturing nature of these black men was amazing. They knew how to appreciate their women to the fullest.

"It doesn't matter now, 'cause he's with us." Marcus smiled a big wide smile while Suave Rob gave him a fist bump. "Suave Rob, let me introduce you to everyone."

"Yes, please do so because we got some news too." I smiled at Siedah; she winked at me and I returned the smile.

"Well, Ladies first." He said giving the floor to Siedah.

"Ok, well we have a new artist, Alicia, that we have just signed and who also has a show already coming up, at a newly opened club." She proudly expressed. Shaunice bumped my arm as I sat next to her taking it all in, it was really happening. I'm living my dream to the fullest.

"That's nice, Alicia. Welcome to the CFE Family." Marcus said, placing his hand over his chest and nodding.

"Wait, did you say she got a gig already at a new spot?" Franklin uttered.

"Yup."

"Damn, how you swing that, Lil' Mama?" They both looked at me, I in turn looked at Shaunice. She smiled and waved her hand.

"By having the best manager ever." I smiled at Shaunice and she blushed.

"This one right here has the hook ups. Her cousin owns the place with her dude." Monica bragged to Franklin about Shaunice.

"Well Ms. Firecracker, you are full of surprises, huh?"

"Yes, Sir." She chuckled.

"Well alright. Well this is my fiance Siedah, and she is Franklin's wife, Monica." He introduced them as he went and shook their hands. "Alicia and Shaunice, this is Roberto 'Suave Rob' Cardenas. I'm sure you've heard of him before. He will be joining CFE." He introduced this fine specimen of a man looking scrumptious and he was making me hungry.

"Nice to meet you ladies," he said, shaking our hands, looking directly into my eyes upon contact.

"Nice to meet you too," I could have sang to him. I wondered if he liked a little meat on his bones. If I was going by looks, he didn't look like the type that would and I would end up with another Maurice.

I'll sit this one out for now. I still gotta close the door on Maurice first and then get my mind right in order to even think about being with another guy. I don't want a rebound dick because that can end up worse than the dick I let go.

"So where's dude at?" Everybody looked at me. I had no idea where he was as I hadn't spoken with him.

"I don't know. I've decided to move on without him." I looked at Shaunice; she smiled at me and nodded her head.

"And that's where y'all come in." Siedah removed Marcus' cap from his dreadlock and let them fall down over his shoulders.

"What do you mean?"

"Wait," Monica sat up. "Do you mind us speaking about this right now?" She said pointing at me. She respected my personal business as Suave Rob was still present.

"Yeah, I'm good." I nodded and she proceeded.

"Well, some things have happened between Alicia and Maurice as she mentioned earlier and she is moving on without him with Shaunice as her manager going forward."

"Ok, that's cool. So where do we come in?" Marcus asked.

"Well, she hasn't told him yet due to the fact of some information she received last night."

"Oh," Marcus responded as Monica held up the picture that was sent to both of them. "Well damn, okay."

"She hasn't told him yet because she hasn't spoken to him. And she feels that he won't take it well."

"Well let that nigga come up on here acting a fool, he won't do it again!" Franklin strongly said.

Just as Franklin finished, Maurice burst through the door.

"Hey, is Alicia here?" He said walking in the door.

"Is that how you come into someone's place? You need to speak first before you go and ask questions, brah." Franklin voiced.

"I'm sorry, my bad. How are all y'all doing?" He corrected himself. Funny how quickly his tune changed when he was put in his place.

"That's better. Yeah, she's here. Wassup?"

"Alicia, I need to talk to you. Can I talk to you?" He stood waiting for me to respond. Shaunice was looking at him but he was ignoring her; he dared not to make eye contact.

"For what?"

"Please, hear me out." Maurice begged. I was tired of him begging and me taking him back.

"Ain't nothing for me to hear. I'm done." I didn't even look at him to acknowledge him.

"You for real? That's how it's gonna be?"

"Yup. I'm tired. And you bogus as fuck to do what you did last night." I yelled at him. He looked at Shaunice who was sticking her tongue out at him. She has no morals when it comes to Maurice. She was ready for him to get his walking papers.

"Shaunice, why you do that shit?" He yelled at her.

"Why YOU do that shit?! I ain't make you do a damn thing! That was all you and you knew what the fuck you were doing so don't try to blame me." Shaunice snapped.

"Why you going in on her? What's sad is that you would rather get mad at her instead of saying you're sorry. You ain't even trying to deny the shit! That's the shit I'm tired of!" I yelled at him. He just looked stupid in front of everyone, still trying to save face. I just rolled my eyes and looked away.

"Alicia, c'mon baby let me talk to you." Maurice begged again. I knew what he was trying to do. He wanted me to believe his sweet talk he always gave me and my ass would always fall for it.

"I'm done Maurice. Ain't no more talking."

"Well what about me being your manager?"

"You've been replaced." I said.

"By who?" He raised his voice.

"Shaunice."

"Dat Bitch!" He said pointing his finger in her direction.

"I got your Bitch Maurice!" Shaunice started to raise up and I grabbed her arm. Marcus and Franklin had already stood up getting ready to control the situation.

"Look brah, we ain't gonna disrespect the females up in here or in our presence. You got that?" Marcus said, looking directly at Maurice.

"Yes Sir." Maurice growled in response.

"Alicia," He called me again.

"Look dude, Alicia seems like she's made up her mind

on the subject and the best thing for you to do is respect her wishes and don't make this any worse than it already is." Franklin said standing in front of him.

"Alicia, that's how it's gonna be?" He asked one last time.

"Yes Maurice, it is." I said looking directly at him. He nodded with anger in his eyes and started stepping backwards.

"Aight, bet." He said turning around and leaving just as quickly as he came in.

"You okay, girl?" Shaunice asked me.

"Yeah I'm good."

"I don't think he is too happy and I'm not sure if he is accepting that you are done."

"True," Siedah said. "Be prepared for him to try and contact you."

"Yeah, he might just try you for real." Marcus said. "Unfortunately, we know too much about that."

"Well, her manager is well equipped to handle her shit." Monica said, nodding towards Shaunice.

"You carrying?"

"Yup."

"Legal?" Both Franklin and Marcus asked simultaneously.

"Of course."

"Well hey, she's ready." Franklin said.

"That she is." Marcus agreed.

"Well Roberto, as you will see, there is never a dull day here."

"It's all good. I'm glad I joined. Y'all seem like family and that's what I want." Rob voiced.

"We are definitely family at CFE." Monica added.

"Well I'm here to stay as long as you will have me." He looked around at everyone.

"If you do well, which I know you will, you will be here as long as you want to be here." Marcus proudly offered.

"I think I'm in good hands," he said looking around the room with his eyes landing on me. "And in good company as well."

"That you are." He smiled at me which made me blush.

"Why don't we get some food up in here so we can celebrate our new artists!"

"I'm on it." Siedah as she opened her delivery app.

I felt that I had made the best decision regarding my future. With Shaunice as my manager and Maurice on his way out of my life, I was looking forward to what tomorrow would bring.

Chapter 5 - Speechless

Maurice

I can't believe that bitch, Shaunice, sent the picture to Alicia! Now Alicia won't have anything to do with me. I've been helping her get off the ground with her singing and Shaunice has single handedly ruined my relationship and my future in entertainment. Shaunice had been filling Alicia with plenty of lies about me and now she's telling me she doesn't want me as her manager. Like she can replace me with Shaunice.

I know she's not done with me. We've been down this road before when she would get mad at me and stop talking to me for a couple of days. Alicia usually comes back around once I lay that good shit on her, I'll have her screaming my name in no time. She ain't going nowhere, she doesn't have a lot of options because not a lot of guys want a big girl. She's fun and cute to have around and all but I ain't that serious like she is.

I get it Alicia ain't had a man like me, so I completely understand why she's stuck on me. I make her thick ass jiggle when I hit it from the back and she can't get enough of my dick, so I let her slide on it every once in a while. Even though I did hook up with the female from the club; Her ass was nice, she had a nice pair of titties and a small waist. That female rode my pole and loved it.

I knew I would get more action when Alicia started blowing up, it was just a matter of time to have all this ass being thrown to me because I was managing her. Now Shaunice has gone and thrown a wrench in my plans; I needed to talk to Alicia and set her straight. Unfortunately, Alicia did this shit in front of everyone and she seemed different this time. She wouldn't look at me. She knew the minute she did, I would have her again. She can't deny me. I am the best thing that has ever happened to her and she knows it.

It's all good, I'll make her talk to me one way or another.

"Dude, damn man. You got caught up!" Calvin laughed on the other end of the phone. I had to clue him in on this shit that I was dealing with.

"She knows she's addicted to me and she ain't gonna get over me like that."

"You know how females are, she probably got someone already." He quipped.

"She ain't got nobody. Ain't nobody hollering at her."

"You think just because she's thick ain't nobody gonna holla?"

"Nigga, ain't nobody gonna commit like me. And she knows it." I said confidently. Alicia and I have been together for almost a year. She ain't going nowhere."

"I'on know man. She might have someone telling her what she wanna hear."

"She ain't got no one, man. She ain't even like that. She

know she got this dick." I uttered.

"Yeah and the other female from the club does too!" Calvin laughed and I joined in.

"Yeah man, she was nice. She knew how to give good ass head too man, damn!" I said, closing my eyes remembering her looking up at me with her mouth full.

"You gonna hit it again?" he asked.

"Hell yeah, that shit was nice."

"Cool, cool. Let me hit you up later dude, my girl just walked in." Calvin said and immediately hung up.

I figured I would call Alicia and try to get her to talk to me. When I dialed her number, it didn't even ring but it went straight to voicemail.

She blocked me? I just knew I was going crazy because Alicia wouldn't do that. I dialed her again.

Voicemail again. Bitch. She's acting up I see. That's cool, I'll let her get this shit out of her system and I'll holla at her in a few days. My phone buzzed as I received a text message.

I smiled because I just knew it was Alicia.

It was not. It was the female from the club.

[Female] Hey, what you on today?

[Maurice] You, if you want me.

[Female] C'mon thru

[Maurice] Omw

It's all good, I'll be preoccupied until Alicia comes back around, like she always does.

Alicia

After dealing with Maurice and finally taking that first step of getting him out of my life, things started moving fast forward. I hadn't spoken with Maurice in a few days with the help of Shaunice and staying busy at the studio. I had to prepare for my upcoming show and I needed to focus. I knew Maurice would try to get in touch with me after everything went down so I blocked his number.

I figured I needed to take that step in order for me to wean off of him because I must admit, I allowed myself to get totally addicted. Shaunice said I should focus on my music and get my songs together because shit was about to happen fast. I was nervous that I wouldn't be able to keep up.

"Hey Beautiful, are you okay?" A smooth and delicious voice sang to my ears as I sat on the couch waiting for Marcus. I looked up and it was Suave Rob. He was gorgeous; his eyes met mine and I found myself staring. He blushed a bit because I didn't blink as I was caught off guard being lost in my thoughts.

"I'm sorry," I blinked and realized I hadn't responded. "I was lost in thought." I was embarrassed and covered my face.

He chuckled and sat down beside me. "You're all good, beautiful. But you look worried, are you okay?"

"Yeah," I trailed off looking down at my feet. "I guess."

"You guess?"

"Well," I said, turning and looking at him. His eyes were intense; his light brown eyes focused on me and the words I spoke. "I've never gotten this far in getting my career off the ground and it's a lot to take in."

He smiled and turned towards me on the couch. I looked at his dark features complemented his light brown skin. The tattoos that donned his face and head make him sexy as hell. His tats alone made me interested.

"You'll be all good Mami, Marcus and Franklin are good people. They will help you."

"I know, I'm just concerned if I will be able to do all of this."

"Listen," he said, reaching for my hands. His hands were soft and warm as he held them between his. "All you need to do is focus on you. The music is inside of you, just tap into it and let it out freely. I know you're nervous, but when you zone into the music inside, you fly gracefully. Just like the beautiful creature you are." He said in a way that made me want to believe him.

"Thank you. And thank you for calling me beautiful." I said blushing.

"I call it as I see it, Mami." Suave Rob kept gazing at me like he was drinking me in.

"I see how you got your name, Suave Rob." I smiled. He blushed and nodded.

"How about you call me Roberto?" He said his name with his Latin accent, with the rolling of the letter 'r' and it awoke something deep inside me that I never knew existed.

"Roberto." I repeated.

"Si, Alicia." He sounded so nice saying my name. I *loved* the way he pronounced it; instead of 'Ah-lee-sha' he said 'Ah-lee-see-ah'. That shit made me want to change my fucking name.

"You'll be fine. Don't think too much about it." He offered.

"Thanks. Can I ask a question?"

"Ask away." I loved the way he paid attention to me when

I spoke. He looked like he was really paying attention to what I had to say. I even noticed him looking at my mouth when I spoke. Each time he did, he would lick his lips and then gaze back in my eyes.

"Why did you leave TS Entertainment?"

"Well, I wasn't getting the attention my boy, Taye, was over here."

"What do you mean?"

"Over at TSE, they are more profit based. I felt like they really didn't care about my well being. They were only worried about how much money and attention I could bring them. It was all about the numbers to them. And I wasn't getting the recognition I felt deserved."

"Damn. I heard they were kinda shady."

"That too. My boy, Taye, told me how he was treated over here and how the contracts supported the artists just as much as the company."

"That's what I heard about them too. I've always liked the artists that had come out of CFE so this was a dream come true for me."

"Well I'm happy I got to experience it with you." He said, looking at me. Roberto was very good at making someone feel at ease; it was easy to talk to him because I felt like I was being heard.

"Yeah, sorry about that. I'm embarrassed by what happened." I winced at the thought of him being there when the shit went down between Maurice and I.

"No worries," He said in a somber tone and shaking his head. "Shit happens. But it's good you found out about dude though. I'm sorry, but it was disrespectful what he did to you."

"Thank you. I know. But I kinda allowed it to happen."

"No you didn't. You ain't to blame for his wrong doing. A real man wouldn't do that to his woman. I know I wouldn't, especially if she looked like you." I looked at Roberto and lost my train of thought. I didn't expect him to be so forward but then again they don't call him 'Suave Rob' for nothing.

I was at a loss for words. He smiled and turned away and I still hadn't responded. My brain went into brain fog and re-played the sound recording in my head with him saying *'if she looked like you'*. I wanted him to elaborate more on the subject but we were suddenly interrupted.

"A'ight Alicia, I'm gonna need you in the booth to run this track. Rob, I need you to go over to Franklin's and run some tracks over there in that studio so we can kill two birds with one stone."

Shit! Rob had to leave. He hadn't heard me sing yet. I wanted to continue the conversation. I had so many questions. Rob was looking at me as Marcus informed us what we were doing for the day. I saw him in my peripheral vision glancing back and forth at me.

"Oh ok, cool." I responded to Marcus.

"Yeah, a'ight brah." Rob grabbed his bag and readied to leave. I stood up to head towards the booth. I looked at him before he headed for the door.

"Thank you Roberto," I managed to get out as we gazed at each other. "You don't know how much your words mean to me. I really need to hear that."

"The pleasure is all mine, Beautiful," He stepped towards

me and tipped my chin. "Keep your head up, you got this." That was the first time I wanted to kiss someone other than Maurice. Roberto smiled, side stepped and walked out the studio.

I turned to watch him walk out the door; Suave Rob was very suave indeed.

Chapter 6 - Getting to Know you

Alicia

The next few days kept me busy with getting ready for the show Friday night. Ironically, I was nervous as if I had never performed before. Maurice was able to get me a few gigs here and there, unfortunately there were no repeats of me going back, it was sort of a one and done kinda thing. I wasn't complaining, someone was getting to see me perform; at least people had heard of me by the time they left the venues.

I was excited every chance I got to record in the studio. They helped me a lot, Marcus knew exactly how he wanted me to sing and I had no problem with taking his direction. He knew what sounded good and he would also challenge me. Siedah was also laying the groundwork along with Monica to get me set up for interviews after the show to promote the new single. I was the new face of CFE and I had to bring it.

The news broke of Suave Rob jumping ship from TS Entertainment and signing with CFE. The social media platforms kept CFE in the news. They wanted to know what happened between Roberto and TSE. Of course, the truth always gets swallowed up by gossip, which is exactly what happened. The reason for the change went from a breakdown in a contract negotiation between Suave Rob and TSE, which was the truth to Suave Rob trying to get up with Tavion's wife, Analia. People love to be messy and will believe the mess over the truth.

CFE took this opportunity to have an introduction of new artists at *Spice*, Dallas' club. Marcus reached out to Dallas' after Shaunice informed them that she had a show set up for me. Marcus was impressed and took it upon himself to bring some attention to the club by using them to showcase some of the new talent that had joined CFE, in which I was included. It was all so surreal; if it was a dream, I would be so pissed if I woke up.

I would perform two songs that I had been working on with Marcus, one was a rendition of *Love by Keyshia Cole* and the other was a rendition of *Too Bad I Forget by Alex Isley*. I loved her songs and I felt that I could really rock my vocals on both of the songs because they allowed me to show my range. Other artists, Taye Mitchell and Analia Cunningham would be there as well, as they were in the process of dropping an EP soon. I hadn't seen Roberto since our conversation was interrupted at the studio. He had been busy as well getting up to speed and laying new tracks because I'm sure TSE didn't release his music to him that he recorded already; after his departure, I'm sure they were shelved.

Siedah called me and asked me to come over to Franklin's house for a get together before the show. It was a tradition as it was a way to relax, be among friends and the CFE family. Of course I called Shaunice to be my plus one; I was so happy to be finally living out my dream with her by my side.

"Girl, this is it! You made it boo! I'm so proud of you." Shaunice said as we walked around their home, drinks in hand.

"Girl, I'm proud of us. You did the damn thang. You've been by my side ever since I said I wanted to sing. You should have been my manager all along. But I'm glad you're here with me now." I held up my drink to toast with.

"The best is yet to come." She said clinking her glass with mine.

We mingled around the huge house looking at pictures of Monica and Siedah. They looked just like Shaunice and I, best friends helping each other to reach our dreams. We walked along another wall lined with shelving holding books, old school records, more pictures with celebrities and the Grammy. Franklin has his on display at the top of the bookcase, looking out over the entire house. I'm sure he was proud of it but needed to make sure it was unreachable to others, without being noticed.

"I want one of those one day." I said out loud to myself. Shaunice looked up and smiled.

"You'll get one, trust me." She had such confidence in me, sometimes more than I had for my own self. She was a true blue friend to the end.

We were sitting around the *'Pit'* talking, which is what Monica called it. It was an area with large couches that were in a semi-circle that had a nice, huge cocktail table in the middle. I noticed a lot of people who were part of the CFE family. My eyes roamed the room looking at everyone when my attention was caught by Roberto entering the door. He was greeted by Franklin at the door who pointed in the direction of the drinks in the kitchen and then pointed to where we were sitting.

Roberto looked over and we connected. He smiled and nodded; I mouthed 'hello' from across the room. He looked good as hell in a pair of faded blue jean shorts, an oversized polo shirt and a pair of clean, white Nike shoes. He fist bumped Franklin and headed towards the kitchen; I watched as he weaved his way through the crowd. I brought my focus back to the group and noticed that Siedah saw me watch Roberto. She smiled and gave me a quick wink; I blushed and turned away, downing the rest of my drink.

"Why don't you go and get another drink?" Siedah leaned over and spoke.

"Nah, I'm good. I need to focus."

"Relax. You'll do good. Don't worry about it, don't even think about it."

"Yeah, I wish it was that easy."

"Then go get another drink to relax. Trust me." She smiled and nodded her head in the direction of the kitchen.

I figured another drink would do me some good and walked to the kitchen. I expected to see Roberto getting a drink but he wasn't in the kitchen. I moved over to the bar and grabbed my favorite, Crown Royal Apple, a few cubes of ice and finished it off with apple juice. I made the drink so good, I downed it right there in the kitchen. I don't know what Siedah was talking about because the more I thought about it, the more nervous I got. I poured myself another drink, this one I was determined to babysit for the rest of the night.

When I returned to the Pit, Roberto had joined the group. Everyone was having a good time, conversing with each other, collaborating on songs and overall enjoying each others' company. Taye and Analia started singing karaoke with music that was bumping throughout the house. They sang so well together. We were all laughing, singing along and having a good time. Then a song by one of my favorite artists, Jhene Aiko came on.

The alcohol kicked in and I was in full throttle. The music was hyping me up and I belted out the song in my own version. Taye and Analia started bouncing their heads to the music as I hit every note and added a few. The flow was so good, I had totally forgotten Childish Gambino had a rap section within the song. And just like a puzzle piece, Roberto picked up the mic and displayed his rap skills. His flow was awesome, with his tone similar to CG's voice. He didn't miss a beat and he knew how to draw the crowd in; he was magnetic. He blended with me so well, we tuned into each other and we made the song ours. When we finished, the crowd went crazy.

"That's the shit!" A random person yelled.

"Damn girl, you liked that song, huh?" Franklin asked from the pit. I smiled hard as I couldn't deny it.

"We gotta get them to do something together because that was Hot." Marcus said, looking at Siedah and the rest of the crew.

I looked at Roberto, who bumped me playfully as we placed the mics back in the holders.

"You got some lungs on you, Mami."

"Thanks, you were spitting good too. I ain't do that by myself, I can't take all the credit."

"Yeah, we had that flow though you know?. You were singing a song I've heard plenty of times so I just had to jump in. It was good though, you made it feel natural. You got a gift, your voice is amazing."

"Thanks." I was flattered but I didn't want to get ahead of myself, especially when it came to Roberto. "I appreciate you coming to join me."

"No problem. Anytime I can be there for you, I will." Without hesitation he spews his confidence so eloquently it completely captivates me without him even trying. I looked at him and nodded in agreement.

We joined the others for the rest of the evening, allowing others to display their skills at karaoke. Shaunice was having a good time as she was having a moment of being in the same room with some of her favorite artists.

"Girl, this is the shit."

"Yes it is. Are you ready to go along with me on this journey?' I asked.

"Been ready." Shaunice replied.

My phone buzzed in my pocket; I received a snapchat message. As soon as I looked at my phone, I rolled my eyes, *it was from Maurice.*

[Maurice] I see you got a gig coming up. I don't know why you acting like this. Call me.

I deleted the message. I didn't want to deal with him and have him ruin my night because it was going so well without him. Of course he heard the news of the upcoming show at Spice, and now he wants to weasel his way in somehow. I hope he doesn't show up and act an ass, but this is Maurice - he *always* acts an ass.

As the party was winding down, I walked out on the patio to get a bit of fresh air. The breeze was warm and touched my skin like warm kisses as I watched the headlights of cars zooming along the expressway. I didn't notice Roberto had joined me on the patio as he stood to the side alone, smoking a blunt. I looked over and smiled, he slowly walked over to the corner of the patio where I stood.

"How's it going?" Roberto asked as he approached. He blew out smoke that just hovered in the hot and humid air.

"It's going. A lot to take in. But I'm good."

"Are you still worried about dude?"

"How did you know?" Was it written on my face? I needed to learn how to give that resting bitch face.

"You looked stressed with a lot on your mind."

"Well," I exhaled. "I'm just hoping he doesn't come to the show."

"You know he will. Guys like that always fuck up and try

to get back in."

"How do you know? Do you fuck up and try to get back in?"

"No, I make sure I don't fuck up a good thing when I see it the first time." He said, looking directly at me without blinking.

"I see you're confident."

"I have to be. I don't want to make mistakes in anything I do, so if I'm going to pursue anything, I have to give it my all, no matter what it is."

"You don't like to fail, huh?"

"There's nothing wrong with failing, a person can learn from it. It's how you come out on the other side."

"Like if you learned something?"

"Right. We all can learn from our mistakes. It's just that some people don't learn and continue to fuck up all the time."

"That's Maurice." I quipped and looked down.

"Do you love him?" he asked.

"No. There was a strong like, but we never got to that point of love. At least I don't think I did." I answered bashfully.

"You would know if you were in love." Roberto answered.

"I don't think I have ever been in love to be honest." I said looking away. "At least, no one has ever told me that they loved me for me to love them back."

Roberto stepped closer as looked away. It was a hard subject for me to talk about. I always wanted to fall in love; I've been in a *hard like*, but not love. I let out a nervous giggle as my tears began to swell up in the corners of my eyes.

"It's okay Mami," Roberto said standing next to me. I could smell his cologne beckoning me to move closer. "Someone will show you what love feels like."

"Thanks. I've heard that before, but it seems to be out of reach for me." I sniffed, wiping away a lone tear that escaped my tear ducts.

"You sound defeated. How can you say something like that?"

"Look at me," I said, looking at him holding out my arms. "I'm not exactly a size 2. Guys usually see me as someone they can play around with and have fun for a while but nothing serious." I looked at him and he looked irritated.

"You just haven't found the right one. There is nothing wrong with your thickness. You're beautiful and you have a beautiful heart with an amazing voice. Ain't nothing wrong with your figure. A real man likes meat on his bones." He smiled and bumped me, making me smile.

"Yeah, I've heard that too."

"It's true. Don't let these fools like Maurice deflate you. You are perfect just the way you are." His words resonate in my soul.

"Thank you." I blushed.

"I'm for real. You are." I looked at him and he gazed into my eyes; it seemed like forever. He bit his bottom lip as his eyes slowly danced over my body.

"You're not so bad yourself, *Suave Rob*." I smiled and he chuckled. He took another pull on the blunt and passed it to me. "You smoke?"

"I've never tried it. My friend Shaunice does though."

"Do you want to hit it?"

"I'll try it." I took the blunt and inhaled slowly, barely lighting up the amber end.

"Inhale harder," Roberto said as I continued to pull on it. Suddenly the smoke hit the back of my throat and it felt like it was on fire.

I started coughing so hard, I felt like a lung was going to appear soon. He patted my back and took the blunt from me.

"Yeah, it takes time to get it right."

"Yeah, I'm not sure about that." I chuckled and he joined in flashing his gorgeous smile. He made me feel better. Shaunice came out onto the patio looking for me.

"I was just looking for you."

"I was out here smoking." I blurted out. She looked at me and then at Roberto. Roberto looked at me and we both snickered. "I'm joking. I tried it, but I'm good."

"Oh my god, don't encourage her. She's more of a drinker than a smoker." Shaunice took the blunt from Roberto and took a long puff. She was the pro between her and I.

"Oh I see." Roberto looked at me and smiled impishly. "A drinker, huh? What's your poison?"

"Vodka, Tequila, Crown, Rum, you know the basics." I laughed. Roberto shook his head and chuckled.

"Wow."

"So Suave Rob," Shaunice chimed in, taking a puff and blowing the smoke in the air. "What's up with you? You got a woman?" she boldly asked, but a question well deserved. I also wanted to know the answer myself.

"Wow, okay. Right to the point huh? I see why they call you Ms. Firecracker."

"You know it. But you still ain't answering the question." She responded by taking another puff on the blunt before passing it back to him.

"Well, if you must know, I'm single." He looked at me making sure I heard clearly.

"Are you gay?" she quickly asked.

"Damn Shaunie!" I hit her arm trying to get her to stop with the interrogation, but yet again, it is a warranted question.

He chuckled and covered his eyes. He was embarrassed by Shaunice's forward questions. I was even getting embarrassed. He smoothed his hand over his face trying to cover up the shocked reaction.

"What?! I'm just looking out for you. I'm your manager and I don't need you hooking up with someone who may or may not have a scandal later on when y'all blow up."

"Wow." Both Roberto and I sang in unison.

"I feel you Lil' Mama. No, I'm not gay. 100% straight. I love women, all shapes, all sizes," his voice mesmerized me with the words that flowed so effortlessly across his lips. "And thickness."

"Mmmm, Okay!" Shaunice bumped me acknowledging his answer. "Well my girl needs a real man, who can handle her not only physically but emotionally as well. You think you're up for it?" I felt like Shaunice was pimping me out. She obviously had had enough to drink as he was being more than just a friend right now.

"Shaunie!" I exclaimed. "I'm sorry, I didn't think she

would..Shit.. I'm sorry." I held onto Shaunice as she giggled.

"It's all good. She's just looking out for her artist and her best friend." Roberto stated. He grinned looking at me. I blushed and looked away.

"She means well, but she can get a little ahead of herself." I admitted.

"I just don't want you to end up with another Maurice. You deserve so much better than that asshole." Shaunice wrapped her arms around me, giving me a tight hug.

"I won't," I looked at Roberto, he gazed back at me smiling a sexy ass smile. "I promise." Roberto nodded.

:

Chapter 7 - Fool

Alicia

I expected the amount of people that showed up at the venue to be crazy but in fact it was insane. The Chicago Police department had to come in for crowd control. Unfortunately, everyone wasn't able to get in due to there being an occupancy limit to which was reached within the first 45 minutes after opening. Ironically, the club owner, Dallas, had anticipated the popularity of his club and installed speakers on the exterior of the building to accommodate those who chose to wait in line to gain access whenever there was room.

Behind the scenes, I was a basket case. It was so surreal, I occasionally pinched my damn self to make sure it wasn't a dream. I had spent hours trying to find the right outfit; I didn't want something too sexy, or too casual, however I wanted to be as comfortable as possible. I decided on a cute outfit that consisted of a red and black vintage, halter-top, lace-up corset bustier along with a pair of black hot pants that showed my thickness in all the right places, fishnet stockings underneath and a pair of platform boots. Shaunice made sure my wig was on nice and tight and looked good with the waterfall curls.

The main members of CFE were in the 'green room' making sure the show went off well. Marcus and Franklin did most of the foot work while Siedah and Monica handled the logistics. It was really happening and I was excited and terrified at the same time.

"How are you doing?" Shaunice asked as I leaned against the wall.

"I'm taking all of this in and it's overwhelming. But I'm good."

"Have you performed in front of a crowd this big before?"

"No, not at all. You know Maurice ain't do anything like this." I quipped. She smiled because it was true.

Suddenly, security comes into the room looking around.

"Who's Alicia?" One security guard asks. My eyes grew large and I raised my eyebrows, trying to figure out why my name was mentioned.

"What's going on?" Monica walked over to the guard.

"There's a guy at the door trying to get in. He said he's Alicia's manager." I knew exactly who the fuck it was - *Maurice*. I had a feeling he would show up, he wasn't going to leave me alone until I talked to him, it was inevitable. Monica turned and looked at me; the security guard glanced in the same direction.

"He's outside, outside?" I asked. Shaunice folded her arms and looked at me. I just wanted to make sure he wasn't outside the green room door.

"Yes."

"He's not my manager, she is." I pointed to Shaunice. She smiled and looked at the security guard. "He can wait in line just like everyone else."

"Duly noted. Have a good show." The security guard left the room.

"Well ok Ms. Thang," Monica sang. "You handle your business, girl." She smiled, patted me on my arm and went back to finalizing everything.

"I'm so proud of you!" Shaunice grabbed me and wrapped her arms around me tightly.

"I said I was done. I'm tired of him telling me what he thinks I want to hear with no truth to it."

"Besides, you can add a little Latin flavor to your recipe." Shaunice grinned.

"Girl, that sounds all good and all but I don't want to rush into anything, not now. And besides, who says he's interested?"

"He did!"

"Did he though?"

"He said he liked meat on his bones."

"I don't know."

"What is there to know?"

"I don't know. I just need to focus on my music. I got sucked up with Maurice and overlooked a lot of shit because he said all the right things. Who's to say Roberto ain't doing the same shit?"

Shaunice was quiet for a moment because she knew I was right. "But he seems nice and honest."

"They all do, at the beginning." I replied. "Maurice was the same way. You thought he was cool as hell when we first got together. Then as time went on, shit started happening and I just overlooked shit because I had an intimate relationship with a fine ass man who paid attention to me." I uttered.

"Yeah but,"

"But what? He's different? Time will tell. I ain't in no rush. If it's supposed to happen, then it will. I'm not trying to rush and make something happen. I want a real relationship with a man I can trust. That shit comes naturally; it can't be forced." I felt as if I had unloaded some deep shit that I had been holding onto for a while. Shaunice nodded with understanding.

Shaunice reached in her back pocket, pulled out my phone and showed it to me - it was Maurice calling. I sent his ass to voicemail. Of course he called immediately back; I repeated the same move sending him to voicemail two more times before he stopped calling and resorted to sending text messages.

[Maurice] Pick up the fucking phone!

[Maurice] I know you ignoring my calls. Pick up the fucking phone!

[Maurice] Why you gotta be a bitch about this shit?

I knew it wouldn't be long before the insults started. They always did.

[Maurice] Why you listening to Shaunice ass anyway?

[Maurice] I can't believe you let her be your manager after all I have done for you! Bitch!

[Maurice] Answer the phone!

[Alicia] Leave me alone Maurice!

I handed the phone back to Shaunice who shut it off. She smiled at me; I smiled weakly thinking about Maurice. I didn't want him to create a scene and ruin the show for everyone.

"A'ight y'all," Marcus said as he entered the room. Everyone turned and gave him their full attention. "We are about to start this show. I want everyone to have fun, relax and just let loose. I know all of y'all ready so go out there and leave it all on the stage. Make yourselves proud that you did your absolute best, a'ight?"

Everyone cheered loudly making the backstage just as loud as the front of the house. Franklin led us with a prayer before we hit the stage and let loose. Butterflies instantly filled my stomach as reality stepped in and I had to focus on the task at hand.

The show went off without a hitch; everyone performed and left all of themselves out on the stage just like Marcus requested. We had the crowd going crazy, they loved every artist. When I finally got on stage and performed I didn't want it to end. It seemed like the songs went too fast, but it was just because I was in my element and I rocked the hell out of it. I had the crowd singing right along with me; I was having a great time singing my heart out.

After the show, we were all sitting in the VIP area, when a security guard approached us yet again. I had just finished a glass of wine when he walked up as we were all sitting, laughing and talking; enjoying each other's company.

"I got a guy saying that he's Alicia's manager trying to get into VIP. Is this accurate?" I looked at the VIP ropes and there was Maurice standing at the entrance. This motherfucker had made it into the club.

"No it's not." I yelled. "My manager is here already." I pointed to Shaunice who sat next to me. Shaunice waved while taking a drink.

"Understood." The security guard left and returned to the entrance shaking his head.

I could see Maurice get upset as he frowned as he yelled at the guard, while picking up his phone. He just wouldn't stop. Roberto came over with a few shots for the table and sat down on the other side of me.

"Shots?" He offered, handing me a shot glass.

"Sure." I took the shot as he passed one to Shaunice and then walked around the area passing out shots. I saw Maurice getting extremely upset because I wasn't answering my phone due to Shaunice turning it off. I was determined to not have him ruin a special night for me and he was just as determined to do the opposite.

Roberto returned after passing out all of the shots, leaving two for him. "How's it going?" He sat down next to me.

"It's amazing. I'm having a good time. You did well out there. You're a good rapper." I smiled.

"Thank you. I've been known to do a little somethin' somethin' here and there." He smiled and threw back one of his shots.

I picked up my shot and looked around for a beer as a chaser. By the smell of it, it was tequila which would have my ass on the floor in the morning but I was celebrating my debut. Roberto noticed me looking around and jumped in.

"Looking for a chaser?"

"Yeah, I need a beer." He picked up his Heineken and handed it to me.

"Thanks." I smiled, throwing back the shot and chasing it with the beer. I felt exhilarated. I was finally having a good time. The waiter came back over to the area to get more drink orders from the crew. I ordered two more shots and two more Heinekens.

Yet, it never fails, Maurice demanded my attention. It was then I realized he'd kept me around for his own pleasure because I made him feel important with all of the attention and dependency I gave him. I felt stupid but I was glad I had clarity.

"Yo, Alicia!" Maurice had moved to the side of the ropes yelling from the edge trying to get my attention. Roberto and Shaunice looked at him like he was crazy.

"Go away Maurice!"

"I ain't going nowhere! I own you!" He yelled. I looked at him like he was fucking crazy. I stood up and damn near lost it.

"Who the fuck are you talking to? You don't own me nigga! I own myself, what the fuck is yo' deal?"

"Bitch, I own you. If it wasn't for me, your ass wouldn't have even met them!"

"Bitch you don't know shit!" I yelled back. Roberto took hold of my wrist and tugged gently, trying to get me to sit down and ignore him.

"Mami, don't fall for his games. He is trying to get you upset and ruin this for you. Don't let him. Just sit down and ignore him. Be in *'this'* moment." Roberto said, pointing around the area. He was right, I needed to not let Maurice push my buttons. I sat down and took a swig of my beer.

"I got you noticed!" He yelled again. Shaunice stood up and got involved.

"Nigga, you ain't do shit. She's the one with the talent, you ain't got shit cuz you a piece shit!"

"Fuck you Shaunice!"

"Fuck you Maurice! Yo' ass mad cuz she doin' this shit without your sorry ass. With your bitch ass! "

Maurice looked over at the table and I was taking another shot with Roberto. I was ignoring Maurice because I knew Shaunice could handle him for me, but as always he resorted back to the insults.

"Fuck you and your bitch ass friend with her big ass!"

"Get the fuck from over her Maurice!" Shaunice yelled back.

"Alicia, you was a good fuck but that's it. You're fat ass ain't gonna get anyone to fuck you like I did." He yelled.

I tried to raise up and Roberto grabbed my arm; I looked at him and he just shook his head 'no'. I wanted to respond to him but I understood what Roberto was trying to say. Shaunice was able to handle it because she was management, but as the artist, I would be in the tabloids for sure. I was now the face of CFE and I had to prove that I could handle the negative side of it.

"Don't let him get to you. I know it's easier said than done, but he's attacking you to get a rise out of you. Don't give him that power." Roberto suggested. I nodded in agreement and settled back on the couch next to him. He held my hand for a sense of comfort as we sat trying to ignore the idiot at the ropes.

"Oh I see how it is, you got someone else huh? Cool, I didn't like your fat ass that much anyway, I got what I needed from you and the pussy wasn't all that!"

"Motherfucker, don't you get the fucking hint? You need to step away from this area otherwise I will get your ass removed from the building." Shaunice yelled back.

"You ain't gonna do shit!" Maurice retorted. Shaunice stepped back looking bewildered at Maurice acting like she was bluffing.

"Watch me." Shaunice said confidently as she walked over to the security at the VIP entrance. She spoke to one of them; the guard nodded and waved to a few people in the crowd.

Instantly two guys, dressed like normal patrons of the club walked over to Maurice who was still near the ropes. They talked to him and looked back at Shaunice. Shaunice tilted her head, gave an impish grin and waved at Maurice. He was shocked at the pull Shaunice had as he was not prepared for Shaunice to come through on her words.

"Alicia! Alicia!" Maurice yelled as the guard motioned for him to leave. "I know you hear me!" I refused to even acknowledge him as the guards had now laid hands on him.

When they finally got him to leave the area, I watched as they weaved through the crowd over to the door and escorted him out of the building. I let out a sigh of relief, but I also knew it wasn't going to be the last time I would hear from Maurice.

"You okay?" Roberto asked.

"I will be eventually. I don't think he's done though. He seemed pretty pissed off."

"Oh yeah, he's really pissed off."

"I'm sorry about all the stuff he was saying." I felt so embarrassed because I know others heard him as well.

"I wasn't listening to the shit that came out of his mouth because it's just another tactic to get you to respond. Don't worry about him and don't apologize for him being stupid. That's not your fault."

I looked at him and thought, Roberto might not be so bad after all. Yet I didn't want to fall for someone just because they were nice.

I deserved more than that.

Chapter 8 - Blocked

Shaunice

I figured that idiot would try something at the event, I'm glad I was able to handle it before shit got too serious. It was embarrassing because Maurice was acting a total ass in front of EVERYONE but they let me handle it and keep it under control. I treated Maurice so quickly he didn't expect that I would have the connections I did, but he knows nothing of me knowing the owner of the establishment.

Alicia did a great job and I was happy with the situation with Maurice not ruining it for everyone. To my understanding he wasn't able to get into the place until well after Alicia performed; he wasn't able to heckle her from the crowd and everyone loved her. She did fantastic but she always does when she's in her element. Marcus and Franklin were impressed when she blew at the house but she really let loose on stage.

A few days had gone by before Alicia told me that Maurice tried to contact her again. We don't live together, but I told her that she needs to have me stay over for a bit until Maurice gets the fucking hint that Alicia is done with him. But he seems like he wants her to tell him directly, just so he can play those mind games with her. I told her not to meet up with him alone because he might be on some crazy shit. Both Alicia and I work at O'Hare airport as janitors. The pay is damn good and we get to work independently emptying trash bins and cleaning up here and there. It's a pretty good job, no one bothers us as long as we do what is needed.

We were on our lunch break when Alicia started getting bogus ass text messages from an unknown number. We both knew it was Maurice's stupid ass. She just ignored it; she was finally done with him and healing. I was happy for her.

"So you think you'll get up with Suave Rob?" I munched on a walnut apple salad and a fruit smoothie.

We only had an hour for lunch but trying to compete with the travelers in the airport along with figuring out what we wanted to eat, cut our time down to about 30-40 minutes. We had to practically scarf the food down and taste it later.

"I don't know yet. His name is *Suave Rob*." Alicia said.

"He is Suave." I smiled.

"Yes, he is." Alicia smiled too. "But that's the problem, he's too suave. I'm mean, I don't know what to believe. Maurice was the same fucking way in the beginning. I don't know."

"Ok, true. He was, but you were with him. You saw things I didn't see, those are the things you need to be looking out for. You never called Maurice on his shit because you were dickmatized."

"Bitch," Alicia laughed and tapped my hand.

"Bitch you know I ain't lying, but still I understand, when that shit is good..,"

"Girl." She closed her eyes as if she was in the moment.

"Ok, stop. I don't need you going back because you need some dick." I quipped, looking at her as I stuffed a forkful of lettuce and walnuts in my mouth.

"See, that's why I don't need to be hooking up with anyone else right now. I don't want to fall for some good ass dick again just to forget the other stupid motherfucker and be back in the same shit I just left."

"I feel you. But I don't think Suave Rob is that way. But time will tell like you said. I'll wait. My vote is for Suave Rob." I smiled, scraping the bottom of the to-go container.

"How do you know he's a good guy?" she asked.

"Because I know. I have a feeling." I didn't know how to explain it but I feel Suave Rob saw Alicia for who she really is. "He must have some kind of morals by taking a chance and changing entertainment companies. I mean he couldn't take any of his music he made with TS Entertainment. He has to practically start over with CFE."

"That's true."

"So don't overthink it. I didn't say you had to marry the guy. I said just let nature take its course."

Alicia looked at me as we went to throw away our trash. Lunch was over and we had to get back to the break room to clock back in for the remainder of the day.

"I feel you. I'm gonna focus on my music and let whatever happens happen. I'm not expecting anything but my music career to take off for now and nothing else."

"That's fair."

Maurice

I shouldn't have gone in on Alicia like I did but she pissed me off listening to Shaunice and leaving me behind after everything I've done for her. I got so mad too because she was all hugged up with some dude thinking he's all that. Suave Rob ain't gonna hit that, I'll make sure of it. I already had a meeting set up with TS Entertainment because they have a bit more exposure than CFE and I think she would do better with them.

I had been trying to tell her that I was sorry for blowing up but she seemed to have blocked me so I'm just gonna have to show up at her place and let her know. I went to the meeting with great expectations to get Alicia signed with TS Entertainment.

"Thanks for seeing me today, I appreciate it." I shook Tavion's hand as he sat at his desk.

"So here's the thing. I just heard that Alicia Givens has debuted with CFE. Is this true?" He looked at me with a serious face that I couldn't tell if he was upset or not.

"She did a show recently, but she did not sign a contract." I lied. I had no idea if she did or not as I was not included in the matter.

"Are you sure?"

"Yes. I'm her manager, I would have known if she signed."

"Why did she perform at their show?"

"She performed to get some exposure with CFE. I wanted her to expand her horizons, so we are hitting up a few entertainment companies to see who is gonna give her the best contract."

"Understood. Well I would like for her to come in and audition for us and then we can discuss the contract terms."

"What are we talking 'bout when it comes to the contract?" I wanted to know what I could bring to Alicia that proved had been working my ass off for her.

"Normally we do 80/20 since we are putting up everything up front, like promotional tours, interviews and spots on radio as well as creating music videos and spots on Instagram and other social media platforms. But if you say she is as good as you said she is, we are willing to go to 70/30." He stated. I figured that would be a great deal for Alicia since I'm sure she didn't get a deal with CFE.

"Oh ok, bet. When do you want her to come in?"

"Let's get her in here tomorrow," Tavion said looking at his laptop. "It looks like we have some studio time around 11 AM. Will that work for you?"

"That will work, I'll holla at her tonight to let her know. Thanks again for the opportunity."

"No problem, brah. Just as long as she shows up, we can do this deal. As soon as she signs, we will get her started with interviews and a few minor shows in which she will be opening for a few artists that have debuted already." Tavion mentioned.

"Cool, cool. Thanks again." I said standing up and shaking his hand again.

I left the office and tried to call Alicia. She still had me blocked, which meant she was going to see me tonight. I'm sure she's been missing this dick too. All I gotta do is lay it on her real good and she will be eating out of my hand yet again.

Alicia

After work, I decided to stop by Harold's Chicken shack and pick up a 3 piece wing, fried hard with mild sauce on the fries and a grape pop before heading home. I kept getting notifications of voicemails but totally ignored them because I knew Maurice had been calling me all fucking day trying to apologize for how he acted at the show. I was completely done. He embarrassed me so much, I wanted to walk out, but Shaunice handled it; Roberto was helpful as well. He was so calm and collected, he didn't let Maurice bother him at all. Even though it wasn't Roberto who Maurice was talking shit about, but Roberto helped me keep my cool.

I had just finished my shower and was ready to get my grub on when my phone vibrated again. I had received yet another voicemail from Maurice. I didn't even bother listening to it. I just deleted it before I even heard it. Just about 20 minutes later, my doorbell rang. I frowned because I had no intention of having company; I figured someone was looking for a different apartment and they were seeing if someone would just buzz them in the building.

I didn't budge from the couch as I watched my favorite movie, *Love and Basketball* on BET. I hadn't seen it for a while and I had turned it on almost at the end of the movie. I checked the guide to see what movie would be next as I relaxed. *ATL* was the next movie after *Love and Basketball*; it was like a movie marathon of oldies but goodies.

Suddenly there was a knock at my door.

"Who is it?!" I yelled because I knew I wasn't expecting

anyone. I just knew this was the wrong apartment they were looking for.

"Open up the fucking door, Alicia!" Maurice yelled from the other side of the door.

No, this motherfucker didn't just show up at my house unannounced.

"I just know you got the wrong motherfucking door. You need to leave."

"C'mon girl, let me in."

"I ain't got nothing to do with you. You need to just leave because you were not invited."

"Wait Alicia," he begged. "I'm sorry. I'm sorry for what happened at the club. I just got jealous seeing you with dude and you weren't tryna talk to me. I just wanna holla at you real quick."

"Nigga you got issues. They make doctors for that shit! I'm done with you Maurice."

"Alicia, I got you an audition with TS Entertainment! Tomorrow!"

"And what does that got to do with me? I'm where I want to be. I already signed with CFE."

"Aw man, no! I have an audition with TS Entertainment tomorrow morning at 11."

"Well, looks like you gotta tell them you were wrong. Bye Maurice!" I said, stepping away from the door. He stayed at the door begging me to let him in.

"Alicia, let me talk to you. Open the door."

"No!" I yelled from the couch.

"Why is you acting like a Bitch?!" Maurice yelled. I could tell he was getting angry.

"You da motherfucking bitch, Bitch! Get the fuck away from my door before I call security."

"Why you tripping?" he asked.

"Why can't you take a fucking hint, Maurice?!"

"A'ight Alicia. I see how it is. You got some dick up in there, huh?" He was fishing for information and was trying to manipulate the conversation to make me offer up something.

"Why you worried about it? You got enough pussy to keep you busy. Why don't you go lay up in one of them bitches you left me for?!" I snapped.

"I ain't got no bitch!"

"Keep looking, you'll find one." I laughed as I sat my happy ass on the couch while he was at the door. It felt kind of good to be honest, having him begging; I was getting some sort of sick and twisted joy out of it.

"A'ight Alicia. I see you playing games."

"Whatever." I answered. I decided to fuck with him. "Hey, did you find it? 'Cause I can't find it?" I asked.

"You can't find what?" He answered through the door.

"I can't find the 'fuck' I don't give?" I laughed out loud and he hit the door hard, making me laugh harder.

"Fuck you Alicia." he said.

"Not anymore!" I laughed again and damn near peed on myself.

"I see you got jokes. A'ight. I'll holla." Maurice finally got the hint and left.

I shook my head and went back to watching my movie that actually went off during the entire conversation with Maurice. I finished my food, threw my trash away and decided to retire for the evening.

I couldn't wait to get into work the next day to tell Shaunice what this fool did.

Chapter 9 - Denim Knight

Alicia

I woke up to a text message from Siedah giving me a schedule for a few radio interviews she had lined up for the week. She has been hustling for me since day one; I appreciated CFE so much because they took a chance and invested in me therefore I needed to show up and shine. It was my day off and I didn't need to be in the studio until later on today; so I had the day to myself.

As I walked out the house, a car and driver were waiting outside my building. The driver got out of the car and walked around to the back passenger door.

"Ms. Givens?" He called my name. I stopped suddenly in my tracks wondering who this person was and how did he know my name?

"Who's asking?"

"I'm from the entertainment company, I was told to pick you up and bring you to the studio." he replied.

I thought I wasn't supposed to go to the studio until later on but I could have gotten the schedule wrong. I figured it might be better to have the afternoon off, I could still run my errands afterwards. I smiled and walked towards the car; the driver opened the back door and I stepped in. I felt it was important that they would send a car for me; it was nice to be appreciated.

I sat back as he closed the door and walked around to the driver's side, got in and we were off. After we had driven for a little bit, I noticed we were nowhere near CFE Studios. I figured we were going to the other studio and relaxed as the driver started going in the same direction. I was getting excited as we approached the exit towards the studio until the driver kept going and made no attempts to get off at the exit. It was then when I realized something wasn't right and I started feeling uncomfortable.

"Sir?" I asked from the backseat.

"Yes, Ma'am?" He answered looking in the rearview mirror quickly.

"You said we were going to the studio, correct?" I needed clarity on what I thought I heard.

"Yes, Ma'am, that is correct. We should be arriving at TS Entertainment studios shortly." he said.

"TS Entertainment?!" I yelled. I smelled Maurice all over this; That conniving, little motherfucker!

"Yes, Ma'am. Mr. Sanders is waiting for you as we speak." He said exiting the expressway.

I sat in the back fuming at the audacity of Maurice; trying to force me to audition, well he had another thing coming. The driver pulled into the parking lot of TS Studios. Don't get me wrong, they were doing very well as the competition, but this was a *dick move*.

Everyone knew I debuted with CFE so why are they trying so hard to steal new artists? Especially after Suave Rob left.

The driver opened the door and waited for me to exit the vehicle. I stepped out and there was no Maurice in sight as he was the first and only motherfucker I was looking forward to seeing.

"You can go through those doors. They will lead you to the lobby. Go to the reception desk and they will take you to Mr. Sanders." He pointed to two huge frosted glass doors.

"Thank you." I smiled and walked with a vengeance through the doors.

On the other side of the doors was a long, white corridor leading to another door at the end. It was like a space portal and my walking never seemed to end. All of the walking allowed me to get even madder; I could have been running my errands instead of going on a wild goose chase looking for a stupid motherfucker so I could kick his ass.

I finally reached the last door and exited the hallway; the lobby was huge and immaculate. The TS logo hung from the ceiling in the middle of the room. There was a modern black and gold reception desk with a cute girl working behind it. I walked over to the desk as instructed by the driver.

"May I help you?" The girl said without looking up. She looked to be about my age rocking a nice lace front wig.

"Um yes, I was told to come to the desk as I have a meeting today?" I replied. She looked up and her eyes grew huge.

"Oh shit! Alicia!" She squealed. I looked at her quizzically. "I was at your show! The one at Spice!"

I was flattered, I hardly met many people after a show to tell me they enjoyed it other than friends and family. "Thank you, I'm glad you liked it."

"Girl, you can blow!" She smiled. "But, wait. What are you doing here?"

Trust me, I was asking myself the same thing. "There has

been a mistake. Someone booked me to come here without my permission."

"Without your permission?" she asked, tilting her head. Suddenly, Maurice and Tavion Sanders showed up behind me.

"Alicia Givens?" I turned to see Tavion walking up to me with his hand extended; Maurice was walking just behind him with a grin from ear to ear. I instantly set my target.

"I'm sorry Mr. Sanders but you have been informed incorrectly."

"Excuse me?" He stopped in front of me.

"Alicia! Let me holla at you real quick." Maurice tried to push me to step to the side.

"No Maurice! I'm tired of your shit!" I yelled, pointing directly in his face in front of everyone. I didn't care if it drew attention, I needed him to get the fucking hint.

I turned to Mr. Sanders to explain. "I'm not sure what you were told, but I can only assume you were under the impression that I would come here, willingly to audition. Am I correct?"

"Yes." Mr. Sanders turned towards Maurice. "That is correct."

"Unfortunately, this asshole has informed you of this, I take it?" I pointed at Maurice.

"That is correct. I was informed that you hadn't made any decisions and you were still trying to find an entertainment group to join."

"That is incorrect, unfortunately. I have signed with CFE Entertainment Group. I debuted not long ago. I'm sure he didn't inform you of this either."

"Again, you are correct, Ms. Givens. I do apologize for your time. I will have the driver take you wherever you need to go." Mr. Sanders walked over to the reception desk and spoke with the girl.

"Alicia, why didn't you go along with it?! Can't you see I'm trying to be a good manager?"

"Maurice, you are so fucking stupid! You ain't my manager anymore! Why would you do this?" I started to panic, I needed to get some damage control as I saw people with their phones out, I'm sure it will be just a matter of moments before this shit hits TMZ.

Suddenly security came to the lobby and Mr. Sanders pointed towards Maurice.

"Mr. Gibbs, we have been ordered to have you removed from the premises." The guards stood waiting to escort Maurice from the building.

Mr. Sanders walked over to me shaking his head. "He informed me that he was your manager and you hadn't signed yet. I do apologize for all of the confusion."

"I am too. I removed him as my manager not long ago due to conflict of interests."

"Understood. Nice meeting you. The driver who brought you here is waiting for you in the parking lot to take you wherever you need to go." He said.

"Thank you, but no need. I'll be fine. Thank you anyway."

"Alicia," Maurice called my name.

"Leave me alone Maurice." I said turning around and

walking past the reception desk and out the front of the building.

Outside, I called the studio to inform Siedah of what happened. I didn't expect Roberto to pick up the phone.

"Hola Mami, how's it going?"

"Not good. Is Siedah there?"

"Naw, they stepped out for a minute, what's going on?" he asked.

I watched as the security guards escorted Maurice from the building. "You ain't gotta stand so close!" he yelled.

"Mami, where are you?" Roberto asked.

"TS Studios." I winced.

"What?! Why?"

"Alicia, why couldn't you have gone along with it!? You bitch! You ain't never satisfied! You fucked everything up! I was doing this for you!" Maurice yelled.

"I fucked everything up! You the stupid motherfucker who set this shit up! And then to kidnap me to come to an audition?! Who the fuck does that?!" I yelled back, still holding the phone to my ear.

"You could have still auditioned for them. They would have given you a better deal!"

"How do you know? You don't even know the fucking deal I got already! You're a fucking joke!"

"I'm a fucking joke?! You're a fucking, ungrateful ass bitch!" he yelled at me and walked off.

The outside drama didn't help at all as people were recording the entire confrontation.

"Hello?" I returned the phone to no one. Roberto had disconnected the phone call.

It was around lunchtime in Chicago, which meant the price for a ride share was practically doubled and I didn't want to pay the prices. I figured I would walk around for a bit before I would try again, hoping the fares would go down shortly after lunch. I scrolled on my phone for food in the area as I figured I might as well grab a bite to eat since I had some time to kill.

By the time I found a place within walking distance, the sound of a motorcycle came roaring down the street pulling up in front of TS Studios. The cyclist pulled off his helmet - it was Roberto! I was shocked to see him; he smiled as he walked over to me.

"Roberto, what are you doing here?"

"Are you okay? Where is he?" he said, looking around for Maurice. He had come to rescue me, without hesitation.

"He's gone. He got pissed off and called me an ungrateful bitch."

"I'm sorry," Roberto said, coming over to me giving me a hug. "I would have been here sooner but I got caught by a little traffic."

"I didn't expect you to come. I appreciate it."

"Well I got you now, so if that motherfucker comes back, I'll handle him." Roberto looked at me lovingly in my eyes as he caressed . I blushed.

He came to my rescue. He earned some major brownie points.

A shutter sound drew our attention as there were people who were taking pictures of Roberto and I, in front of TS Studios. That alone was an entirely different story. We needed some serious damage control.

"Let's get back to the studio. We need to keep this shit on the low." He grabbed my hand and walked me to his motorcycle.

I knew nothing about motorcycles as I had never rode one before, this would be my first time. Roberto handed me a spare helmet, which he helped fasten to my head. He looked sexy as fuck in his jeans and leather boots with a jean button up, opened to reveal a wife beater underneath.

"Have you ever been on a bike before?" he asked as we stood in front of the motorcycle.

"No, I haven't."

"Okay. I'll get on first then you get on behind me, you think you can do that?"

"Sounds easy." I admitted. He gave me a thumbs up and hopped on his bike. He started it up and motioned for me to get on. He pointed where I could step to hoist myself up and leg over. It was different for sure.

"Hold on to me here," He said, wrapping my hands around his waist. I laced my fingers and leaned against his back. He patted my hands and smiled. "Close your legs on mine, just like I'm giving you a piggyback ride."

"Understood." I closed my legs and held on for dear life.

Roberto put on his helmet , revved the engine and we were off.

He wasn't my knight in shining armor, he was my knight in denim.

Chapter 10 - I Appreciate You

Suave Rob

Alicia was on the back of my bike, holding me tight. I didn't know the entire deal with her and this dude, Maurice, but I think it's time for me to make my interests known. What I do know is that she was with this dude for a bit and apparently he helped her with getting her music career started. From what I understand, they had a relationship, but he wasn't or hasn't been too faithful which is why I didn't understand why she stayed with him.

As we drove along Lakeshore Drive, she laced her fingers across my stomach with her head laying on my back. I could get used to having her holding on behind me. She's a beautiful woman who I feel has been taken for granted because of her weight. I could tell she was self-conscious about it, but she needs to know how to love herself. I've never had an issue with a woman with meat on her bones, I actually enjoy it. It's way better than grinding on bones up against my skin, that shit ain't sexy. I'm attracted to all of her curves along with her adorable personality. Alicia is attractive, has a great sense of humor and the woman can sing her ass off.

Some guys don't know what they have until it's gone. Maurice is gonna have to find out the hard way Because I have my sights set on making her mine in due time. I don't want to rush into anything with her because she just let this fool go and I don't want to be a rebound. Therefore, I'll just keep being me and I'll show better than I can tell her. First off, I'm already making her think because I picked her up in a time of need. I got upset hearing that nigga call her a bitch, I was ready to pop his ass when I got there, but he was gone before I arrived.

Rage ran through me just hearing her mistreat and talk down to her, he was glad I wasn't there because I wouldn't have held back, I would've whooped his ass up and down the fucking sidewalk. He didn't have the right to disrespect her or any other woman with his bitch ass. We finally pulled into the parking lot in front of the studio and I turned off the bike. I took off my helmet and turned to see if she was okay.

"Hey Mami, you good?" She lifted the helmet off her head and smiled.

"Yes, I'm good. Thank you for coming. I appreciate it."

"Anytime." I helped her off the bike and jumped off myself, kicked out the stand and took her helmet.

"Why did you come?" She asked. I could tell she's never had someone to show that they cared for her.

"You needed me. So I came." Simple as that. I didn't need any other explanation.

She looked at me amazed by my answer. "Ok," she smiled. "Thank you." I had left her speechless.

"Like I said, anytime." I looked at her and she blushed. "Hey just in case he tries something again, let me give you my number."

"Oh ok, yeah." She stuttered at me offering my number and not asking for hers. She pulled out her phone, went to 'Save New Contact' and handed her phone to me.

I smiled and proceeded to save my number in her phone. I handed it back to her. She looked at my name and number, she looked at me and smiled. She dialed me and my phone rang. I pulled my phone out, showing an unregistered number.

"This you?"

"Yup. Now you have my number."

"Cool." I smiled at her as we started walking to the door. I opened the door to allow her in first, with me following directly after. The cool air felt good against my skin when we entered the studio.

"Where y'all been?" Marcus asked. "Didn't I leave you here Rob?"

"Yeah, but Lil Mama had a little incident that I had to help her with." I looked at Alicia who was looking at Marcus.

"What happened?"

"Maurice, is what happened." she stated.

"What the fuck that nigga do now?" Marcus sounded upset. "It seems like he just wants to be a mosquito on my ass."

"I thought you guys sent a car to pick me up from my place this morning."

"Why would you think that?" Franklin said.

"Well, the driver said he was from the entertainment company to take me to the studio."

Marcus and Franklin both looked at him. "Who was it?"

"Maurice had set up an audition with TS Entertainment."

"Are you serious? That lil' motherfucker is getting on my last motherfucking nerves."

"Trust me, I know."

"So how did you come into this, Rob?" Siedah asked.

"I was here when she called looking for you. Maurice was going off on her outside, calling her names, so I just went and got her." I said standing confidently.

Siedah smiled and bumped Monica. She looked at me and winked. I smiled because she knew what I was on. Siedah be on some shit, she peeps out a lot; she likes to sit back and observe, watching people when they don't know it.

"Ok, good. Well I'm glad you went and got her. But that lil bitch ass nigga needs to be dealt with." Marcus said, pacing back and forth.

"Marcus, calm down." Siedah said, catching his arm as he walked past. Marcus stopped and looked at her. She caressed his face and he totally melted in her hands. "Breathe."

"I'm good baby." He said giving her a quick kiss and rubbed her protruding belly.

"Where's Shaunice?" Monica asked.

"She had some things to do today with her family." Alicia responded.

"She would've taken care of him for sure."

"Yeah, but we don't need her in jail either, so maybe it was a good thing she wasn't around." quipped Siedah. Everybody nodded in agreement.

"Well, I'm glad you're okay. But I think Rob needs to hang with you for a while, just in case that fool tries something again." Marcus said, sitting down at the soundboard.

Alicia and I looked at each other simultaneously. We gazed at each other for what seemed like a few minutes before Monica chimed in. "Well, there you go. You two are stuck together until further notice."

"We don't need any other shit going on with anybody else." Franklin said. "We had enough over a year ago with these two over here." He said, pointing to Marcus and Siedah.

Everyone knew what happened to Marcus and Siedah. It was all over the news when they got viciously attacked. They survived and came back stronger than before. Shortly after Marcus and Franklin won the Grammy for their song putting CFE on the map.

"Yeah, unfortunately we don't take shit like that lightly." Marcus looked at both of us. "Y'all cool with that?"

"I'm good." Alicia said, looking at me. She blushed and looked away, making me smile.

"I'm definitely good." I answered finally.

"Good. Now get y'all asses in the booth. I wanna try something with y'all." he ordered.

"Back to business people!" Franklin said, sitting down at the soundboard. Monica and Siedah left the area and sat down on the couch further away and flipped on the tv.

Alicia and I walked into the studio and closed the door behind us. She looked nervous as she stood nearest the microphone. I walked over to her and grabbed her hands. She looked at me with her doe-like eyes. She was so beautiful and insecure.

"Breathe. You got this."

"I know, it's just.." I looked at her, still holding her hands. I massaged the back of her hands with my thumbs. "I get little nervous just before, you know."

"It's all good. This is family. Don't be nervous."

"Yeah I know. Shaunice is usually here when I get this way."

"Y'all good in there?" I heard over the speaker.

"Yeah, just a minute." I looked at the window raising my finger, and then looked back at Alicia.

I held her hands and stood closer to her. She looked at me as if she was about to have a panic attack. She looked down trying to hold it together. Everybody has their thing when it comes to singing. Some people float right in and let everything flow while others get sick right before performing.

"I'm here with you. I'm not going anywhere. Just like earlier, I'm here. Okay?" She nodded and held my hands. I smiled, making her smile. "I got you."

"Thank you," she took a deep inhale, closed her eyes and exhaled. "I appreciate you." I let her hands go and grabbed a pair of headphones.

"I know." I laughed, making her giggle. She bumped me with her arm.

"You something else."

"Yeah, I know. But you like it." I said. She gave me a shocked look and playfully hit me. I looked at the window and gave the thumbs up. "We are good to go."

"Cool. Siedah sent the lyrics to the tablet. Check it out while I play the track." Franklin uttered over the speaker.

Alicia grabbed the other set of headphones as the music pumped through. It was a nice beat that had us bouncing in no time. It was a hot piece but I should have known because it was the talent of Marcus and Siedah. She was perfect at writing songs and Marcus was amazing with adding music to her words.

Alicia sang along and I jumped in, rapping here and there; it was like putting the icing on the cake, our voices blended so well together, the beat was tight and the words were magical. We had everyone in the studio bouncing. By the time we finished, Monica and Siedah had joined the others at the soundboard.

"That's the shit I'm talking about!" Marcus yelled excitedly, standing up and giving a high five to Franklin.

"Y'all did the damn thing. I think we got a real hit, for real." Franklin acknowledged.

Alicia and I exited the booth and joined the others. I was happy they were happy with our outcome. We did sound good together. I'm sure we looked good together too.

Alicia

Roberto and I sang together and hit it out of the park. It was absolutely amazing. He had been showing up and showing out and I didn't know how to thank him for doing what he did for me earlier in the day. Since the issue with Maurice was real, they didn't want to not take him seriously after the incident therefore they paired me with Roberto to make sure I was safe when Shaunice wasn't able to be my bodyguard.

"You ready to go?" Roberto asked as he grabbed his helmets.

"I am, but I want to thank you for earlier." He looked at me confused, trying to figure out where I was going.

"You did already.."

"Yeah I know, but..." I hesitated. "Are you hungry?" I asked. He looked surprised, he wasn't prepared for me.

"I could eat, yeah. Why wassup? You wanna feed me?" He said playfully.

"Yes. Yes I do." He looked at me and stepped back.

"Ok, cool. Feed me then. Do I need to stop at the store to let you pick up some stuff?"

"Nope, I have everything at home."

"Well let's bounce then." He started walking towards the door. "A'ight y'all, we outta here."

"A'ight y'all be careful." Monica sang out as we walked out the door.

On the ride over to my house, I was thinking about what to cook Roberto; I had options but I wanted something quick and good, just like a booty call. Roberto followed me into my apartment and looked around as he removed his shoes. I thought that was very respectful of him; another brownie point for Suave Rob.

"Where's your bathroom? I want to wash my hands."

"Down the hallway, first door on the left." He smiled and left. I quickly went into the kitchen and looked in the fridge. I had already taken out chicken breasts and ground beef. I was very indecisive this morning as to what I was going to have for dinner, so I always gave myself options. I had a nice, chilled bottle of wine on the door calling my name. It would pair well with Chicken Alfredo. I checked the freezer and had garlic bread as well. I had made my decision and grabbed the ingredients out of the refrigerator as Roberto came around the corner.

"You need some help?" He rolled up his sleeves.

"You cook?"

"I'm a single man, of course I cook. I need to survive."

"I see you're a smart ass as well." He chuckled.

"I'm just giving you a hard time. But yes, I can cook."

"Good to know."

"Again, need some help?"

"Sure, you can cube the chicken." I handed him a bowl of thawed chicken breasts. He looked around at all of the ingredients as he walked into the kitchen.

"Chicken alfredo?" He asked.

"How did you know?"

"Again, I cook."

"And a smart ass." I laughed and he smirked.

"Yes. So you know how to make your own alfredo sauce too?"

"Sure do. I didn't get this thick on nothing." I said smartly.

"Ain't nothing wrong with that. I love a woman that knows how to eat." he said as he cut up the chicken.

"No salad women for you?"

"Well, I like the occasional salad, but I need more, you know?"

"I feel you. Salads are good, at the beginning of the meal."

"True."

"You drink wine?"

"Yes, I do. What did you get to drink?"

"A nice bottle of Sweet Red."

"Aww, that's nice. Okay, I see you." He chimed in.

"I told you I had everything I needed at home."

"Were you planning on having someone for dinner?"

"No, I just meal prep for the week so that's why I have so much out." I answered

"Look at you being all economical."

"Shit I live alone, I need to stretch my dollas." I beamed. I was being totally honest. If he hadn't come over, I would have this good ass meal for the rest of the week.

The food was so good, we practically ate the entire pot full. We opened the bottle of wine with dinner, leaving only about 2 glasses for both of us after dinner. We sat in the living room finishing the wine and the *'itis'* started kicking in big time. Roberto yawned as he sat comfortably on the corner of the couch.

I watched him periodically; he looked so damn sexy. He licked his lips making me want to know the softness of his lips. We sat talking as if we were in high school, talking about everything from how Shaunice and I met all the way down to me starting my music career. Roberto made it so easy to talk to, I felt like I could tell him anything. I sat quiet looking at him, he moved closer to me, making chills roll across my skin. Just as he moved closer again to me, the doorbell rang.

I frowned and looked at the time, the clock read 10:30 pm. I already had an idea of who it might be and now wasn't the time for him to try and apologize again.

"Are you expecting someone?" he asked.

"No, I'm not. But I don't plan on answering it either." I said gulping down the rest of my wine.

"Why not?"

"Because I know who it is."

"Who?" he asked. I gave him a look and he knew instantly. "Oooo, please can I answer the door." He smiled slyly.

"You're bad." I said, shaking my head and smiling.

"Yup, but you like it."

Chapter 11 - Waiting Game

Siedah

I feel this baby is going to be huge. It's hot and it feels like he is forever on my bladder. I'm glad I'm doing this with Monica because there is no way I could be doing this whole pregnancy thing without driving Marcus crazy. But then again the way he seems excited, always rubbing my belly each and every time he sees me. It's like his hand has been permanently attached to my belly.

He's cute though, I wouldn't have guessed it by looking at him. He has a playboy look, without the mentality. He makes being pregnant fun, always kissing and talking to MJ. Marcus practically has bought every possible toy for him, he wants to be a great father, and I do believe he will be.

"Hey babygirl, how you feelin'?" Marcus sat down next to me on bed and massaged my feet. My ankles were swollen again. I really need to watch my sodium intake and stay off my feet.

"I'm feeling alright, I guess." I leaned back against the headboard and rubbed my belly: MJ kicked at my touch." "Ooo, Lil' Man, not so hard."

"You guess? What's on your mind?" He grabbed the

Palmer's Cocoa butter jar off of the side table. He took a small amount, rubbed it in his hands to warm it and massaged the back of my legs, ankle and the heels of my feet.

"Well, I've been thinking about Alicia. She's dealing with that idiot Maurice. I just have a funny feeling about it." I didn't want to say anything to Marcus, but he knows me and I remembered what we went through, all because we didn't take someone seriously.

"I feel you, that lil nigga is getting on my nerves. And Alicia shouldn't have to deal with him for much longer." He said after he finished my legs, ankles and feet.

"What you got planned?"

"Nothing yet, I'm just trying to get prepared. I don't need a repeat," Marcus hesitated, he remembered too. "I got too much to lose." He grabbed the Palmer's Stretch Mark Tummy Butter off of the table.

"I know baby," I said, getting emotional, tears started building in my eyes. I sniffed as one tear fell down my cheek. "I feel you."

"Well, Suave Rob is gonna hang with her until we come up with something better." He said rubbing tummy butter on my belly. He had it glowing like a shiny bowling ball.

"Yeah, we can have both of them promoting together, that way we can kill two birds with one stone. Suave Rob is with her and both of them are out promoting their single, once it's ready."

"That'll work. Suave Rob ain't gonna let anything happen to her, for sure." Marcus smiled at me. He knew something that I didn't know.

"What? You know something." I said leaning down, trying to make eye contact with him. He looked at me and made a face. I rolled my eyes and he chuckled. "Tell me." I sang.

"A'ight. Well he peeped her out since he came on with CFE. He told me he was feeling her when they met at the studio."

"For real?"

"Yup. But he didn't want to holla at her because she was just ending it with dude."

"I get that. That's the last thing a woman wants is another man to try to talk to her when she just finished dealing with a nigga. That just ain't cool."

"Right?! So he was like he would just let her get to know him and make her own decision."

"I'm surprised that he didn't have a woman already."

"Naw, he had the sort of the same situation I had with Justine."

"Aww damn."

"Aww damn is right. He caught her fucking Tavion."

"Damn! Shut the fuck up!" Marcus shook his head confirming he was not playing, he was being totally honest.

"I know. Tavion is something else."

"All of them are something else. Do you not remember Isis? His wife? With Darius?"

"Aw shit, that's right!"

"Right. They just fucking everybody with no regards." I said as he placed the tummy butter back on the side table. He leaned over and kissed my forehead and then my belly.

"Are you hungry?"

"Yeah," I said, putting a couple pillows behind my back.

"What do you want me to get you?"

"I want the Shin Spicy Ramen noodles with kimchi."

"I thought that spicy foods give you heartburn. You sure you can eat that?"

"Yes, it doesn't give me heartburn, I don't drink the broth that much. Besides, I thought it was the baby's hair that's giving me heartburn."

"Then he got a whole lotta hair."

"I know right." He leaned down, placing a kiss on my lips.

"I'll be right back with your food babygirl. Watch something on Hulu." He said handing me the remote control.

He was going to pamper me since I wasn't feeling well. I couldn't complain, I knew there were a few pregnant women who would love to have someone like Marcus. Marcus was happy to become a father; he has been ready and waiting. He has been on point since I told him New Years. I was happy we moved into a new place a while ago to give us more room to expand our family; MJ being the first to arrive. Marcus had his room ready and stocked; it's just a waiting game at this point. I just need to get through these next few months with no stressful shit happening.

Suave Rob

"C'mon, let me answer the door. I promise I won't make a scene." I begged. I could see that sparkle in Alicia's eye; she knew Maurice would be upset with me answering the door.

Apparently, someone had granted him access and he was knocking on the door. He knocked like he was impatient, calling her name periodically.

"A'ight, just don't beat his ass, okay?" She asked, raising her eyebrows.

"I promise." I held up my hand. "I swear. I just want to see his face when I answer the door."

"You are silly as all get out." I smiled a smile as big as the Cheshire cat. "I'm going to the bathroom. Please don't fight and get the police up here."

"I won't." I replied as she walked to the bathroom.

I took off my button up shirt and my wife beater and threw them on the couch. I unbuckled my belt and unbuttoned my pants just enough to show the top of my underwear. I adjusted myself and then opened the door. The look of surprise filled his face as I opened the door; he stared at me shockingly as I pretended to pull my pants up.

"Uh, whatchu doin' here?" He asked, getting irritated and I hadn't said a word.

"I should be asking you that question, brah." I said standing firm.

"Where's Alicia at?" He said, trying to look past me into

the apartment.

"Who is it baby?" Alicia played along as she yelled from the bathroom.

"No one special Mami." I said looking at him. "Wassup, whatchu need, brah?" I could see the anger grow inside of him as I casually called her 'Mami'.

"Tell her to come to the door." He demanded.

"Well she's busy right now, so you can tell me what you want or you can bounce." I stood confidently at the door. I made full eye contact so he knew he was not about to boss anyone around, not today.

"I need to speak to Alicia."

"I'm sorry, bro, that ain't happening today. Besides, it's kinda late and we're about to go to bed."

He scoffed and shook his head. He was hot; he was so mad beads of sweat started forming on his forehead. He tried to stare me down as if to intimidate me. I chuckled and stepped towards him.

"Listen brah,"

"I ain't yo, brah." Maurice interrupted. I smiled and shook my head. I promised Alicia that I wouldn't and I was going to keep that promise, but this fool was really asking for it.

"Listen Brah," I spoke clearer and louder making sure he understood my tone. "Alicia is incapacitated at the moment and she's not coming to the door, especially not to see you."

Maurice scoffed again in disbelief. He pulled out his phone and dialed a number. Ironically, Alicia's phone started ringing on a small table nearest the door. It seemed to make him angrier because he couldn't have his way.

"Like I said Brah, either you tell me what you want or you can bounce." I folded my arms in front of me.

"So y'all together now? That's what you're saying? Is y'all like together now?" He asked, trying to understand how I had so much rank in Alicia's life.

"Well, that's none of your business, now isn't it?"

"Oh I get it, you famous and shit so now she's with you, huh?" He asked sarcastically.

"Wouldn't you like to know?" I asked. His lips got tight; I could tell the more I stood my ground the more irritated he got. "So who you with?" The question threw him off.

"What the fuck?"

"Exactly. Don't worry about what we doing up in here. This ain't got nothing to do with you." I said, stepping back and closing the door.

"What the fuck?! Alicia!" He said knocking on the door again. I quickly opened it up.

"Listen *pendejo* (stupid), I done already told you, she ain't coming to the door and she shole' ain't about to talk to you after you done showed your *culo* (ass) in the club."

"Nah, nah brah."

"Oh now I'm yo brah? Listen, I already promised her I ain't gonna make a scene so do yourself a favor, step on up outta here before I break my promise." I said in a tone that he could understand. Maurice looked at me with so much anger; he bit his lip and backed away.

"A'ight," He said, backing away a little farther. "I see how it is. Bet." He nodded, turned and walked down the hallway to the elevators. I closed and locked the door. Alicia came out of the bathroom as I walked back to the couch.

"Damn," she said looking at my chest. "Y'all got that damn heated?" I laughed.

"Thanks for playing along."

"I figured it would piss him off if I called someone else baby instead of him."

"Oh ok, I see." I smiled putting my t-shirt back on. "So what are you going to call me?"

"I ain't figured that out yet." Alicia smiled. She liked what she saw and was impressed with how I handled Maurice.

"That's cool Mami, I'll wait for you to come up with one." She blushed and rolled her eyes. "Do you mind if I crash here tonight? I'll sleep on the couch."

"I don't mind. I think it would be good, just in case he decides to come back."

"I was thinking the same thing." Alicia chuckled.

She moved the cocktail table from in front of the couch and pulled the bottom of the couch out. It was a futon and storage was at the bottom with pillows and extra bedding. She pulled out everything and extended the back of the couch down which opened up to a full size bed.

"This shit is tight!"

"I know right. I saw it and I had to get it just in case I had people who wanted to stay."

"Oh ok, cool."

Alicia prepared the bed making it look so comfy and inviting.

"Thanks again Roberto, I truly appreciate you."

"The pleasure is all mine, Mami."

"How can I repay you, again?"

"I'll think of something." I said smiling.

Chapter 12 - You Make Me Feel

Alicia

The craziness with Maurice finally died down after the incident with him coming to my home. I couldn't imagine what I would have done if Roberto hadn't been there. I had never seen Maurice get so angry, but since I dropped him entirely, he seemed to have gotten a bit more irritated and has been directing it towards me. With Marcus suggesting Roberto and I promote together, it was like I had my own bodyguard; he was a fine ass bodyguard to be honest. I caught myself thinking about how he could protect my body, with his.

I hadn't paid attention, just lost in thought sitting in the lobby of the radio station where Roberto and I were waiting to be interviewed. Being out with him seemed like a fun, long lasting date; we would go to various places to promote our music almost every other day. It was a new experience for me as it was my first time doing all of this ground work, whereas Roberto had experience from dealing with TS Entertainment.

During our interviews, the radio hosts would always bring

up the drama, it's inevitable - people love messiness. First they start off with Roberto and they travel on over to me. We were at Hotness 97.5 with their disk jockeys, Roddy Rick and Chantelle Lafonte. I was in shock when I first started doing the interviews because the radio personalities looked NOTHING like the individuals I created in my head; I only heard them on the radio therefore my mind made up a full damn person just by their voices alone.

"So Suave Rob," Roddy spoke into the big ass mic hanging in front of him. He resembled Future without the dreadlocks. "So you have jumped ship from TS Entertainment and gone over to CFE Group, what's up with that? Why you leave TS brah?"

"I would say, it was because of collective differences, to be honest." Roberto answered smoothly, I loved his calm swagger.

He held his shit together well, he was determined not to let anyone see him sweat. I took a sip of my water and nodded slowly, not putting my two cents into anything I knew nothing about. It was a well thought out answer to a very intriguing question.

"Well that's understandable. E'erbody gotta be on the same page. So I feel you on that."

"But you know on TMZ," Chantelle chimed in. "You know they're saying that it was much more personal than that, which is the reason that the collaboration didn't work."

"Ahhh, so what are they saying Ms. LaFonte?" Roddy boosted her from the mic.

"They're saying that Isis Bradley had a part in this. That she was the reason it wasn't working out." she responded. Roberto scoffed and just looked at them. The sound guy played the music from the movie, Jaws.

"So brah, why is TMZ saying the breakdown has something to do with Isis Bradley?" Roddy asked.

"First of all, TMZ loves drama because it gets attention. Secondly, I know what went on in the boardroom because I was present, TMZ was not," Roberto stated his facts confidently and professionally. "And lastly, Isis is not my type." The sound guy played back the recording of Chris Tucker saying *daaaayum* from the movie, Friday.

"Well!" Roddy stated. "Brotha said, 1, 2 and 3!"

"Yes he did, yes he did!" Chantell sang. We all chuckled at the facts that Roberto had laid out for everyone to hear.

"Ok, I appreciate that brah," Roddy and Chantelle were still laughing at the delivery. Roberto smiled looking at me; I instantly blushed. "You said Isis is not your type, huh?"

"No, she is not." he proudly stated again.

"And what exactly, *Is* your type?" Chantelle said, leaning into her mic hanging in front of her.

"Yeah, what is your type?" Roddy added.

Roberto leaned into the mic on the stand directly in front of him. "Unmarried." He said looking at Roddy. He turned and looked at Chantelle and spoke, "Unattached." "And Single." he said looking at me.

"Wooooow!" Both of them sang out. I blushed as Roberto smiled; he was just adorable and genuine.

"Okay! I likes that in you man!" Roddy said getting hyped and giving a bump to Roberto. "Man said, unmarried, unattached and single. Ya' heard it right here folks, directly from the man himself." I smiled, enjoying the entire atmosphere.

"Yes sir, but did you peep what I peeped, though?" Chantelle asked Roddy as she looked directly at me and Roberto.

"Nah, nah, what did I miss?" He asked, looking at Roberto.

"When Suave Rob gave his types, he looked directly at Alicia over there when he said *'Single'*. Ain't that right Ms. Alicia?" A lump formed in my throat. The tables had turned on me so quickly and I had to handle it.

I leaned towards the microphone sitting in front of me. I saw Roberto looking at me in my peripheral; it was like he was channeling his calmness to me. I spoke softly, "I don't have a clue as to what you are talking about Ms. Chantelle." I said, raising my eyebrows and pursing my lips together, not saying a word.

"A'ight, she done got tight lipped on you Chantelle, real quick!"

"I feel you though, girl. It's okay. Keep it tight, keep it right." Chantelle said, shaking her head. "So Alicia, you signed with CFE Group as well, congratulations to you on that."

"Yes, I did. Thank you, I'm excited."

"This is your first time with an entertainment company, correct?" she asked.

"Yes, it is." I was doing leg work with Maurice.

"Okay, so you have signed with CFE Group; you found a home and you are doing some things, okay I see you." she said smiling.

"But this is not your first time out, right. You've been around but under a different promotion, correct?" Roddy asked, bursting my bubble. I knew they would bring it up, it was just a matter of time.

"Uh, yeah. I was under different management, but we parted ways." I answered, trying to stay cool, calm and collected. Roberto leaned against me, giving me a boost.

"I can't even imagine trying to get your foot in the door and you having to move around so much with management."

"Yeah, it's hard when all you want to do is share your talent." I answered honestly.

"True, that is true."

"So, who were you with before?"

"I think it was Maurice Gibbs, right?" Chantelle said looking at a blue sheet of paper with most likely tidbits of information about us.

"That is correct." I answered.

"Oh, that's right. I saw the recording! Y'all was in the lobby at TS Entertainment." Roddy shouted out.

"That's right!" Chantelle sang. "Alicia, girl, you were giving him the business. What happened?" she asked.

The moment came flooding back, I was so embarrassed. Maurice had not only kidnapped me but he had Tavion under the impression I was interested in joining his company. I shook my head as I remembered going off at him in the lobby and then again outside.

"That was a disaster, is what it was. I decided to end it as we were going in two different directions."

"Understood. But y'all were dating as well, right?" Roddy asked me. I knew it was going to come out, but with Roberto by my side, I felt his energy. He made me feel at ease as he didn't get flustered at the rounds of personal questions they threw at us.

"I think the key word here, Roddy, is *were*. As in past tense. There is no more *us* as in a business or personal relationship."

"Ok, shut it down!" She laughed loudly. "She was like, let me get this straight right now!" I smiled.

"Ok, okay. But my man, Suave Rob came to the rescue, did he not? Of course, the video went viral of you being whisked away on the back of Suave Rob's bike."

"That is true. I picked her up and we went back to CFE Studios, where we are now."

"Swooped in like Superman!" Roddy waved his hand in the air. "And picked up this beautiful *Single* woman!" I blushed and Roberto smiled, turning his gaze towards me. I bumped him and the hosts picked up on it.

"Awww, look at them. We got something in the making here y'all! So if it happens, It happened here first! At Hotness 97.5!" Chantelle shouted into the mic. The sound guy was on point with the applause going on.

"Yes Sir, and so both of you are out here promoting together. Both of you have singles coming out, right? Y'all just doing it, ain't they!" Roddy mentioned.

"Yes." We replied in unison.

"So what is next for you two? Suave Rob, Now since you've switched companies, you were not able to take your music with you, correct?" Chantelle asked.

"Unfortunately no, I was not able to do so. But it's all

good. People know who I am because of it, so I can continue making more music with CFE." Roberto's words flowed out of his mouth so easily, he was ready for every question.

"Nice, nice. Brah, well take it and run. I'm excited to hear your sound come out of CFE because they have been crushing it!"

"Yasss they have," She sang as she danced in her chair. "My girl, Analia, has been hitting it for real though. I'm so glad she got with them."

"Yeah and don't forget Taye, he has been killin' it!"

"Yeah he has." All of us agreed.

"Well, good luck to you Suave Rob and Alicia, I'm anticipating your music to come out soon from both of you. Ma'am. I heard you at Spice."

"Did you?" I replied. It happened so fast and there were so many people, that entire night was a blur to me. "Thank you so much."

"Yes Ma'am, you can blow, girl. And I love it, you rocking out for us thick sistahs out here."

"Yes she is, Looking all cute." Suave Rob quipped on a low tone.

"Yep, even my man had to chime in on this." Roddy Rick added. It was the first time I saw Roberto blush; it made me smile.

"Thank y'all. I really appreciate it."

"Now y'all got a single out now too, right?" Roddy asked.

"Yeah, you know how it is, we're out here getting busy for real. Both of our singles are out separately but we also have a single together called "Lights Out, that's out right now. So go listen to it." Roberto chimed in. I was glad he was with me, he made learning the ropes of this entertainment shit look easy.

Maurice had no skill in this. He was probably a good promoter, but not manager. He didn't ever get me a gig like this. And he didn't take the time to teach me about the business and my image. Roberto helped me with that for the first time we did the debut show together at Spice. When he held my hand, holding me back from slapping the fuck out of Maurice, he showed me how to stay calm within a storm. He was my safety net.

"Cool cool, so I know y'all gotta bounce, but we wanna thank y'all for coming out and hanging with us."

"Yes thank you for coming to see us."

"Thank you for having us," We said.

"Check them out, Suave Rob and Alicia, they have singles out now wherever you get your music. Check them out! Show them some love for our talented people!" The sound guy ended with a round of applause.

After the show, we scored some merch, took a few pictures with the staff and said our goodbyes. It was our last interview of the day as we had some time in between to kill before heading back to the studio.

Suave Rob

"You wanna get something to eat? I'm hungry." I asked as we left the building walking over to the parking lot.

"Yeah, I could eat. We've been going strong all day long."

"I know right. How many spots have we done today?" I asked.

"Shit at least 4 or 5. I lost count."

"I know right. Well let's get some food, I'm famished." I said walking over to my bike. Alicia looked cute in her royal blue shorts and halter top. It was perfect for the weather because Chicago was burning up, the summer season was in full swing.

I handed her a scarf to protect her hair while wearing the helmet. After I helped her put on the helmet, she clipped the strap underneath her chin while I put on mine. I hopped on my bike and revved the motor; she sounded good purring like a kitten. Alicia grabbed a hold of my shoulder and straddled the seat like a pro. She leaned against my back, wrapping her arms around my waist. I patted her hands to let her know I was about to take off. She nodded and off we went.

I decided to go to Chinatown to a nice Vietnamese spot called Ocean Grill & Bar. It's like a hidden gem in Chicago like so many other small places off the beaten path. It wasn't crowded, so we entered and immediately grabbed a seat farthest away from the door, for a bit of privacy.

"I've never been to this place before." Alicia said. She was still wearing the scarf on her head. She looked so natural and beautiful, it matched her outfit perfectly.

"I found this spot a while ago, they have really good Pho here."

"Mmm, that sounds good. What else do you usually get?"

"I get a bit of everything. They have a really good selection of meat here so you can get something different every time."

"I wouldn't know what to order."

"Let me order for you. I promise you'll love it all."

"You promise?" She smiled and leaned in. I leaned in to match her energy. I gazed directly in her eyes, Alicia's dimples in her cheeks made her even cuter.

"I promise."

"Ok, I'll hold you to it." She said, I figured she would.

I wouldn't make a promise that I couldn't keep with Alicia. I didn't want to be that person that she had already dealt with. She needed and wanted someone she could depend on and I was determined to show her that I was that person.

After the waitress took our order we sat at the table stealing looks from each other. She was quiet but cautious. I wanted her to know she could open up to me and she didn't have to worry about me making her feel vulnerable.

"You did good at the station." I placed my phone face down on the table. It was a gesture of me letting her know, she had my full attention. She took her phone and did the same; leaning forward and gently placing her hands on the table, lacing her fingers together in the middle.

"You think? I didn't say much though." She tilted her

head looking at her hands, probably trying to remember the entire interview.

"Trust me, you said a lot. Less is always more." I gazed at her, she smiled bashfully.

"I guess, if you say so. I just followed your lead. You're helping me more than you know."

"So it's a good thing Marcus and Siedah put us together, huh?"

"Yeah, you're helping me to learn the ropes. Especially on dealing with that idiot." She frowned while mentioning him.

"Well, we ain't gonna talk about him," I said gently, putting my hands around hers, holding her softly. " You did really well today. Sometimes the radio hosts can be a little pushy trying to get you to insinuate something."

"You mean like twist my words up and shit?" I nodded.

"Exactly. But you did good." I patted her hands, she smiled and caressed part of my hand that her thumbs could touch.

"Thank you. Yeah they really get a hold of a lot of information about stuff quickly."

"That's because they hire people to dig up shit. They don't care as long as they get some shit to spread about someone."

"You did good too. Especially with them mentioning the switch from TS Entertainment to CFE Group." I looked at her hand and massaged her hands between mine.

She unlaced her fingers and laced them with mine. It was nice holding her hands, they were soft and small. I got lost in thought holding on to her.

"Thank you, I appreciate that. I'm kinda used to it

though. It's hard sometimes when people think they know you, but it's really what they expect from you. People live for drama and all that messy shit. I'm not like that. I'm a lover not a fighter."

"I like that." She smiled. "A lover not a fighter." Alicia repeated softly underneath her breath.

"But I will fight for love." I confessed. She looked at me surprisingly just as the waitress returned to the table.

The waitress came back with glasses of water and a few side dishes, we parted and sat back as she continued to place dishes on the table. Alicia kept her gaze on me after the woman left.

"Is that so?" She had been holding on to that question, waiting patiently for the woman to finish.

"Always, if the person is worth it."

"Can you say you have ever fallen in love before?" She asked. She looked as if she wanted an honest answer to give her the slightest bit of hope.

I don't believe she has ever felt real love. I know for damn sure she didn't get it from Maurice.

"Yes," I answered honestly and carefully. I didn't want her to lose hope because of what happened to me. "I had fallen in love before, just with the wrong person. But I do believe it's still possible for me to find my person."

"I believe that too. I mean, it took me a while to figure it out, and I feel stupid that I wasted time on that," She started.

"Nope, we are not mentioning that person." I interrupted. She stopped abruptly and smiled.

"I'm sorry."

"It's all good, Mami. But when you're with me, we ain't

gonna mention him, okay? He's not worth us talking about him."

"Understood."

"Good. But I feel you. I felt like that too. But use that energy to grow from it, because we all make mistakes and sometimes we become impatient,"

"But good things come to those who wait." Alicia finished. I gazed at her smiling back at me.

She made me blush, which has been a while since I had someone to make me feel shy.

"Yes, they do."

"Are you willing to wait for someone?" she asked.

"If I feel she's my person, I'll wait forever."

Chapter 13 - Take Care

Shaunice

I was so happy Alicia was out doing her thang. She hasn't gotten to the point where she can quit her job but she's well on her way. I had been missing in action for a while as I had to take care of a few family matters but I was able to be with Alicia at work.

"So have you heard from that fool? It's been a minute, right?" I asked as we sat down for lunch.

"Not since he showed up at my place and Roberto answered the door." She smiled, stabbing her fork into her salad.

"Girl, I would have paid a million dollars to be there to see his face when Suave Rob opened the door." I laughed, throwing my head back; I'm sure Maurice was not expecting Alicia to have moved on.

"So, y'all an item yet?" I winked at her, giving her a sly smile.

"No, not yet." She blushed talking about him. "I'm taking it slow and he's willing to wait."

"Well that's when you know he's a good one. He ain't tryna pressure you into anything." I sipped my drink.

"No, he's not. But damn girl, I swear, I'm having feelings each time we're around each other."

"But isn't that like every day? Ain't y'all promoting together?"

"Yes, girl. But girl, when I ride with him on that motorcycle, I just want him to turn around and let me ride him."

"Aww shit, your ass is getting all hot riding behind him!"

"Girl, shit. Then he holds my hands and then flirts with me. I don't know how much longer I can hold out."

"Shit, why are you holding out? You should've given him some *good-good* the time he scooped you from TS Entertainment."

"Shaunice, you're so bad." She giggled.

"Girl, I'm for real." I smiled. "So when is your next show?"

"I don't know yet, Monica and Siedah had been working on getting us the next gig, but they hadn't told everyone yet. I think it's gonna be a big one."

"I hope so, because you deserve it."

"Thanks girl, I'm glad I'm doing all this shit with Roberto. I get to see how to respond and how to ignore some of that negativity that comes with it."

"Girl, Suave Rob is definitely on the path of teaching you a few things."

"Well, I'm ready to learn." We laughed and finished out lunch before heading back to work. The day went by faster than expected and before I knew it, we were at CFE Studios, this time it was at Franklin's place.

Alicia and I walked into the studio, to what seemed like a very important meeting. Analia, Darius, Taye were already there along with Jacobi, a new singer who had just signed with the company shortly after Alicia did. We squeezed in next to Suave Rob sitting on a bench located on the side opposite Marcus and Franklin.

"Thank you all for coming, I know it was last minute but we just received the information and confirmation." Franklin spoke loudly to make sure everyone could hear him.

"We just received confirmation for our next showcase," Marcus chimed in. I looked over at Siedah and Monica, they looked hot as they fanned themselves with their hands. "CFE Group will be in the house at the Taste of Chicago!" He yelled. Everybody cheered loudly with excitement.

I looked at Alicia and she was hugging Suave Rob, smiling hard. She looked at me and waved me over, giving me a hug as if I was going to perform.

"Oh my goodness, The Taste?!" She screamed, holding me tightly.

"You're on your way girl!" I screamed and we jumped up and down in place. Suave Rob smiled as he watched Alicia get excited.

"Ok so, we have the lineup for the showcase and who will be closing out the show. Information about CFE Group owning a stage at the Taste should be going out now on the radio station so you will start seeing ads for showcase running asap." Franklin yelled. Everyone clapped and cheered as music started playing; people started dancing, bouncing to the music excited about the upcoming show.

"Wow, y'all about to blow up just so y'all know." I said pointing to Alicia and Suave Rob.

"Man, that's crazy, yo." He said, shaking his head and smoothing his hair to the front of his head.

I think it was the first time I really paid attention to Suave Rob, he had a nice faded haircut with his hair smoothed to the front ending with a nice trim. The brotha was fine as fuck and Alicia hadn't sat on that face yet.

"It is, isn't it! Oh my goodness. I gotta find out the line-up." Alicia said, walking over to Siedah and the group.

"So what's up with you and my girl?" I asked.

"Whatchu mean?"

"I see how you look at her." Suave Rob looked at me; he looked away blushing. "She likes you."

He looked at me and nodded. "I like her too."

"Good." I said still being her best friend in the world with the best intentions. "Don't fuck her over." He looked at me, nodded and smiled.

"I don't plan to." He responded sincerely. I believed him and I believed he would be good for her.

"Take your time, but don't wait too long." I suggested.

"Thanks for the heads up." He looked at me holding out his fist for me to bump. "Good looking out for your friend."

"I have to, until I find someone who can." I

"Well I'm here, you can stop looking." Suave Rob stated without blinking. My heart flipped for Alicia; this man was going to show her what love really is.

"Cool." I pulled a blunt out of my stash and lit it up. I inhaled pulling hard before passing it over to Suave Rob.

"You don't have to worry about your girl, I'm for real. I have no intention of playing games with her. I've been on the other end of that, I know how it feels."

"Good. Thanks for telling me." I said looking at him. "Just so you know, you had my vote at the beginning." I playfully bumped his shoulder. He chuckled and pulled on the blunt.

"Well thank you for putting in a good word for me."

"You just keep on doing what you're doing, she'll let you know when to make the move." I held out my fist and he bumped it while handing back the blunt. I was happy for Alicia, she was finally living her dream and she had a growing relationship with a good man who wanted to see her flourish.

Siedah

I was happy we landed the gig with The Taste of Chicago; that showcase will really put CFE on the map. Monica and I worked our asses off trying to get that gig. The footwork we put in, the phone calls we made and the money we put down to get an entire stage in downtown Chicago for the Taste was a big deal.

The Taste of Chicago was one of Chicago's biggest events that ended just around the 4th of July holiday. It's a food festival that lasts about 2 weeks and features food, music and all around fun for everyone. People come far and wide to tempt their taste buds with the fabulous flavors of Chicago. Concerts are held on various stages throughout Grant Park located near the lakefront of Lake Michigan. There is something for everyone. What better place to showcase our new talent and get more exposure for the CFE Group, showing that we are serious participants in the entertainment business!

I was happy we finalized everything and we were able to tell everyone because that would give them a month to prepare. Marcus and Franklin were in charge of the line-up because Monica and I managed to pull a needle out of a haystack and landed a stage at the Taste before TS Entertainment could. I knew once we got a spot, they wouldn't attempt to get one because it would seem as though they were imitating us.

In the midst of getting everything set up, I had been ignoring a few noticeable things when it came to my body.. I didn't want to keep things a secret but I just wanted to finish what needed to be done so I could take a small break before the showcase. I sat back on the couch trying to catch my breath. It seemed as if MJ was laying on my lungs as he was making it difficult to take a deep breath.

"How are you doing over there? You're not looking so good." Monica turned to the side on the couch and faced me.

"I'm good," I said breathlessly. "MJ is sitting high today. It's like he's on my lungs. I just need him to move around a bit." I said, trying to tap him to make him move around. I felt him move a bit and readjust but I was still having a hard time. I put my feet up on the table, my ankles were swollen badly.

"Siedah! Look at your ankles.!" She yelled. Instantly I had a pain at the top of my stomach, that felt like no other pain that I had felt before.

My head suddenly felt so much pressure inside, I closed my eyes, wincing in pain. "Aargghh!"

"What's wrong?" Monica scooted over and leaned in.

"I don't know. I'm not feeling well. Something's wrong." I got worried. I didn't want to get upset and lose the breath that I had, but I was about to freak out.

"MARCUS!" Monica yelled. Everyone in the close vicinity turned towards Monica who was looking at me.

"Yo! Marcus!" Someone yelled opposite us.

"Aye Yo Marcus!" Someone screamed again, over the music.

"MARCUS! IT'S SIEDAH!" Monica yelled again. She touched my head as I held my stomach trying to figure out why I was having pains. It wasn't time for MJ to come, not yet - it was too early!

Marcus showed up quickly at my feet on his knees. He looked worried which in turn made me worry; tears started streaming down my cheeks. He rubbed his hands over my belly; I held his hand as he took control of the situation.

"It's okay Babygirl, I'm here. Little man ain't ready yet. Let's go to the hospital, right now!" He said taking off my shoes and throwing them on the floor. "Can you walk?"

"I think so," He slowly took hold of my hands and pulled me up while Monica helped me by pushing my bottom. A pain raced across the top of my belly which made me bend over and try to catch my breath.

Marcus caught me as I was about to go down. "Aye, yo Franklin!" He yelled and Franklin rushed over to help him.

"Get the door man, I got her." Marcus picked me up in one fell swoop and we were off.

I wrapped my arms around Marcus's neck as he whisked me across the room over to the door; Franklin held it open as we walked out to the car.

"Where's the keys?" Franklin said, following closely behind.

"Front right pocket." Franklin grabbed the keys out Marcus's pocket and opened the door.

Marcus placed me as gently as possible in the car and slammed the door. Monica came behind him, opened the door, handing me my wallet and phone.

"Call me when they check you out." I gave her the thumbs up as Marcus started the car.

She quickly closed the door and stepped away from the car. She wrapped her arms around her belly looking at me while we pulled off, racing to the hospital.

Chapter 14 - Unexpected

Maurice

Alicia was tripping and she needed to understand what I had done for her. I didn't expect her and that dude to be close so soon, so I'm gonna have to step my game up to let her know that I'm not going anywhere. She knows she wouldn't be with CFE without me and now that she has a contract, she just forgot about me! But I wasn't not having it, She owes me and she's gonna listen to me, I'll make sure she does.

"Hey Bruh, what are we doing tonight?" Calvin asked as we left my apartment. "Are we going to Spice?"

"Yeah, but I need to make a stop first."

"You know I heard Alicia got a gig at the Taste this year."

"Yeah, I heard." It irritated me when I heard CFE got a line-up for the Taste of Chicago and she was featured. I should have been there with her.

"She's doing it man," He laughed. "Without you! She got up with CFE and just dropped yo' ass!" Calvin laughed as we got in the car. He wasn't making it any easier to deal with either. I don't know why I even hung out with that fool.

"Man I know, that shit ain't right." I was getting heated thinking about how easily and quickly Alicia replaced me.

"Naw it ain't right. She knows she's wrong for doing that. She needs to be put in her place, dude. I'm surprised you ain't slapped the shit out of her yet."

"Man, she's been on some shit man. I went over to her house the other day and she had that nigga answer the door." I hit the expressway, weaving in and out of traffic, lane by lane.

"So what are you gonna do man? She's still your bitch right? I would have fucked him up right there."

"It's all good, I know where she's gonna be and she's gonna be alone."

"Oh ok, I'm liking how you thinking, my nigga." He said. "How you know she's gonna be alone?"

"I've been listening to 107.5 WGCI and they had been saying she was coming down there today. They didn't say Suave Rob would be with her."

"Oh ok, she's be hanging with Suave Rob?!" Calvin said excitedly. "Damn man, she done stepped up!" He laughed which irritated me.

"Dude! Who's side are you on my nigga?" I asked loudly.

"I'm just fucking witchu man! I know you care for her man. She'll come back."

"That's the goal man, she's my ticket into the entertainment industry and she needs to understand that we had a verbal agreement."

"So what about Suave Rob, how you know he ain't gonna be there?" he asked.

"'Cause 96.3 B96 has been boosting Suave Rob on their channel. He's supposed to be there at the same time Alicia is doing WGCI."

"Aww shit, you been doing your homework."

"I told you I know what I'm doing. I'll catch her as she leaves the station, she ain't gonna have a choice but to talk to me."

"Yeah, 'cause she ain't gonna have her bodyguard with her." Calvin laughed.

"Exactly. That fool is gonna be busy with his own shit." This was my opportunity to speak with Alicia without Shaunice or Suave Rob.

"Ok, I see you now." Calvin nodded in agreement as we drove over to the station.

I got a chance to visit the radio station a few times when I was doing the footwork of getting Alicia known; I would hit up the radio station trying to get them to just listen to her music. Upon my many visits, I noticed that the talent or visitors of the station would come in a special entrance which was located at the back of the building. The front of the building was usually offices of people who are actually running the station, but the actual radio studio is located in the middle of the building on the second floor, nearest the back of the building.

Even though the building had a lot of entrances and exits, they normally had the guests of the show enter through the back to avoid fans depending on the personality that is showing up for the show. We were able to park in the back; a few of my boys worked the security gate and gave me access through the employee entrance.

I parked away from the building; I didn't want Alicia to notice my car, I wanted to catch her by surprise. It was late in the evening for her to be doing an interview, I didn't know what was going on with CFE scheduling their talent so late in the day when most people aren't listening that much to the radio.

"Man, you think she's gonna listen to you?"

"She'll listen. She still likes me."

"You sure? I mean," Calvin said, raising his eyebrows. "You said Suave Rob was at her crib. I'm just saying."

I got frustrated. "You saying too much!" Calvin just rolled his eyes and scoffed.

"That's yo' deal man. She ain't gonna try to hear, nothing yo' ass is spittin.'"

"Oh, she'll hear it." I said stepping out the car at the sight of Alicia walking slowly out of the door.

She was looking at her phone and slowly stepping down the stairs as I swiftly ran through the parked cars, keeping my eyes on her. She stopped on the last stair, still looking at her phone; I took the opportunity to make my way to the row of cars directly in front of her. She raised the phone to her ear and started smiling. I walked slowly over to her, glancing around to see if anyone else was present in the parking lot.

We were alone and she was clueless as I began crossing the parking lot towards her. Just before I reached her, she glanced my way. I kept walking over, I saw her look at me trying to figure out if it was me or not. As I briskly walked towards her, she looked surprised as she realized it was me.

"Maurice?!" She yelled as I stepped to her, slapping the

shit out of her. Her phone dropped from her hand as she stumbled in confusion.

"Bitch, what the fuck!" She shouted charging at me. I swung again and slapped the shit out of her again, striking her enough to make her fall.

"Bitch, you fucking with the wrong Nigga!" I said, standing over her as she held her face. "We ain't done yet. This ain't over Alicia. You owe me! You ain't getting rid of me. Tell dat nigga to watch his back!"

"Fuck you Maurice!" Alicia said, getting up off the ground. I rushed her quickly and grabbed her neck. She was swinging and clawing me, trying to reach my face.

"Bitch, I could end you right now!" I said squeezing her neck, she was struggling to breathe when Calvin showed up and grabbed my arm.

Anger pulsated through my hands, the more I stared at her the more I remembered how she just left me out there to fend for myself after all I've done for her. Alicia was clawing my hands and hitting my arms but I zoned out, I was thinking about her fucking Suave Rob which made me even more upset.

"Nigga! You can't beat the fuck out the bitch out here in the open! Dude, we need to bounce, right now!" He said, trying to pull my hand from around her throat. "You is doing too much right now, fool." Calvin shouted. A few people started exiting the building and I instantly let Alicia go. She collapsed on the steps and we took off.

Calvin and I ran through the parking lot and over to the car. We started it up and left out the same entrance we entered located at the back of the parking lot. On the way out,

I noticed people had stopped near Alicia, seeing if she was okay. I knew she had gotten the hint that I was not fucking around anymore.

"Nigga," Calvin said trying to put on his seat belt as I was driving fast as hell through the streets. "What was you tryna do? Kill her?"

"I wanted to," I responded. "But I didn't. I just wanted her to see that what she did was wrong."

"I feel you man, but you need to think it through first,"

"What you mean?" I said stopping abruptly at a red light; I scared a person crossing the street as the front of my car was a bit in the crosswalk.

"You need to get her alone, where nobody knows y'all there and they ain't just gonna walk up on you." he mentioned. He was right, I needed to catch her when she least expected it.

Alicia

I couldn't believe what happened. I was in a fucking daze. It was like I was dreaming and I really wanted to wake up. A woman was standing over me; I looked at her and saw her mouth moving but I didn't hear the words coming out. I licked my lip and felt a liquid with a copper taste, *this motherfucker busted my lip!* Finally, I heard the woman talking softly to me as I tried to get up.

"Sweetheart, do you want me to call the police?" She asked in a sweet tone as she helped me up. I looked around and saw another woman holding my hand bag and phone.

Shit! I was on the phone with Roberto when Maurice slapped the shit out of me. Roberto is going to be so pissed,I'm sure he's already on his way to find me. The woman handed me my handbag and phone as I heard the growl of Roberto's motorcycle coming down the street. There was a man holding my arm along with the first woman who was talking to me, holding my other arm. I walked over and sat on the steps, waiting while I heard the rumble from Roberto's motorcycle get closer and closer. Suddenly, he came racing into the parking lot, barely stopping the bike before jumping off and running over to me.

"Alicia," he said, jogging over to me. "Where is he?" He said angrily.

"The guy just ran off that way," The woman pointed towards the parking lot.

"It was two of them. They jumped in a car and left through the employee entrance." The guy said standing next to the woman.

Roberto looked around the parking lot, pacing back and forth and then came over to me. He kneeled down and looked in my face. I could see the anger on his face along with a look of devastation masked on his face. He carefully touched my face and flinched when winced in pain.

"I'm sorry, Mami," he said softly. I loved when he called me Mami. I could hear his little Spanish accent when he called me by his pet name. "I should have been here with you." He held his lips tight as he fought with his emotions.

"You didn't know. I hadn't heard from that fool in a minute. He caught me by surprise too." I said, tears falling down my face.

Roberto softly caressed my face, wiping away my tears with his thumbs. I looked in his eyes as he looked at me. His eyes began to gloss over and swell up with tears. He inhaled deeply as he held my hands, kissing them as they lay on my lap. He held me close, wrapping his legs around mine.

"It looks like he'll take care of you sweetie." The woman said. "Make sure she gets checked out, because she hit the ground hard."

"Thank you, Ma'am. I'll see to it she's taking care of properly." Roberto said, holding back all but one lone tear drop that streamed down his cheek. He dared not face her directly, he was trying to control his emotions. He turned his head slightly and waved towards her.

I looked at her and waved. "Thank you Ma'am. I'm good. He'll make sure I'm okay." I said looking at Roberto.

I touched his shoulder and he lowered his head again to my lap. The other two individuals slowly walked away leaving me alone with Roberto. He raised his head, sniffling, struggling to speak.

"I'm sorry." He raised his head and looked at me. "This won't happen again. I should have been here."

"It's okay. I'm good." I whispered. My throat was kinda scratchy from Maurice choking me. I thought I was going to die at the hands of this motherfucker.

"We gotta tell Marcus and Franklin." Roberto said standing up; he held out his hand to help me up.

"I know."

I took his hand, he pulled me up and straightened my outfit. He stood in front of me, holding my hands. He laced his fingers with mine, stepping forward and planting a warm kiss on my forehead. I leaned into his lips, bringing me warmth as he wrapped his arms around me, holding me tight.

"I'm sorry again, Mami. I should be your protector and I wasn't there." He kissed the top of my head leaving his lips pressed against me. "It won't happen again." he whispered.

I closed my eyes and pulled him tighter against me. I smelled his faint smell of Axe body wash and Burberry cologne. My body wanted to have him hold me entirely. I hadn't felt secure in a while. He was beating himself up about not being with me, but this was the first time in a long time since we were separated while promoting. There was a schedule mix up between the two stations and both spots got booked at the same time, which caused us to be separated.

"I know." I softly replied.

He stepped back and gazed into my eyes. He tipped my chin up and smiled softly while tracing my bottom lip with his thumb. I gazed into his eyes as they met mine; Butterflies instantly filled my stomach as he lowered his mouth over mine. His lips were electric, sending a jolt deep inside my cavern. His lips were moist and soft as he gave me a small, sweet, wet kiss. We parted, our noses hovering close to each other while our breath mixed between us.

"You're staying with me tonight." He stated. He gave me a look as if it was not up for discussion.

"Ok. But what about clothes?" I asked. He smiled at me as if I wouldn't need any, I swore I could've read his mind.

"Can you tell Shanice to bring you some clothes?" He asked, lacing his fingers with mine. He walked me over to his bike, handing me the headscarf.

"I can, but if you got a t-shirt I can just wear that." I suggested.

"I can see what I can do." He helped me put on the helmet, snapping the clip underneath my chin.

Roberto quickly put on his helmet and jumped on his bike. He started the motorcycle, the rumble of the bike resonated in my body. I held his hand as I swung my leg over the bike and straddled the seat. I closed my legs tightly against his as I wrapped my arms around the front of him, lacing my fingers together. He gave me the usual pat on my hands, signaling he was taking off. I knew he had me, he was determined to make sure I wouldn't have another confrontation with Maurice. I felt safe and secure as he held my hand periodically against his chest while we rode over to his place.

Marcus

I raced to the hospital, disobeying all traffic laws within reason; It wouldn't have been beneficial for us to get involved in an accident on the way there. I pulled up to the emergency room door and ran in looking for help.

"Help! My girl, she's pregnant and she's hurting." I grabbed the first person in scrubs walking past the door.

The person looked at me, seeing the panic in my eyes. "It's okay, let me take a look at her." I could only assume he was a doctor as he seemed to be in complete control.

He followed me out to the passenger side of the car. I opened it and Siedah looked like she was in so much pain, I felt helpless not being able to take her pain away. I didn't know what to do, I just didn't want to lose both of them. My life would be over.

"What's your name?" He said, pressing on her belly. Siedah closed her eyes in pain as he pressed.

"Si..e..dah." She struggled to breathe.

"Ok, Siedah, let's get you into an emergency bay okay?" He said looking around and two orderlies walked out the door. "Guys can you get me a wheelchair quickly, she needs to go in now!"

One guy raced back in and returned with the wheelchair as I helped the doctor get Siedah out of the car.

"Dad, you go park your car then come back in." He said, spinning her around and through the doors. I saw my life roll away in his hands and I felt completely powerless.

Chapter 15 - Such A Thing

Suave Rob

I hadn't told Alicia about my anger. It wasn't like I would lose control and go the fuck off for no reason. But I have a hatred for men that lay their hands on women. I completely understand, a female may get a man upset; there have been times in which some females may even take it a step farther, knowing their guy won't hit them, and will hit him instead, trying to get him to react so she would have a reason to call the police. But even in that type of relationship, a man should walk away. Even if the female is calling him out of his name, he still needs to walk away.

That is one of the characteristics of a Real Man.

I've been in that type of situation before whereas the woman I was dating got upset because I caught her up in her own shit and she wanna turn it around on me. No matter how mad I got, I walked away. That makes me the bigger person in the situation, that makes me the adult in the matter. But it irritates me when a man gets so mad that he hits a woman. I had enough of seeing that growing up. When I was little, my father was a bad drunk as he would want to fight all the time when he got lit. And of course, he took it out on my mother, that was until she got tired of his shit and beat his ass. He was never right after that, my mother gave him a concussion. But one thing did come of it, my father never hit my mother again. In fact, he stopped drinking altogether.

It hurt me to my heart and soul to see Alicia beaten like she was. I normally don't get emotional but seeing her like that, I did. If that motherfucker crosses my path, he might as well wish he was dead. Her beautiful face was bruised and her lip was busted by the powerful strike against her face, but I had her now with me. I held her hand as I pulled into the underground parking lot of Trailhead Apartments near Humboldt Park; the rumble of the bike echoed throughout the lot alerting everyone of my arrival. I backed my bike in my spot and turned it off. I held my hands against Alicia's as she was still holding on, with her head laying against my back. I loved when she held onto me; it was a surreal feeling.

I pulled off my helmet and hung it over my handlebars as Alicia sat up, unfastening her helmet and removing it. She still looked beautiful, her spirit was still there, just broken a little. She glowed as she looked at me, I knew she could feel what I'm sending out; she knows it's real. I took the helmet from her and helped her slide off the bike. I kicked out the stand and got off the bike. She stood looking cute as ever with the head scarf still on her head waiting for me to lead the way. I took her hand, lacing my fingers with her and pulled her along with me to the elevator bay.

She stood next to me, holding my hand quietly as we waited for the elevator to arrive. I turned to her and adjusted the scarf on her head. I stood a few inches above her; she looked adorable looking up at me, her eyes meeting mine. We gazed into each other's eyes which felt like hours, building the sexual tension between us. I looked at her lips slightly parted as she got lost in my gaze; I wanted to take her pain away and make her forget all about him. I didn't want her to have to worry about him ever again. I squeezed her hand and she smiled, bashfully.

The elevator dinged, breaking our connection. We walked into the elevator and I pushed the button to my floor. We arrived at my apartment, I opened the door and let Alicia in first. I flipped on the light and closed the door. My apartment wasn't much, but it was enough for me. It was pretty much an open concept with a bar area pass-through from the living room to the kitchen.

Alicia took off her shoes and walked around the apartment, settling on the big, comfy couch nearest the patio doors. "Your apartment is nice. I wouldn't have guessed you lived here."

"Why not?" I said getting the first aid kit from the hallway closet.

"I guess it's because you ride a bike, I assumed you would have more workshop or motorcycle related decor going on in your place."

I laughed and shook my head. "Naw, I love my bike, don't get me wrong, but I also need a place of peace and a place to be centered, and that is my home."

"I like that. You amaze me." She smiled and gazed at me.

"That's because I'm amazing," I said playfully. She giggled and pursed her lips up.

I opened the first aid kit and sat next to her on the couch. I opened the antiseptic, placed it on a mesh pad and dabbed it on her lip. She watched me as I took care of her wounds.

"Thank you Roberto." She said softly. She held the back of my hand as I dabbed the dried blood off of her lip.

I melted looking at her, she had me wrapped and she didn't even know it. I loved the way she looked at me, she made me feel special and I hadn't had that feeling in a long time. I wanted someone who needed me along and wanted to be with me genuinely. I wanted to make her mine since I laid eyes on her, I just needed her to trust me with her heart.

"You're welcome, Mami." I wiped her face and winced seeing the bruises; he literally left his hand print across one side of her face. Her left eye looked as if it was part of the blow he struck against her face as it was bloodshot on one side of it.

She held my hand and traced my fingers with hers as she sat forward. I smiled at her, she blushed making me fall for her even more. I felt my heartbeat pound in my chest as I tried to contain myself and be a gentleman. She held my hand up to her face as she laid her cheek in the cup of my hand. She closed her eyes, enveloping my touch against her face. Her caramel skin glowed as she looked at me with her eyes so bright. I slid my hand back cupping the back of her head pulling her lips to mine.

I kissed her slowly, feeling her exhale as I inhaled; her lips were soft and moist and luscious. I could hear her moan softly as I explored her mouth. She tasted sweet just as I figured she would. We parted slowly with soft kisses, me gently holding her face and giving her gentle kisses upon her lips. I opened my eyes to hers staring back at me. We had a bashful moment, got a bit embarrassed and started laughing.

"Um, let me get that shirt for you to wear."I said, leaning back from her. I needed some space as my soldier was awake and trying to figure out who the new person was waking him up.

"Yeah, I'll need that." She smiled and sat back on the couch.

"You want something to drink or eat? Are you hungry?" I asked, walking to my bedroom right off from the living room.

"I could use both." She answered.

"Cool, let's order some food that way after you take your shower the food should be here." I yelled from the bedroom. I returned with a Golden State Warriors jersey and a brand new pair of boxer briefs. "I hope these will do." I said holding it in front of Alicia.

"I'm sure they'll work." Alicia said looking at the articles of clothing. "How about a towel?"

"Towels are in the bathroom in the cabinet. Everything else is located in the bathroom too. Oh, and shower caps are in the drawer."

"Damn you got everything, huh?"

"I like to be prepared." I said smiling.

"I bet you do." She said walking off to the shower.

Alicia

"Order anything you want, I'm sure it'll be good." I yelled out to Roberto as I closed the door to the bathroom. It was surreal as I looked around, still thinking about the lingering kiss he planted on my lips.

He kissed me! I was floating.

"Ok." I heard his muffled answer.

Here I was, taking a shower at Roberto's place! He had come to my rescue once again, making me realize he wanted to make an effort to be there for me no matter what. I'm sure he had told me before, but if it was not for him coming to scoop me up on the bike before, this solidified it for me for sure. He wasn't on time to catch Maurice in the act, but it wasn't his fault. Both of us were out there promoting ourselves and it was just a mix up in scheduling. Roberto came as soon as he could knowing he must have been worried the entire way after hearing me scream.

The shower felt good against my skin as I had the water run down my back, filling my body with a warm sensation. I lifted my face to the shower stream, the water stung as it sprayed on my face. I'm sure my face was swollen and bruised, which didn't help my already chubby cheeks.

I smiled and touched my lips, thinking about our first kiss in the parking lot. I closed my eyes remembering the way he looked at me as he kissed me. I could tell he cared for me just by the look he had in his eyes when he saw me all bruised and battered.

After my shower, I dressed in the jersey and a pair of his boxer briefs, which astoundingly fit rather well. I was nice and comfy, sans a bra when I walked out of the bathroom. Roberto was just closing the door from grabbing the delivery. He placed the food down on the huge cocktail table in the middle of the living room.

He brought over two small chairs that had no legs, just the seat and back of the chair. He left again and brought back four Coronas and a container of sliced limes. He smiled as he pulled out a small chair for me to sit.

"These are Japanese chairs," He said pointing to them. "You won't fall back, so no worries. But it's easier to reach all the food on the table while sitting on the floor." I smiled and sat down on the floor, scooting onto the chair.

"So you like Japanese culture? I noticed a few paintings of what look like Japanese letters on your wall." I asked.

"I do, I admire all cultures honestly." He said, sitting down on the chair and opening the containers. "And this food represents my Puerto Rican heritage, so I hope you enjoy it."

"Oooo, I'm excited." I said looking at all of the food on the table. "What place is this from?"

"El Mofonguito. It's authentic Puerto Rican cuisine. Just like my Abuela (grandmother) used to make." He said, swiping a piece of beef from one of the containers and holding it to my mouth for me to taste. I opened my mouth and he placed it on my tongue; the meat was so tender and delicious. It was as if it melted in my mouth and it was cooked to perfection.

"Mmmmm! That is delicious." Roberto smiled at my appreciation of his selections.

"I'm glad you love it, let me set your plate up with a bit of everything and you tell me what you think."

"Sure." I said looking at him as he enjoyed fixing my plate for me to eat. He placed a loaded plate in front of me, opened a Corona, slid a few limes in the bottle and placed it next to my plate.

I watched and waited until he fixed his plate before I ate my food. I wanted to thank the Lord for the meal and the day I had. He placed his plate down on the table and looked at me, a bit confused.

"Is everything okay?" He asked, wondering why I wasn't eating yet.

"Everything is fine, I just like to pray before I eat. Do you mind?"

"Not at all." He agreed. I held out my hands and he took hold of them, closing his eyes and bowing his head. I was impressed, he might not practice his faith all the time, but he was fully aware of assuming the position.

"Thank you Father for this food we are about to eat, for the nourishment of our bodies. And thank you Lord for Roberto, I appreciate him more than he knows. Amen."

"Amen." Roberto smiled and opened his eyes. "You know, you're remarkable. I've never met anyone like you."

"That's because God broke the mold when he made me." I smiled and picked up what looked like a fried, mashed banana.

"That He did." He said responding to my sassiness. "And that's tostones, it's fried plantain."

"Okay, interesting. Never had it before, but everything looks so good, I'm about to smash this."

"Good, eat up." He said, stabbing his fork into his plate of food.

Chapter 16 - You Got Me

Alicia

Dinner was amazing, Roberto had picked a great selection of food from carne frita (fried pork), pastelillos de pollo (chicken patties) , pincho (pork on a stick), sorullo (corn fritter cheese), maduros (sweet plantains), tostones (fried plantains) and pollo sopa (chicken soup). I was so full , I wasn't sure if I would be able to get off the damn floor!

I helped clear the table as Roberto collected all of the empty takeaway containers to throw away. I sat on the couch flipping through channels waiting for him to tell me where I was sleeping. I figured the couch would be fine, it looked as if it was big enough for two people to sleep comfortably with the chaise on one side.

Roberto came from the hallway and placed bedding on the end of the couch along with a pillow.

"I'll be back, I'm going to run the trash down to the bin." He said holding a huge bag of trash.

"Sure, I ain't going nowhere." I said smiling. He smiled, winked at me and left to dump the trash.

I helped myself to the bedding and spread out the flat sheet over the chaise part of the couch, threw down the pillow, sat down and covered myself with the comforter. I was engrossed watching American Idol and didn't realize Roberto had returned.

"Mami?" he said standing in my view of the television to get my attention.

""Huh?"

"I didn't put this out here for you." He said pointing to the bedding.

"What do you mean?" I was so confused.

"I didn't put this out here for you. You're not sleeping out here."

"Oh, well where am I sleeping?" I asked as I wondered who he laid the bedding out for. He smiled, walked over and held out his hand for me to take.

I took his hand and he pulled me off of the couch behind him and across the living room to his bedroom.

"You are going to sleep in here, in my bed." He said, looking at me. He was being so sweet, offering his room for me to sleep, but I didn't want to impose and make the man leave his own bed.

"But where are you gonna sleep?"

"On the couch."

"I can't let you do that. I'll be fine on the couch."

"I'm not allowing you to sleep on the couch." He stated. He was adamant about me not sleeping on the couch.

"But I can't just let you sleep on the couch, this bed is big enough for both of us." I said looking at him, hoping he would take the hint that I was giving. He looked at me, blushed and turned away.

"Naw, I'm good. You can have the bed." I was disappointed.

"Why? You can sleep with me in your bed, it's big enough. I don't bite, I swear." I said playfully tickling him.

He chuckled and smiled at me.

"Yeah, I know, but," He hesitated. He gazed at me and caressed my face.

"But what?" I said, stepping towards him. I wanted a real reason why he didn't want to sleep in the bed with me. I'm sure he was just trying to be a gentleman but I was the one offering.

"Mami, it's not you I'm worried about." He softly whispered. Roberto had a look in his eyes; he looked as if he wanted to completely devour me. He licked and bit his bottom lip, shaking his head and smiling.

"What are you worried about?" I asked, wishing he would reconsider.

"I'm worried, I won't be able to keep my hands off of you." He stepped to me. I held his waist as he smoothed back my hair from my face.

"What if I don't want you to keep your hands off of me?" I said, smiling impishly. He raised his eyebrows and smiled.

"Mami, do you know what you're saying?"

"Yes, I only had two beers. I'm not intoxicated." I answered. He smiled looking longingly into my eyes.

I was excited to be able to be wrapped in his arms, feeling his skin against mine. My secret garden quivered at the thought of the pleasure he would deliver to my body. Roberto tipped my chin up, gazing into my eyes one at a time. I could feel his breath softly move across my mouth as he lowered his mouth. I closed my eyes as I felt his lips press against mine. He inhaled deeply, cupping my face in his hands, pulling me closer to him.

I slowly slipped my hands underneath his wife beater,

gliding my fingers across his well sculpted chest, across his nipples and around to the small of his back. My light touches across his skin made him slowly moan as his tongue danced with mine. I grabbed the end of his shirt and pulled it up, indicating to him that I wanted this article of clothing removed from his body.

He paused from kissing me and removed his shirt. He body was so fucking amazing. His honey butter skin tone perfectly accented mine as I ran my fingers across his chest while he held my hand. He watched me drink him in as he directed my hand across his satin skin. I blushed and he snickered; we acted like teenagers about to have sex for the first time.

"You sure, Mami?" Roberto whispered, holding my hand against his chest. He wanted to make sure before he crossed the imaginary line. He wanted reassurance that what he was about to do was fully accepted.

I looked at my favorite part on a man; On Roberto - it was fucking gorgeous. I don't know why, but this part of a man, turns me on so fucking much. It's the man's pelvis cut, the area just under the stomach on both sides, just above the hip. This part is so sexy to me on a man and when it's on a well sculpted body, I just want to lick it.

Call me crazy, but it makes my vajayjay shudder at just the thought. Everyone has quirks, I just own up to my shit. I was about to lose it when he lowered my hand to that area. I touched the other side of him and ran my fore finger tracing the muscle lightly. He flinched and giggled a bit; I knew it was a ticklish spot, it normally is for everyone. I heard him blow out air through his nostrils when I touched him again as he smiled.

I glanced up to meet his eyes. He was still smiling, a small hidden dimple showed itself nearest the corner of his mouth making him even sexier. His hazel brown eyes danced with mine as I watched him slowly lick his lips while he traced my lip slowly with the tip of his thumb. A year ago, no one couldn't have told me that this was part of my plan. He wasn't even seen in my cards until he walked into my life the day I let that idiot go. I leaned forward and planted a soft kiss upon his chest.

He stared at me wantonly. "Yes, Papi. I'm sure." His eyes widened as he inhaled. His mouth dropped open as I gazed directly into his eyes.

Now I might be a hefty girl, full of voluptuousness in all the right places, but this motherfucker bent down and picked me up with the quickness and carried all of me, with my legs wrapped around his waist, placing me on the bed with no struggle at all. His platform bed had a brown leather cushioned headboard attached with huge fluffy pillows and a soft white comforter. I watched Roberto close the door and lowered the light switch, setting the ambiance in the room. The entire room was white with a light yellow glow from the lights running along the ceiling. He switched on his soundbar, stepped out of his basketball shorts and walked slowly towards the bed in his sexy ass boxer briefs. Kehlani started singing *Everything* from across the room. It was the *Everything* for me too.

Roberto sat on the edge of the bed, facing me. Our legs were entangled on the bed as he pulled a few strands of my hair through his fingers. I watched him as he crossed his legs over mine moving closer to me, I could feel the warmth growing between us. He was going to take his time with me, Roberto was most definitely *Suave*.

"You are so beautiful, Mami." Roberto softly slid his fingers across my thighs, tilting his head slightly.

"Thank you," I said looking at him. "Papi." Roberto smiled. He leaned over, grabbing the end of the jersey pulling it up over my head revealing my twins in all of their glory.

I felt a chill grace my body, chill bumps ran across my arms up to my shoulders. My nipples grew instantly hard; Roberto pulled the cover up and moved into the bed next to me. He laid down with his arm extended across both pillows.

"Ven aquí Mami.*(Come here Mami).*" Hearing Roberto speak in his native tongue made my shit instantly squish. I looked at him waiting patiently for me to comply. " Por favor no me hagas esperar. *(Please don't make me wait).*" he pouted.

"What?" I asked, not understanding one word. I heard *aquí* and I know that means *'here'* but that's it. I was fucking stuck just on hearing him speak Spanish. The words rolled right off of his tongue and sang to my uterus. I was so fucking horny, I just wanted to sit directly on his face.

"Por favor, no me hagas rogar, te deseo. *(Please don't make me beg, I want you).*"

I shook my head, "I don't understand, but is sounds good as fuck." He waved me to come over.

"Come here, Mami. Ven aquí Mami." He repeated as I moved my body closer to his. I pulled the cover up to my chest as he turned to the side watching me getting cozy next to him. I felt my girls lay against his chest, warming instantly.

"What else did you say?" I asked, laying my head on his arm. He smiled as he smoothed my hair behind my ear.

"I said, Por favor no me hagas esperar. Please don't make me wait." He repeated. I grinned, his accent was so fucking sexy along with his velvety low tenor voice, he could read the damn phone book and I would get fucking hot.

"What else did you say?" I said propping myself up on my elbow, leaning in and kissing him on his chest.

He inhaled deeply as he wrapped his arm around my waist, grabbing a handful of my ass cheek. He squeezed it, moaned while I steadily kissed up his neck; he adjusted his soldier in his briefs as it had grown tremendously. He grabbed my thigh and pulled my leg across his; I could feel his manhood pulsate underneath my garden. He grinded himself against the briefs I wore, making them stick to my wet fleshy folds. I creamed the moment he told me to come to him.

"Por favor, no me hagas rogar, te deseo. Please don't make me beg, I want you." He whispered gazing at me, our faces millimeters away from each other, I felt his hot breath enter my mouth as I inhaled.

"Oh." I whispered looking at his lips as he licked them again.

"Yeah." Roberto replied. I nodded and he instantly kissed me so passionately, I moaned as he broke away and kissed along my neck and across my collarbone.

I threw my head back and closed my eyes as I felt my body succumb to the pleasures this man was giving my body. Chills crossed my body, and my nipples grew harder as he had taken both of them and proceeded to suck on them simultaneously.

"Aaaaa...Mmmm," I moaned softly. I gushed between my legs as I felt my nectar oozing between my petals as he rubbed his member hard against them through the briefs. I knew he felt the wetness, there was no denying.

Electric jolts pulsated throughout my body, making me shudder as I anticipated each touch and feel of him. I wrapped my leg around him and beckoned him to lay on me, he obliged with ease as I opened my legs allowing him to lay between my thickness. He kissed me deeply as he held my hips, grinding his rock hard dick against my mound.

"Mami," Roberto whispered my name between kisses.

"Yes?" He stopped and looked at me. I watched his eyes dart back and forth from one eye to the next. His eyes were beautiful, I would get lost each time I took a deep dive into them.

"Quiero que seas solo mia." I looked at him, listening to his words as he softly touched my cheek with the back of his fingers. "I want you to be mine only." He said hoping I'd say yes.

He had me, no questions asked.

"I'm yours Papi, all yours." I responded slowly. He kissed me deeply and passionately, filling my entire body with a desire that burned for him throughout. This was like nothing I had ever felt before.

"Un momento por favor." He pulled away from me and quickly jumped out of bed; He held up his finger as if asking me to wait while he walked over to the dresser across from the bed.

He pulled out what looked like gold medallions attached to each other and closed the drawer. He stripped down, pulling off his briefs showing me his well toned ass. His ass cheeks were perfectly round looking like a small teardrop. He turned around, with what I realized were magnum condoms hanging from his mouth; And by the look at his member, he needed every inch of a magnum.

Roberto came to the edge of the bed, flipping back the comforter exposing my semi-nakedness underneath. He leaned down, taking hold of my briefs, looping his thumbs around the edge, pulling them down. I raised my ass to assist him; I watched as he slowly removed the briefs and threw them on the floor. He watched me as I watched him open one of three condoms and roll it on his thick, meaty shaft. He rolled it all the way to the base of his member, almost running out of latex.

"¿Estás lista para mi, Mami?" he asked and smiled. He knew I didn't understand but loved to hear him speak. "Are you ready for me Mami?" Roberto asked again.

"Oh, Si Papi." I answered. I knew he loved when I called him Papi, he always had a reaction. He smiled hard and gently crawled back into position, laying on top of me.

He kissed me, sucking my tongue into his mouth, driving me crazy as I wiggled beneath his weight. I could feel him relaxing as his body felt heavy as he laid across me, I caressed his head, raking my fingers across his wavy low cut fade as he laid on me. He kissed down my neck and across my chest, giving attention to my twins individually. Roberto's kisses felt so soft and meaningful as he lightly ran his fingers along my arms to my hand, lacing his fingers with mine.

Roberto moved south, kissing me around my belly, then hovering just above my mound. I watched him between my legs; I felt his hot breath blow across my vajayjay. He released my hands and grabbed a hold of my ankles, spreading them apart, revealing my secret garden. He buried his face against my mound, licking softly across my fleshy folds. I closed my eyes enjoying him licking my slickness, but I wanted to watch him as well.

"Mmmmm...." I moaned softly.

I opened my eyes and lifted myself up to my elbows to see him enjoy his meal. Roberto's head looked like a sun setting between two thick, mountainous thighs. He watched me watch him as he flicked his tongue quickly across my bean, filling my body with electrodes arching my back. I dropped my head back when he began sucking my engorged clit between his lips. I could hear him lapping my nectar as he closed his eyes and pressed his mouth against my wet pussy. I was ready to feel him, as my body permeated with a fiery desire.

"Aaaaa....ooooo that feels so good." I softly spoke.

Roberto slowed from licking my juiciness, kissing me along my thighs; his face glistened with my wetness as he kissed along my body upon his return. I could taste my nectar when he kissed me longingly; I felt him position his manhood - the tip of his head touching my cavern door. He wrapped my legs around his waist, sucking my tongue into his mouth as he pushed himself through my doorway and into my honey pot.

"UUUuuuuhhhhh!" We both moaned loudly simultaneously. I held his waist as he pushed himself deep inside me, stretching my walls and filling me completely to the end.

"Mmmmm, you feel so good Mami." He said as laid atop me kissing me slowly.

"You do too." I whispered between kisses. I crossed my ankles behind the small of his back as he slowly started pumping in and out of my spot.

"Mmmm..." A deep groan echoed from him with each slow stroke of his gyrating hips. He relaxed a bit more, holding himself up above me on his elbows as he buried his face between my neck and shoulder.

He felt so good inside me, I felt his thick shaft throb within my satin walls. He wasn't in a rush, I felt like he wanted to savor this moment of us making love for the first time. He was taking his time, enjoying every bit of ecstasy pulsating between us.

"Am I too slow for you Mami?" He whispered in my ear as he grinded his pelvis against mine, pushing him deeper inside.

"Aaaaaaa," I moaned with pleasure. "No, not at all."

"Good. I don't want to just *fuck* you," He said stopping for a moment looking me directly in the eyes. "I want to make *love* to you."

"Yes, make love to me." I said breathlessly.

He moved his mouth over mine, I bit his bottom lip as he kissed me. He smiled a small smile and rubbed the tip of his nose against mine. I gazed into his eyes and immediately felt a warm feeling take over my body, I was falling for him. He was truly Suave Rob.

I heard Saint Joshua singing *Devil's in the Detail,* from the soundbar. I had to agree, Roberto was definitely paying attention to the details as he was determined to take his time. He made sure to please every part of my body as a man should while he made love to me all night long. Roberto made me feel wanted, needed and loved. There was no comparison to the passion between us as we created a connection that felt unbreakable. He made me feel like I could love again.

Chapter 17 - Nothing Feels Better

Suave Rob

Waking up with Alicia in my arms gave me the most remarkable feeling, one that I could definitely get used to. Last night, Alicia and I crossed that line; we made love and it was magical. We could have just fucked each other's brains out but our connection was special, I didn't want to just fuck her the first time out. I'm sure I'll get the chance to find out how wild she can get in the bed, but for our very first time being intimate with each other, I wanted it to have a purpose and meaning and it be meaningful for both of us.

She submitted herself to me and I to her while I took my time in exploring every part of her ravishing body, pleasing her fully to the utmost of my delight and hers. I made sure she was absolutely satisfied and more. She was still sleeping peacefully with her head on my arm, her head wrapped in the very same scarf she used for the helmet. I smiled as I watched her breathing; she was amazing and addictive. She paid attention to detail as she pleased me fully as well. I can say I am absolutely satisfied and most likely stuck on her.

We also became a couple. I didn't want her to have to worry about being with another, as I plan to be her one and only as well as her last. She pulled me into her soul as a smoker would pull on a cigarette; deeply and filling up completely. I had no intention of breaking her heart as I didn't want mine broken as well.

Alicia moved a bit as I touched her cheek with the back of my hand, her skin was so soft and supple, I could hold onto her forever. She accepted me 100% and I will do everything I need to do to prove to her that I'm in this for the long run. I kissed her forehead, she hummed at the gesture as she awakened to my smile.

"Morning Beautiful," I said looking into her barely opened eyes. Our bodies were still naked and entangled as we were completely exhausted after our lovemaking. I loved the dimples in her cheeks, she yawned quietly covering her mouth triggering me to yawn as well.

"Morning," She threw her arm up while she stretched, arching her back looking heavenly. "Mhhmm, what time is it?" She said scooting closer and wrapping her arm around my waist, her leg across the top of my hip and burying her face into my chest.

"It's about 7:15 in the morning," I kissed her gently on the top of her head. "Are you hungry, Mami?" I spoke softly, rubbing her up and down her back from her shoulders to her round, juicy ass. That's what really drew me to Alicia, it was her ass. I admit it, I'm an ass man and she has a lotta ass. I loved the way she backed that ass up last night, it was everything I could have imagined and more.

"Mhmmm, too early. Why are you always trying to feed me?" Her muffled question echoed between us.

"So you can keep that ass." I said palming it with my hands, kissing her on her forehead. She raised her pouting lips up, I smiled and kissed her. She set my heart on fire.

"Oh, it was the ass that did it for you, huh?"

"Si Mami, tienes culo para días." I mumbled and kissed her again.

"Uhn-uhn, what'd you say?" She giggled, making me laugh.

"I said, you got ass for days Mami." I chuckled and kissed her again.

She kept her eyes closed as I kissed the tip of her nose, her smile widened as kissed her eyelids, then her stomach growled loud as hell.

"Damn! You are hungry." I playfully patted her ass. She sucked her teeth and playfully pushed me away. She turned around, placing her ass right against my sleeping member - apparently she wanted him to wake up. "Aye yo, you putting your ass this way is gonna start something." I mentioned. She quickly turned around and faced me again.

"Food first, then." Alicia said into my neck as she nuzzled her head underneath mine.

She was a perfect fit for me, I could wrap my arms around her and embrace her fluffiness, I loved it. Her curves gave her a uniqueness that many women don't have. Her curves create a sexiness that I can't get enough of as I would to melt into her if I thought it would be possible. I held her close to me, feeling the body heat between us before leaving the bed to make breakfast.

The phone rang loudly on the dresser across the room. I dared not move just to answer the phone at that moment, I wanted to stay with her as long as I could. I allowed the call to go to voicemail and heard the notification that one was left. However, the phone rang again. I let the voicemail pick it up again, yet this time, no message was left. Instead, the person immediately called back.

"I think someone is trying to get a hold of you." Alicia said, rolling over onto her back.

"I agree." I kissed her lips quickly and got out of the bed grabbing my briefs as I walked over to my phone. It was Franklin calling.

"Hello?"

"Hey Rob, listen, they are keeping Siedah at the hospital. Something to do with the baby, they are trying to make sure she and Lil' Man are alright."

"Oh ok, understood. Thanks for filling me in."

"Yeah, so Marcus and Siedah won't be at the studio today. In the meantime, do you know where Alicia is? We've been calling her and she hasn't answered her phone." I looked at Alicia who had just sat up in the middle of the bed, holding the cover over her breasts. She looked cute as fuck laying in my bed.

"Oh Um, she's with me." I hesitate to admit Alicia was with me at such an early time in the morning.

"Oh, okay."

"Um yeah, some shit happened yesterday," I hesitated to speak, I didn't want to relive it all but Franklin had a right to know.

"What happened?" Franklin sounded concerned.

"That motherfucker got a hold of Alicia, man. He attacked her."

"He attacked her!" Franklin yelled. "How? Weren't you with her?"

"Usually I am, but yesterday there was a mix-up in the times for the interviews so we had to split up because they were at the same time at two different stations."

"Oh shit. Is she okay? Where is that motherfucker now?"

"She's okay, I had her stay with me last night, given the fact that he knows where she lives."

"Smart. Keep an eye on her. I see we are gonna have to deal with this bitch ass nigga." Franklin sounded irritated.

"Yeah pretty much."

"Do y'all have any shows to do today?" He asked. I checked our schedule quickly on my phone and we actually had the day off. That made me feel even better that I would be able to spend the entire day with Alicia.

"Naw, we got a day off today."

"Well good. I'll keep y'all posted about Siedah if anything changes."

"A'ight, Thanks Bruh."

"A'ight, holla." And just like that, Franklin was gone.

I turned and walked back over and sat down on the edge of the bed. Alicia scooted closer to me; I leaned forward, rubbing the tip of my nose with hers. She was making me fall hard, I had never felt this way with anyone - not this soon. It made me feel scared and excited at the same time which made me want her even more. She made a fire burn deep inside my soul that I didn't want to be without her.

"That was Franklin. They are keeping Siedah to make sure her and the baby are okay."

"Oh good, I hope everything turns out okay."

"I also told him about what happened between you and that bitch ass nigga." I blurted.

"Yesterday was a fucking mess." She sadly said, grabbing my hand.

"Well, yesterday *was* messy, but something good came out of it, you think?" I laced my fingers with hers and she smiled.

"Yep, something perfect." She blushed. I cupped her face and kissed her softly.

"Absolutamente perfecto." I leaned my forehead against hers, still cupping her face. Her stomach growled loudly again.

"My bad," she giggled.

"It's all good, Mami. I'm about to go cook some breakfast." I said kissing her forehead raising up off of the bed.

"Okay."

"Hey, also, I found out that Marcus and Siedah aren't going to be in the studio today and we have the day off today, so do you want to hang out with me?" I asked hoping she would.

"Hang out here?" She said pointing down on the bed.

"Yeah, you okay with that?"

"Yes, I'm more than okay with that."

"Cool, let me get some food for you Mami. Mi casa es tu casa." I smiled and she smiled back.

"I'll call Shaunice to bring me some clothes over here, if you don't mind."

"I don't mind at all as long as you stay here." I replied.

"I'm not going anywhere." She ginned. I nodded and left

the room.

Alicia

I couldn't wait to call Shaunice and tell her about the shit that I had gone through since Marcus and Siedah left the studio. Throwing the comforter off I realized I needed to get clothes first as I was totally naked. Everything seemed surreal to me as I looked around his room looking for the garments I had on prior to the events that had taken place. Roberto and I took our friendship to an entirely different level; we made love and it was phenomenal!

I was walking on air as I stepped out the bed grabbing the briefs and the jersey that had somehow landed on the opposite side of the room. Roberto made love to me like no other man has ever done; this motherfucker got me hooked. He asked me to be his and only his, I have absolutely no problem with that. He took his time with me and made sure I was fully satisfied - *and I was*. I smiled and blushed as I looked at the bed; moments in time flashed in my memory as I saw what we did and how we did and how we looked doing it.

I walked out to the living room to grab my phone out of my bag. Roberto was in the kitchen wearing earbuds, singing and cooking in just his briefs, with his fine ass. His back was turned towards the living room therefore he had no idea I had entered the room. I grabbed my phone, shuffled back to the bedroom, sat on the bed and dialed Shaunice.

"Where in the hell have you been? I've been calling you for the longest. I'm gonna have you share your location with me from now on."

"I know I've been missing in action,"

"Yes," she interrupted. "Yes you have. Maurice has been trying to get a hold of me, for what I don't know, I won't answer his calls, it seems like he's trying to find you for some reason."

"Fuck that motherfucker. He jumped me yesterday, outside the radio station." I said growling.

"What the fuck?! Are you fucking serious?" She snapped.

"Girl, I *wish* I was lying."

"That motherfucker done put a target on his damn head." She said with such anger in her voice.

"I know right. Roberto told Franklin so CFE knows." I said, wincing because I didn't tell her I was with Roberto yet.

"Well that's good. Wait, how did Roberto know? He was with you?"

"Now Bitch, you now betta than that. You think if Roberto would be there, Maurice would have attacked me?"

"You right. But how did Roberto tell Franklin?" she asked.

"'Cause I was on the phone with him when it happened. I had just finished the show and called him to see if he could come and scoop me."

"Well damn. And all this happened yesterday?"

"Yup."

"Well I can only assume, you are alright because I would hope yo' ass would have called me a lot sooner than this." Shaunice said sarcastically.

"Yes, I would have, but I'm okay."

"So you were with Suave Rob last night?"

"Yes."

"Y'all do it?" I was waiting for her to ask that question. She always does. It's our thing, we're stupid but it's us.

"Yes. Gurl, oh my goodness."

"I knew it. He looked like he could take care of the bizniz." She said laughing. I could just see her dancing in her apartment with her tongue hanging out, rotating her hips like she normally does when we talk this way with each other.

"Well I'm glad y'all have cleared the air. It's about time."

"Yeah I know. He asked me to be his girl."

"Shut the fuck up?! Well damn, I'm proud of you bitch, that's what I'm talkin' 'bout." She chuckled proudly. She made me smile because she always said he was a good guy and to give him a chance. I'm glad I listened this time.

"Yeah, so I need you to do me a solid."

"Whatup?" She answered. "You need me to shoot Maurice in the balls?"

"As much as that sounds interesting, no. I need you to go to my place and grab me some clothes."

"Damn it's like that? I should have known. Okay, I'll call you when I get to your place. Send me his address."

"How'd you know I was still at his place?" I asked.

"Why would you not be?" She responded sarcastically?"

"Shut up." Shanice snickered on the other line.

"A'ight girl. I'll call you when I get to your place."

"A'ight, holla." We disconnected.

Chapter 18 - Happy Thoughts

Suave Rob

Alicia came out to the kitchen while I cooked, looking bootylicious in my Golden State jersey. That ass has gotten me mesmerized. I smiled as she rounded the corner pulling out my earbuds.

"I would've come and brought it to you Mami," I wrapped my arms around her as she embraced me in hers.

It was like we were long lost lovers who had found each other again. Once I was given permission to place my hands upon her, I was addicted. I told her in advance, I knew I would have no control. I couldn't and didn't want to keep my hands off of her. She looked up to me, laying her chin on my chest.

"Do you need help?" she asked, looking cute as ever.

"You wanna help?" She nodded. "Sure Mami, you can cook the eggs."

"Ok, I gotchu. Do you like cheese in your eggs?"

"Yes, I knew I liked you." I walked over and kissed her on her forehead and returned to my chorizo in the skillet.

"Well I'm glad you did. You're the first guy who has ever cooked for me."

"Really? Oh man, baby I gotchu," She placed the eggs on the counter as I came up behind her and wrapped myself around her ass. "I gotta make sure you keep this right here." I said as I grinded up against her.

"Now you gonna start something," she said, moving her ass back against me. I laughed and patted her ass walking back to the skillet.

"Food first, we need energy."

"Besides, we have all day. I'm enjoying myself with you." I turned and looked at her. She was already special to me, I'm sure she felt it.

"I'm glad Mami. Did you get a hold of Shaunice?" I removed the chorizo from the skillet and finished the fried potatoes.

"Yeah I did," She said, scrambling the eggs and adding seasonings. I knew she could cook, a woman with her voluptuousness should know how to cook, not just eat. She was toned in all the right places, just thick and beautiful. I absolutely loved it. "She's gonna call me when she gets to my apartment."

"Oh good."

"She told me that he has been calling her but she hasn't been answering him. She thinks he's looking for me." My anger started to build quickly just by her mentioning the likes of him.

"She ain't gonna tell him where you are, is she? I mean, I know she's your girl and all but,"

"I know, calm down," Alicia interrupted. "Don't worry, she is definitely not going to tell him anything. She hates him. She asked me if I wanted her to shoot him in the balls."

"I like her."

"See!" She said pointing at me and smiling. "Besides, he doesn't know where you live anyway."

"True, so you know what that means right?"

"What?" She said bringing the egg mixture to the stove. I placed a cast iron skillet for her to use on the stove.

"It means you need to stay with me for the rest of the weekend until we figure something out about that bitch ass nigga." I tried to smile, thinking about the best outcome of that statement.

"Aww," she said, holding my face. "I can see you are upset just mentioning him. I know and I completely understand, trust me, I of all people know exactly how you feel."

I nodded and looked at her, she smiled a small smile and kissed me quickly on the lips.

"But if it weren't for him, I wouldn't be with you." She softly said, melting my heart even more for her. She knew how to see something beautiful out of something so terrible.

"I feel you. Thank you for being a beautiful person." She pouted her lips and I kissed her quickly.

"Trust me, it took work for me to get to this place in my life." She said, grabbing the butter from the fridge. I leaned against the counter as she turned on the stove to finish the eggs.

"Yeah, but I have some issues when it comes to a man hitting a woman." I folded my arms in front of my chest, trying to contain myself.

"What happened? Your father?"

"Yeah, from when I was about 4 years old to about when I was maybe 10 years old."

"Wow." She looked at me to see if I was okay. "You good? We don't have to talk about it."

"I'm good. Seeing you just brought back flashbacks, you

know?" She stirred the eggs in the skillet, her ass shaking as she moved them around. Her body was so fluid and I wanted to feel it on mine.

"I can understand. I saw it at home too." I looked at her, she was focused but still smiling. She finished the eggs and placed them in a dish I had set out.

"Enough of that." I said walking over to her and wrapping myself around her. "So whatchu wanna do today?"

"I don't know, what are you thinking?"

"I don't know. Why don't we grab our food and then scroll on Instagram to find some places, I'm sure there is some shit somewhere for us to get into."

"That sounds like a plan and fun as hell!" She yelped. She was excited, I was happy and excited myself.

I wanted to spend some quality time with my woman.

Mi Preciosa (My Precious).

Marcus

When I returned, Siedah was hooked up to a machine monitoring MJ's heartbeat, along with a mask for oxygen. I walked in and she held out her hand, I immediately grabbed it and kissed her forehead.

"Hey Babygirl, how are you feelin'?" I was trying not to worry but I would be lying if I wasn't.

"I'm feeling a little better," her voice muffled through the oxygen mask. "My blood pressure is too high, they need to get it down." Tears started flowing from her eyes. She was just as afraid as I was. With this being our first pregnancy we wanted to make sure MJ was alright. I wanted both of them to be good, honestly.

"Oh good, You were able to find her." The doctor said as he returned and walked over to the bed. "How are you feeling Siedah, better?"

"A little." she responded.

"I understand. We will get a full blood work up and we are going to start some IV meds to get everything under control." The doctor informed us.

"Is the baby okay?" I asked.

"So far, the baby's heartbeat sounds good, but we want to make sure Mom is okay as well. With her blood pressure being high, she is in the early stages of preeclampsia. We want to get that under control as it may have some serious effects if it is not. Did your obstetrician inform you about your high blood pressure?"

"She did, but she said it was borderline at the time. I had an appointment to see her tomorrow." Siedah said softly.

"Understood. Well, we are going to have you stay here for a few days because I want to make sure we get your blood pressure under control. I don't think it would be best for you to go home just yet as we want to monitor you and the baby as well."

"Do what you have to do Doc. This is my life right here," I said, holding Siedah's hand with my other hand on her pregnant belly. "I just need them to come home, eventually." My voice was shaky as I fought to hold back tears.

Siedah squeezed my hand, which made tears fall from my eyes. I needed both of them, I wouldn't know what to do without them.

"Understood. I will make sure BOTH will." He said putting his hand on my shoulder. "I will see to it personally. In the meantime, the nurse will come in and collect some blood and we will get a room ready for you. And Dad, you are more than welcome to stay."

"Thank you," I said, holding out my hand. "I appreciate it." The doctor shook my hand and smiled.

"Everything will be okay." He reassured me as he headed for the door. "By the way," he said, stopping just before exiting. "I love your music." He was a fan of my music.

"Thank you." He smiled and disappeared out the door. I'm sure he made everyone feel as though he was going to do everything in his power as he could, but I felt with him being an admirer of my music, he was going to go above and beyond.

About an hour later, Siedah was resting comfortably in a private room on the Maternity floor. I was able to tell Monica and Franklin, who said they would reach out to everyone and give them an update. As I sat in the room, with MJ's heartbeat reverberating throughout the room, I sat in the chair watching her sleep. Siedah was my heart. She had me fully from day one and I haven't looked back since. Each day of my life is better with her in it. I wouldn't know what to do without her and honestly, I wouldn't want to do anything without her. The more I think about our situation, I think about how quickly things could change.

I slept as much as I could, with the beeping noises from the machines, and medical staff periodically entering the room to check Siedah's vitals as well as MJs. A member of the staff was kind enough to place a blanket over me while I slept in the hospital recliner that sat next to Siedah's bed. I held her hand all night as I slept. Morning greeted us as the sunrise peeked its head over the horizon, filling the room with a bright, orange hue.

I checked my phone and noticed Franklin had called. I decided to step out of the room while Siedah slept peacefully to catch up with whatever I missed.

"Hey Brah, wassup? I missed your call." I walked out into the hallway and stood against the wall as I spoke softly with Franklin.

"Hey Man, how's Siedah and MJ?"

"They're doing good, Siedah's still sleeping."

"Good to hear, Man. Monica is too. We both were worried last night, but it's good to hear they're doing good."

"Thanks man, I appreciate it. So how's things going?" I asked, rubbing my eyes, trying to wipe away the morning sleep.

"Well, I've told everyone so far that you won't be in the studio today, but everyone has their agendas for today. Oh, and we gotta do something about dude fucking with Alicia man."

"Whatchu mean? What happened?" I asked, being more alert.

"Man, that fucking idiot attacked her yesterday when

she left the radio station."

"What?!" I yelled and covered my mouth forgetting I was in the hospital. "Are you fucking kidding me?"

"I wish I was, dude. This motherfucker is getting bold and we need to put his ass in check."

"That motherfucker has gotten on my last damn nerves. A'ight, this asshole has another thing coming. How is Alicia? Where is she now?"

"She's with Rob. He said he was on the phone with her when Maurice jumped her. By the time he got to the station, dude was already gone."

"Okay, she's in good hands. Rob will take care of her. We need to find out where this nigga lives and send him a fucking message."

"Already on it. In the meantime, Rob and Alicia have the day off, so she's staying with him."

"Good."

"When I get the dude's location, I'll let you know." Franklin quipped.

"Cool. Keep me posted." I disconnected. I couldn't believe that asshole had the nerve to jump on Alicia.

That guy was causing more trouble than he was worth. He was affecting my business in more ways than one which makes me involved because Alicia is my artist. I understand that dude is upset that she dropped his ass like a hot frying pan, but that nigga needs to get a fucking life. No worries though, once I get done with him, Alicia won't have to worry about him darkening her doorstep anymore.

Chapter 19 - Consequences

Siedah

Being in the hospital was not what I had expected, especially since I wasn't in labor. But it seems as though my blood pressure was the reason they decided to keep me for a few days. The doctor said I was in the early stages of preeclampsia and he needed my blood pressure under control before I would be allowed to even leave the hospital. He mentioned after the release, I needed to stay off my feet and have bed rest for at least 30 days!

Monica and Franklin decided to stop by the hospital to fill me in on everything and to help with the upcoming event. I hoped I would be able to attend, as long as my blood pressure is under control, everything would be fine.

"Hey Honey," Monica said as she walked into the room. "You're getting all that rest in here."She hugged me and laughed.

"I was about to say, you know damn well you don't rest in the hospital." We chuckled and she sat down next to the bed in the recliner.

"I know right. So what did the doctor say?"

"My blood pressure is too high. I'm in the early stages of preeclampsia."

"Oh shit. I read about that in my baby books."

"I did too. That was the last thing I was worried about.

Usually my blood pressure is normal."

"Well at least he caught it early and can turn it around."

"True." I replied. Franklin and Marcus came over to the sides of the bed; Franklin rubbed Monica's pregnant belly and smiled. Marcus kissed my forehead and held my hand.

"So how're you doing girl?" He asked.

"I'm good Franklin, thanks for asking."

"She gotta stay here for a lil bit but she'll be out soon." Monica chimed in.

"Good, we gotta make sure y'all ain't doing too much." Franklin responded.

"True, maybe we should hire a bit of help, for the both of you." Marcus suggested.

"Yeah, but who can we get to trust to help us?"

"Right, we need someone who can get the job done and we can depend on."

"Hey, how about Alicia's manager? Shaunice?" Franklin asked. We all stopped and looked at each other. Shaunice was a good choice; she made sure Alicia had a spot at the club even before she was signed with us.

"I think that she would be great." I said.

"I agree, plus she ain't gonna let anyone fuck her over at all." Monica chimed in.

"You got that right." Marcus uttered. "We should have sent her with Alicia and she probably wouldn't have gotten hurt." I looked confused at everyone while they nodded.

"Wait, Alicia got hurt?" I asked.

"Oh, you were sick girl, so we didn't need you getting your blood pressure higher than what it was already." Monica sat up in the chair.

"That fool Maurice jumped her outside the radio station." Franklin said.

"What?! How is she? Where is she?" I blurted.

"She's with Rob. He was able to get to her just after it happened." Marcus said. He smoothed my dreadlocks back, checking in on me as I was getting riled up.

"Oh ok. Did he beat her badly?"

"Rob said she's okay but that asshole hit her pretty hard. She has some bruises."

"Oh my goodness. Where is he?"

"We got eyes on him, babygirl. Don't you worry about him." Marcus reassured me. I knew when Marcus said he had eyes on him, I was put at ease. I knew I had nothing to worry about.

Marcus and Franklin were both businessmen who knew how to get shit done without getting their hands dirty, so I had no reason to believe that idiot wouldn't be taken care of. Sad thing is, that fool didn't know what was coming for him.

"Good to know. We need to get a hold of Shaunice so she can meet us at the studio to go over a few things."

"We'll take care of that, you just rest and get better. We don't need you in the hospital." Monica said, rubbing her huge belly.

"I know and I will," I said, holding Marcus's hand. "But y'all make sure she's okay, please."

"We will babygirl, don't worry. He ain't gonna try it again. He ain't gonna have the opportunity to."

"How can you be sure?" I asked. Franklin smiled at Marcus and shook his head. "What? What is it?"

"Well it seems as though the unfortunate incident has

solidified their relationship." Franklin quipped.

"Shut up!" I looked at Monica and she was nodding in agreement. Suave Rob and Alicia got together.

"She's been staying with him since it happened. Which is good because that fool knows where she lives."

"Rob ain't gonna let anyone get to her. I can promise you that." Marcus stated.

"Well at least she's safe. So what are y'all gonna do with that motherfucker because he is messing with our money." Marcus smiled and kissed my forehead again.

"See, I knew you had some *'hood'* in your ass."

"The *'hood'* has always been there, it just takes some stupid shit to bring it out. So what y'all got planned?"

"The less you know, the better." Franklin quipped. I looked at Monica who nodded again in agreement.

"Girl, you don't wanna know." she said.

"Do you know?" I asked.

"Nope, and I don't want to. If they said they are handling it, let them deal with that. We got too much shit to handle already. They got that shit under control." Monica said. I looked at Franklin and Marcus were smiling and nodding. They were handling it.

Maurice didn't even know how fucked he was.

Alicia

I had an amazing day with Roberto, I couldn't have planned it better. After Shaunice bought my clothes over, Roberto and I went out to have some fun as a couple. We decided to hit the streets to see if we could catch up on some festivals while we got to know each other a little bit better. It was like a breath of fresh air, slowing down and getting to really know someone.

I used to think that I had to sleep with the guy in order for him to like me. I thought once I did they would want to be with me. Normally the guy would stick around because what guy wouldn't - *it was free pussy*. It was when I noticed they only wanted to see me at night or at my house, was when I realized that wasn't the case. No one wanted to be seen with me; no one wanted to be caught off guard of having to explain who I was and why they were with me.

Spending time with Roberto was enlightening; he wanted to be with me, he showed me he was proud to be with me. He didn't hesitate to hold my hand or wrap his arms around me. Roberto called me ' Mi Preciosa', I was precious to him. I felt my heart dance as I felt the feeling of someone who really cared for me. He made me feel special 'showing me off' to everyone.

We found out about some Umbrella Sky art exhibits in Elmhurst and Roberto was excited to go and see it. It was a nice day and I felt cute as ever in my blue jean shorts, showing my thick thigh just right, a white crop top with a light blue button up smelling good with a splash of body spray and a pair of white Pumas to finish off my look.

Roberto looked good in almost anything he wore because his body wore everything well. But he looked good, getting as close as possible to my color scheme. He wore a nice pair of jean cargo shorts, a wife beater and a navy blue short sleeve button up. He wore his motorcycle boots so as to not mess his kicks up when he rode the bike; I carried them in his backpack so I could hold him close as we traveled.

We hit up the West Loop and walked around a vintage flea market. I felt myself watching him as he walked along the tables holding my hand, fingers laced with mine. He would turn and look at me periodically and drink me in.

"What are you thinking about when you look at me like that?" I asked. His gaze made my heart beat faster. It was like he was in deep thought when he looked at me.

"How beautiful you are and how lucky I am." I said pulling me over to him. We were so close, our breaths mixed. His hazel brown eyes always made me melt.

I blushed as he gazed in my eyes. "Thank you, but I'm lucky too." Roberto smiled. He planted a sweet small kiss on my lips.

In public. In the daytime. In front of everyone. I was in heaven.

"You don't mind all of the PDA do you?" He asked as we walked along the tables of wares and creations of the vendors.

"Not at all. I never really had anyone who *wanted* to be seen with me." I slowly stammered. Roberto stopped and turned towards me.

He held both of my hands, lacing his fingers with mine and gazed into my eyes. Roberto was serious in a way that was genuine as he lived his life as honest as possible.

"I'm sorry Mami, you had to deal with assholes. But you ain't gotta worry about them anymore. I'm your man now.

And you are a beautiful and magnificent woman who I am proud to be with. I won't hold back from letting anyone and everyone know that you are my woman - *Mi unica y exclusiva, My one and only.*" He spoke profoundly.

My heart skipped a beat. I was in awe, I hadn't had anyone step to me like that. My heart was overjoyed, it was information overload. I was stunned, my brain had shut down while thoughts raced wild in my head. He said words I've always wanted a guy to say to me.

"Oh, I love you," I slowly said out loud - *outside of my brain.* When I realized - it was too late! "I mean! Shit! Um! Fuck!" I uttered repeatedly. Roberto cracked up laughing, letting out a laugh that caught the attention of a few people walking by.

He wrapped his arms around me as I buried my face into his chest. It was the most embarrassing moment and I wanted to disappear. Although, I felt as if I cared for him because he was saying and doing all the right things. I'm sure he wasn't perfect and those flaws are yet to show themselves. But, I didn't want to admit my feelings until I had seen everything I needed to see in order to make that decision.

"It's okay Mami," He held me close to him. "It feels like that, I know. Trust me, I know." He blew out air from his mouth and chuckled. "If anybody knows, it's me. But let's not rush, we just started our relationship. Let's just enjoy this feeling before putting a name to it. How about that?" Roberto had the best way of knowing how to talk to me. He knew how I felt.

"Thank you, I appreciate that. " I said, looking up at him.

"You know you're special right." He released me slowly as I leaned back.

"Whatchu mean?"

"They don't make men like you anymore. God broke the mold when he made you." He blushed and kissed my forehead.

"Come on, let's get something to eat."

"Here we go, feeding me again." I giggled.

"You'll need your energy for *later*, Mami." Roberto whispered as he palmed my ass. I smiled the biggest smile as we walked back to his bike. I was ready to go back, fuck getting something to eat.

On the way back to Roberto's place, we stopped by my crib for me to gather more clothes. Shaunice conveniently only bought one outfit because she said I couldn't make up my mind when I had her go to my place. Roberto suggested we could stop by and grab a few items since I was planning on staying the weekend with him. As we reached my apartment door, there were two bouquets of flowers that had been delivered.

"Oh Shit." I said as I reached my door. I knew exactly who they were from, I just shook my head because this idiot was ridiculous.

"I just know this fool didn't."

"He did. He always does." I replied as I opened the door to my apartment.

"He's laid hands on you before? Mami, please tell me he didn't." Roberto spun me around as we entered my apartment.

"Once before." I was ashamed to let Roberto know that I stayed with Maurice after the fact.

Roberto's face changed, he turned dark and very serious. This was a side I hadn't seen and I wasn't sure if I wanted to see it.

"Mami," He looked at me, slowly caressing my face. "I will never raise my hand to hit you. I'll spank you ass, playfully. But I'll never strike you, ever. I promise." Roberto uttered.

"I know, Papi."

"Please don't tell me anything else about this guy because I will do something that I'm not proud of."

"As long as you don't kill him, I'm good with whatever."

"Bet." He kissed my forehead quickly. "Go grab some clothes for the weekend. I'll come back and stay with you next week."

"Good." I left to grab clothes as Roberto took the flowers and threw them in the trash.

While I grabbed a few outfits, I overheard Roberto on the phone with someone that seemed to be making him upset.

"That has nothing to do with me Marisol." He stated. I didn't want to listen, *but I wanted to listen*. Whomever she was, he was not happy; Roberto's voice had totally changed. "You should have thought about that before you did what you did."

I grabbed my duffel bag and threw everything in it and headed for the bathroom. I stood nearest the door grabbing my toiletries while still trying to listen to his conversation.

"No, you can't come and see me. I've moved on. You made your bed, now lay in it." He disconnected as I heard movement heading down the hallway.

"Hey," He said as he peeped his head in.

"Hey," I said looking at him. "You were on the phone?"

"Yeah, it was my ex. She said she's pregnant." I turned and looked at him.

"Yours?"

"No, most like Tavion's." Roberto blurted. My mouth dropped open in disbelief.

"Tavion? As in Tavion Sanders? As in TS Entertainment?"

"The very same one."

"Well damn."

"Damn indeed. She was part of the reason I left TS Entertainment." Roberto mentioned.

"Wow."

"Exactly. I caught them in bed together. Now she's claiming she's pregnant and not sure whose it is."

"Are you sure it's not yours?"

"Positive. I always used a condom with her. I just had a feeling I needed to, at least until we got tested."

"Interesting."

"I have no doubts whatsoever. I promise."

"What did I hear about her coming to see you?"

"She wanted to come and try to convince me that she's changed and we could work through it."

"Oh." I didn't expect an ex to pop back up in the mix, but it seemed as though he was handling it well.

"Mami, you don't have to worry. I am done with her and I am with you, 100%. I'm your man, yours and yours only."

"I like that." I walked over to him and kissed him deeply. He was my man. Mine and only mine.

"Mmmm, you ready to go? I want some dessert." He said, slipping his arms around my waist pulling me closer to him.

"Yeah, I'm ready. You want to stop for dessert?" I responded.

"Nah, you got what I want to eat, Mami." He said licking his lips. He smiled and placed a small kiss on my lips.

"Alrighty then, let's bounce." Roberto grabbed my bag and we were off to his place for the rest of the weekend. I could definitely get used to being with him.

Yet, I still thought secretly - *that baby needed to be tested just in case.* I didn't need to have any surprises later on.

Chapter 20 - Briefing

Suave Rob

I couldn't believe Marisol had the audacity to call and tell me she was pregnant, as if I had anything to do with it. I had no issue in letting Alicia know because I didn't want her to have any doubts about me. Of course I have a past, everyone does but I don't have any baby mama drama and I wasn't about to start. Marisol knows she's not pregnant with my seed, and if I needed to request a test to satisfy any doubts Alicia may have, I would be the first to step up with a sample.

That motherfucker also had the nerve to stop by Alicia's apartment with flowers - Roses at that. I cut them up and put them in the trash and made sure they were out of the apartment by the time we left. I didn't need her to have any memory of him, the guy was psychotic. My plan was to make sure everyone knew she's mine.

The next day, Alicia and I were back together on our rounds of promoting ourselves along with the showcase at the Taste of Chicago. Marcus asked us to come by the station before we headed out to the 102.5 Jamz radio interview. When we arrived, everyone except for Siedah was there. Shortly after we arrived, Alicia's friend Shaunice walked through the door.

"Good, everyone is here." Franklin picked up a tablet off of the cocktail table. " Let's start because we have a lot of stuff to go over. First off, it seems as though you two are quite the item." Franklin pointed towards us.

"What?" Alicia and I asked in unison. Franklin chuckled and looked at Monica who was shaking her head.

"You two were seen out and about , I can only assume it was yesterday, correct?" Marcus asked.

"Yeah, we hung out a bit yesterday. Why? What happened?" I asked. Franklin handed me the tablet. Alicia leaned over and looked at it with me.

Pictures of us had hit social media; as I scrolled there were more and more pictures. We looked good together I had to admit; we looked happy being with each other. The caption was *'Suave Rob and Alicia: Are they an item?'*. There was even a picture of us kissing. Alicia blushed so hard she covered her mouth in awe.

"Wow, okay. I didn't expect that." I said handing back the tablet.

"We did, we just didn't know it would happen so fast." Monica replied. Alicia looked at me, making me smile. I loved the way she looked at me.

"You expected us to get followed?" Alicia asked.

"That too, but we expected you two would get together." Marcus blurted. Both Alicia and I smiled, I felt myself blushing more than I have ever done before in my life.

"So let's just set the record straight - *y'all together now right*?" Monica asked. I looked at Alicia sitting next to me on the couch. I took her hand, laced my fingers with her and kissed the back of her hand.

"Yes. We are together." I said proudly. Alicia smiled and leaned on my shoulder, I could tell she was happy.

"It's about damn time!" Shaunice yelped and everyone laughed.

"Congratulations." Everyone chimed in. It felt good to be part of the CFE Group, it was like Family.

"Well, that radio station, Hotness 95.7 is claiming they knew something was going on before y'all actually started."

"Yeah, I kinda figured. I was in the process of making my move." I laughed and Alicia bumped me."

"Well the news has hit that you two are a couple or the beginning of a relationship, just to give you a heads up when you two go to the station today."

"A'ight cool." I answered.

"Ok next, since Siedah is in the hospital and will be on bed rest when she is released tomorrow, we need someone to help Monica with the logistics. That's why we asked you here, Shaunice."

"Me?" Shaunice perked up when her name was spoken. She sat in the chair across from us.

"Yes, you are the only one we can trust. You know how to handle your business and get the job done and we need you to help Monica and Siedah get the job done." Marcus said.

"Ok," Monica chimed in. "To put it better, we need you to be a stand in for Siedah since she can't be mobile."

"Oh ok, however y'all need me I'll help." She replied.

"Cool, cool. Thank you for stepping in and helping us."

"No problem, I'm sure there will be some kind of compensation, right?" she asked. Shaunice was a hustler, she knew her worth.

"Yes, we got you." Franklin answered. Shaunice nodded and grinned at Alicia. I chuckled watching them get excited.

"Next topic we need to discuss is Marisol." Marcus blurted. I turned and looked at all of them; I closed my eyes and inhaled deeply. I ran my hands across my face and shook my head in disbelief; this bitch just won't go away. Anger crept across me just by the mention of her name.

"Shit." I said lowering my head and not wanting to look at Alicia. This issue with Marisol could give Alicia doubts about me. I knew the kid wasn't mine but does she believe me, is my worry. We just got together and both of us came to the table with baggage, it's just that I knew about her baggage, not many knew about mine.

"It's nothing right now, but she's starting to brew up an audience. Everyone knows she was with you and now with you moving on, people are speculating."

"As they always do." I shook my head. "Y'all heard the last interview when they asked me about Isis right?"

"Yeah, I figured they would go that way. Those two are loose as fuck; shit, she hooked up with one of our guys too." Marcus voiced.

"Yup and got married on his ass too. That shit was bogus." Franklin added.

"Yeah, I remembered that. She tried it with me, but like I said on the show, I don't date attached or married women." I sat back on the couch and Alicia laced her fingers with mine. I smiled and rubbed my thumb along the back of her hand.

"Well you're with Alicia now so, you're off the table."

Shaunice blurted.

"Yes Ma'am and I'm okay with that," I turned slightly towards her. "Te parece bien, Mami? Are you okay with that, Mami?" I spoke softly between us. She turned and smiled.

"Si Papi, I'm down with that." Alicia replied.

"Damn! He got yo' ass learning Spanish already! That's my dude." Shaunice chuckled and held out her fist for me to bump. I smiled, shook my head and granted her a bump.

Monica got up and walked around as Franklin walked with her rubbing her back. She looked like she was in a bit of pain as they walked around the studio.

"Is she alright?" Alicia asked.

"Yeah, Braxton Hicks that's all." Monica yelled back as she waddled slowly back and forth while rubbing along her stomach.

"Braxton who?" Shaunice asked.

"Oh, forgot y'all don't know. It's just my body getting ready for the baby to be delivered, but it's like false contractions. My uterus is just going through the motions to get ready for the real thing."

"Aw damn, okay. No thank you." Shaunice winced at the thought. Alicia laughed at Shaunice, she didn't seem appalled by what Monica was going through. For a split moment, I wondered what it would be like to have a family with her. The thought made me smile.

Alicia

"Ok getting back to Marisol, you know she might come out and say she's pregnant but from what I'm hearing, she's not revealing who the father is."

"Well I know for a fact, it ain't mine." Roberto replied.

"We know it ain't yours, but people don't like the truth, they like the drama. So what we are going to do is pivot the story back on them. From when you left TS Entertainment to the time for her to announce her pregnancy, the timeline doesn't match up. We can go with that because the relationship between you and Marisol was over publicly before the breakdown in talks between you and TSE." Marcus said.

"This is true." Roberto nodded. "I like how you did that. Cool."

"If they want to play the speculation game, let us take control of it and make it a challenge. Now of course they are going to ask you about her and the baby," Marcus mentioned.

"And they will ask you if it's yours. Push comes to shove, you could tell them the real reason of what went down, but that's up to you to let that out." Monica chimed in.

"Yeah I know, I figured that. I'm just tired of dealing with her, ya know?" Roberto quickly got up off the couch and just walked over to the punching bag Marcus had hanging in the corner. "Por qué esta zorra no puede dejarme en paz?! *(Why can't this bitch just leave me alone?!)*"

Roberto was upset Marisol was coming out about her pregnancy and people adding him to the mix even though they weren't together anymore. He paced back and forth along the wall. Marisol was a singer with TSE, who started a bit before Roberto joined. She was established and Tavion was known to promote a lot for her when she started. So much so people started speculating something going on between them. Especially since everyone was aware that Isis and Tavion had an open marriage. When Robert joined, he and Marisol started dating shortly after. I didn't know if Marisol was seeing Tavion on the down low behind Roberto's back or not, but I had a feeling she was.

"I feel you Brah," Marcus said, grabbing a pair of boxing gloves from underneath the cocktail table and throwing them to Roberto. "Take it to the bag man, get it out."

"Cool." Roberto said, catching the gloves. He took off his shirt, put on the gloves and started hitting the bag. He looked sexy as fuck and mad as hell.

"Next topic, Maurice." Marcus said. My heart dropped. I didn't want to talk about him or think about him.

"Shit." I blurted. The tables had turned to me. Roberto stopped punching the bag and looked my way.

"Has he tried to reach out to you?" Marcus asked.

"No." I said softly.

"He tried to reach out to me after the fact, but I didn't answer. I've blocked him since then."

"Mami, tell them about the flowers." Roberto yelled from the other side of the room. He went back to hitting the bag harder than the first time. Everyone turned and looked at me.

"What flowers, Mami?" Monica asked playfully.

"We went to my house to pick up a few items and there were roses delivered to my apartment."

"From Maurice?" Franklin asked.

"Yes."

"This nigga is bold as fuck." Franklin turned around and put his hand on his head.

"Yo' Rob, she's staying with you right?" Marcus yelled back to Roberto.

"Yeah," He said, stopping for a moment. He was glistening from the sweat he'd built up punching the bag. "We're going back and forth between both places."

"Oh ok, cool. If that fool shows up, you know what you gotta do."

"Yes indeed I do, Boss." Roberto answered and attacked the bag like it was Maurice.

Watching him hit the punching bag, turned me on a bit. I zoned out and watched Roberto's muscles flex upon impact as the others started talking to Shaunice about the logistics. Roberto looked irritated, his eyes were focused on the punching bag - whatever he was thinking about had him in deep thought. I just wanted him to look at me, just a glance to let me know he's okay. I knew all of this shit dealing with his ex probably stressed him out, especially since his relationship with his ex was about to go public.

And then he looked at me.

The frown upon his face as he hit the bag, startled me as he gazed at me. I raised up off of the couch and headed towards him as he took the gloves off. He was sweaty, his chest heaving as I approached him. He watched me as I got closer, his gaze softening when I finally stood in front of him.

"Hi Papi, are you okay?" I said, speaking softly. He smiled, and caressed my cheek.

"I'm good, Mami. Thanks for checking on me."

"I wanted to make sure you were okay."

"Si, gracias Mami." He planted a quick kiss on my lips and placed the gloves around the top of the bag. "Ay Marcus, Do you think I could use your shower real quick?" Roberto asked.

"Mi casa es su casa." Marcus gave him the thumbs up.

"A'ight Brah, gracias." He grabbed his shirt before heading to the bathroom. "I'll be back, this won't take long unless you want to join me?" He smiled slyly.

"Yes and no." I replied.

"Another time then?"

"Another time for sure." He smiled, gave me a quick kiss and headed to the bathroom while I went back to join the others.

Chapter 21 - Stay

Alicia

After the meeting, Roberto and I headed out to the radio station. We were prepped for questions they would most likely ask so we were ready for whatever. Roberto held my hand as we walked through the entrance to the radio station. We were meeting Dj Rocket and Fancy Jane of 102.5 Jamz. They were cool people to be honest, I had been a listener for a while and I liked their style because they allowed the artist to have a safe space to offer whatever truth they want the world to know which allows people to hear it directly for the artist themselves.

"Yo, yo, yo! People, we have Suave Rob and Alicia Givens with CFE Group in the House!" Dj Rocket yelled into the mic.

"Yes, yes they are in the house y'all. And they lookin' good and happy!" Fancy Jane said into the mic and the sound guy was on it with the applause; it had us smiling and having a good time.

"Okay, first things first. Suave Rob, it's good to see you man. It's been a minute. You disappeared on me man."

"Yeah, I know. It's good to see you man. Thanks for thinking about me and having me here. Yeah, a lot has changed man since I last saw you."

"That's right, you were with TS Entertainment and you

left due to contract negotiations, is that right?"

"Yes, that is correct." Roberto acknowledged.

"I know there are a lot of rumors out there," Fancy Jane started. "And I want to first, thank you and Alicia for coming to set the records straight."

"It's good seeing you, Fancy Jane. Thank you for having us and thank you for allowing us to do that." Roberto nodded.

"Most welcome, you know how we do it here on 102.5 Jamz, you ain't new. But Alicia is, welcome Alicia!" she yelled into the mic. I smiled at the welcome and the noises the sound guy filled in the dead air.

"Thank you so much for having us, it's a pleasure. I listen to y'all all the time."

"Aww that's so sweet, thank you! We appreciate you too."

"Now getting down to business because we want to put all of the truth out there so we can squash all of the rumors, Suave Rob," DJ Rocket started.

"Wassup?" Roberto responded.

"First, the pictures have been seen of you and Alicia. They hit TMZ but they had no footage," DJ Rocket said.

"Thank goodness, those reporters be on you quick and in your face with the questions and some be out of pocket."

"This is true, but there wasn't any video, just pictures. So you already know what is being said so we are just going to ask," He hesitated making my heart pound in my chest. Rob must have sensed it as he reached over and held my hand, putting me at ease. "Is it true that Suave Rob and Alicia Givens are a couple?"

Roberto laced his fingers with mine and looked over at

me sitting next to him. He leaned towards the microphone, his eyes still on me.

"Yes, we are." He kissed the back of my hand making me blush.

"You heard it here first - Suave Rob and Alicia Givens are a couple!"

"I knew it, I saw them when they walked in the station. They were holding hands, looking in love.Y'all were cute!" I smiled and Roberto squeezed my hand for reassurance.

"When did y'all get together?"

"Not long ago, it's still brand new." I chimed in.

"It's all good, that's when y'all finding out about each other." Fancy Jane added. "I love it."

"Okay so not to change the subject but, Alicia, how do you feel about all this stuff going on with Suave Rob?"

"What do you mean?"

"His ex-girlfriend, Marisol has announced her pregnancy and a hold of her next EP."

"That sounds like she's adjusting her priorities." I answered.

"Good answer. 100 points!" Fancy Jane responded. I smiled. I was determined not to be blindsided by the questions, which was the reason for the meeting.

"Suave Rob, what about you? She didn't reveal who the father was. Do you know who the father is?"

"I know it's not me! I know *that* rumor had been floating around and I wanna squash *that one* right now. No baby mama drama over here." Roberto snapped. I smiled because he said he was going to go all out if he needed to; he wasn't afraid to be honest - it was his truth.

"Ha, My guy said it's not him. I know that's right. Man, he was like *'take me out of the equation'.*" DJ Rocket cackled loudly.

"Yes Sir." Roberto smiled.

"Well, you and Marisol had broken up before you left TS Entertainment, right?" Fancy Jane chimed in.

"Yes Ma'am. We broke up about 3 months before I left TS Entertainment. I remember because my contract was up for renewal in 3 months and I was wondering if I would stay or not."

"Right, I heard y'all were stalled in contract negotiations for at least 2 months, right?"

"Yes we were. It was over the legalities of the contract, you know terms and compensation. " Roberto replied.

"Oh ok, yeah you need that right otherwise you will get screwed." Fancy chimed in.

""True."

"Okay, so do you know who the father is?" DJ Rocket asked. Roberto smiled and looked at me.

"He's not answering people. He's smiling and not answering. Not answering could be an answer."

"This is true." Roberto smiled and sat back in the chair. He handled it well. "I can say this, I have an idea of whose it is. But I'm waiting for the paternity test."

"Aww damn, it's like that? So you know it's going to be a test?"

"I'm just saying." Roberto knew how to stir the pot well to push the negative attention back towards the ones who deserve it. "*Someone* is going to ask for one. That's all I'm saying."

"Wow, okay. Alicia," Fancy Jane started on me. "We had some reports of your ex boyfriend and ex manager Maurice Gibbs attacking you, is this correct?"

"Unfortunately, yes. I had just left an appearance at another station and he caught me in the parking lot." I said trying not to relive the incident; hoping by me talking fast would allow me to get it out without having to lay awake in it.

"I'm sure you can't speak on it because of legal purposes but I *know* CFE is handling it. Marcus is *my guy* and he knows first hand how to deal with people like that." DJ Rocket said.

"That's bogus man. Are you okay?"

"I'm good now," I said smiling and thinking about how I felt. I felt happy I got to wake up with him everyday. "CFE is handling all of it currently."

"She's got Suave Rob, Hell yeah she's good." I smiled and Roberto bumped me.

"Right! And both of y'all are out here to promote your single and your upcoming showcase at the Taste of Chicago, right?"

"Yes! Both Suave Rob and I will be performing our single at the Taste of Chicago - at the CFE Stage. So y'all come out and see us. All of CFE will be there so come and show us some love." I spoke into the microphone.

"That's what I'm talking about, and I love this single. Y'all snapped!"

"Thank you!" We said in unison.

"Alicia, you got some pipes, girl."

"Thank you." I smiled. It was nice being appreciated for

my talents.

"A'ight we are gonna open up the lines for your fans to call in and ask a few questions, y'all ready?" DJ Rocket asked. Roberto and I nodded in agreement.

All of a sudden, the switchboard lit up with people who wanted to talk to us. I felt overwhelmed at the opportunity I was given. We got a few callers congratulating us on getting together and Roberto was happy, smiling each time someone cheered us. He held my hand the entire time making me feel safe and secure.

"We got time for one last call and then they have to bounce so they can promote their single, download it today!"

"Yo, hello?"

"Hello! You are on live with 102.5 Jamz talking to Suave Rob and Alicia Givens of CFE," DJ Rocket stated.

"Yo, thank you for letting me get on cuz I wanna tell Alicia that I love her and Suave needs to watch his motherfucking back! "

"Yo, yo, yo! Dawg, we ain't having that on here, either you got something to say or we dropping you."

"Ok, ok, my bad. Alicia, how you gonna do me like that though. After all I done did for you!"

It was Maurice! He had called the show. I squeezed Roberto's hand and he instantly snapped.

"Yo' Brah, I done told you Cuz. You need to move around Brah." Roberto spoke into the microphone, I was holding his hand with both of mine.

"I ain't your Brah nig.." They cut the line.

"A'ight y'all. E'erbody know, we try to keep things positive and honest. We don't have time for all that drama and negativity, this ain't that show. But Thank you to Suave Rob and Alicia, check them out at the Taste of Chicago on the CFE Stage. And download their single, it's out now, so do it."

"Thank y'all for having us." I uttered robotically. I was just so tired of dealing with Maurice. He was popping up frequently, making me a bit uneasy.

After the show ended, Fancy Jane asked me if I was okay. She saw me tense up when I heard Maurice over the phone. She said she knew what I was going through, she had an ex-boyfriend that stalked her to the point she had to get a restraining order. She told me to think about it.

We arrived back at Roberto's place and I had no motivation to pack my things to return to my home, not after that phone call. I didn't want to be at home just in case he decided to come and stop by.

"Do you mind if we stay here instead of going back to my place tonight?" I asked as I walked in the door and plopped down on the couch.

"You know I don't mind," He said, coming over sitting next to me. "I would rather you stay here with me *until* we figure out what we are going to do with Maurice, instead of us going back and forth."

"After today, I was thinking the same." Roberto leaned over and kissed my cheek.

"No te preocupes mi preciosa, te tengo. *(Don't worry my precious, I got you.)*" Roberto spoke in Spanish, walked around to the other side of the chaise lounge and sat behind me, wrapping his legs and arms around me.

"Thank you for being there for me, even in the middle of

me having all of this drama." I said holding his hands.

"It's my pleasure, Mami. I'm sorry you have to deal with my own shit. I'm sorry I didn't ask you how you felt about it all. I practically didn't tell you anything about it."

"It's okay. It's not always easy to talk about difficult relationships, especially when you're the one being hurt." I reassured him.

"Exactly, but that doesn't mean I'm supposed to lead you in blind into my life. I just don't want you to have doubts about me, especially with Marisol announcing her pregnancy."

"Both of us have our own shit; ironically it brought us together. I believe you when you said you're not the father. I could tell how adamant you are with the condoms we use."

"See, you already know me." He smiled. "I got a question." Roberto's tone changed to serious.

"Wassup?" I leaned to the side and turned a bit to see his face.

"Would you wanna get tested with me?" He was asking me to get tested for STDs. He wanted to remove the condom. My garden quivered at the thought of feeling him naturally - *skin on skin.*

"Sure. I'll get tested with you."

"Wait, what about pregnancy control?" he asked, looking curious.

"I have birth control. I have an IUD."

"Cool, okay. I'll let you know when the appointment is set."

He moved my hair to one side and kissed my neck. "Let's take a shower and then order food afterwards." He lowered his chin to my shoulder and held me gently as he waited patiently for my response.

"I'd like that." I smiled and he kissed my neck again sliding his across my thighs and in between my legs.

"Can we take that shower together?" He asked.

"Si Papi." He cupped my mound as he nibbled and sucked on my neck.

"Me vuelves loco cuando me llama Papi." He moaned softly. "You know you drive me crazy when you call me Papi, don't you."

"You want me to answer honestly?"

"Always." He leaned forward, his cheek touching mine.

"Yes, I know. Is it okay?"

"Oh si Mami, siempre está bien. It's always okay, Mami." I turned to see his face smiling back at me. "C'mon, I wanna see you wet."

Chapter 22 - Shaunice to the Rescue

Shaunice

I was so happy for my girl, Alicia. She was happy with Suave Rob and I couldn't wait to see how far they go in the industry. I was happy I was offered to jump in and help out with CFE and be mobile for Siedah since she had to be on bed rest. If everything goes well, she would be able to attend the showcase at the Taste of Chicago and I may have a permanent position.

I sat in Siedah's bedroom at her desk as she sat in the bed surrounded by documents, a bed tray stand holding her laptop, and her cell phone in hand as she gave me a rundown of the lineup for the showcase.

"We'll have Darius start off the showcase with about 3 songs, then move on to Analia."

"Got it."

"Then it will be Taye who has a song with Analia to come next with about 3 songs as well."

"Got it."

"Okay so then we'll have Alicia sing right before Suave Rob. The last song for Alicia will be the song with Suave Rob then she leaves and he has the stage for 2 - 3 songs." Siedah said looking at her phone.

I wrote down the information on the clipboard for the line up as well as saved it in my organizer app on my phone. "Got it."

"And then we will have Jacobi, with his 3 songs, to come out after Suave Rob."

"Got it."

"Oh, I need Suave Rob and Alicia at the studio today as well, I came up with another song for them. It might be an encore song. It's a sexy song for them."

"I thought Lights Out was good, but you got a baby-making song, huh?" I asked as I pulled out my phone and sent a text to Alicia.

"Girl, it's a rendition but I'm sure they will do it well." Siedah shook her head left and right. "It reminded me of when Marcus and I got together."

"How did y'all meet anyway?" I asked, curious. They seemed to have a very deep connection with each other, un-like I've ever seen. I think Alicia has something like that with Suave Rob.

"We met at a listening party Monica and Franklin were having. Monica asked me to come and celebrate but it was a set up, she wanted me to meet Marcus.

"And you fell for him when she introduced you?" I asked.

"Not exactly. We never were introduced. I never actually *met* him."

"Huh? Well, how did you guys get together?" I was to-tally confused.

"I ran into him at the next listening party, it was there when we finally exchanged numbers."

"Nice." I smiled. It was as if it was a real love story. "So what does the song sound like?

"We are gonna embrace Suave Rob's Latin roots, so it has a reggaeton beat with a mixture of Afro Soul and Spanish lyrics."

"Oh that sounds Hot!"

"It is. Every time I hear it, it makes me wanna dance. It's called *Celebra by Amara La Negra*." she said, shaking her hips in the bed.

"No shaking anything until the showcase." I demanded. She smiled. Siedah looked back at her phone and then her face suddenly changed. Something was wrong.

"Oh Shit," Siedah blurted. "Fuck!"

"What's wrong?" I looked at her shuffling papers on her bed.

"It looks like we did it again." Siedah said, sounding disappointed.

"Did what again?"

"Double booked Suave Rob and Alicia." She sounded defeated.

"Oh Shit." I replied.

"Oh Shit is right." She looked worried; I didn't need her to worry as the entire reason I was there is to make her life easier. "Listen, I'll pick her up after the radio spot and take her to the station."

Siedah looked at me as if I had saved her life. "You think you'll be able to do that?" she asked.

"I should. What time do they need to be at the studio? And what time does she need to be at the station?"

"They need to be at the station by 1:00 PM. They can

come to the studio whenever they finish. Marcus has been staying late to get ready for the showcase. They just need to text him when they are on their way."

"Oh ok." I gave her a thumbs up and sent another text to Alicia about the changes regarding the interviews.

"Shaunice," Siedah started. "I want to thank you for stepping in for me, I really appreciate it."

"No worries, the pleasure is all mine. I'm happy to help the people who helped my girl's dream come true, anytime."

"You are a really good friend to Alicia." She responded.

"Thanks. I try to be. She gets stuck in her head sometimes and becomes self conscious, but I'm glad she finally has found someone who loves her for who she is and opens her up."

"Yeah, she;s had some self esteem issues. But I think Suave Rob is definitely making them disappear."

"I know right?! I think he is good for her as long as he doesn't hurt her."

"Rob's not like that. He's a one-woman man. He was devastated when he found Marisol sleeping with Tavis."

My eyes grew huge, I didn't know the entire story of why they broke up. "Is he the baby daddy?"

"We think so, but we aren't sure of who else she may have slept with."

"Wow." I sang.

"Right. Rob was hurt because he invested his time and feelings into this woman and she was fucking Tavion behind his back."

"That's probably why she was promoted more than Suave Rob?" I asked.

"Yup. Rob speculated that was the case but he didn't have any proof until he walked in on them in the middle of the dirty deed."

"Damn! That's one hell of a way to find out."

"It is. Trust me, I know the feeling oh too well." She smiled and shook her head.

"Ok, so I just received a text from Alicia and she said she was worried about the double booking again but I told her I would be there when she finished. It seems as though Rob was trying to get to her as well."

"I figured as much. He wasn't going to allow it to happen again on his watch."

"So Rob is going to drop her off first and head to his radio spot. I'll meet up with Alicia when she finishes, wait for Rob to come and get her and then they will come to the studio together." I said reading the text message on my phone.

"Oh, you're not bringing her?" Siedah asked.

"Well it seems as though they have a previous engagement they have planned but she said it won't take long and they will be at the studio shortly after."

"Ok, that's fine. As long as they get to the studio tonight because the sooner they learn the song, the better." Siedah said leaning back against the headboard, she rubbed her pregnant belly as she exhaled.

"Is there anything I can do for you, or get for you?" I asked as I started packing up my things.

"No, I'm good, just getting tired of being pregnant. I'm ready for the little man to be here. I'm tired-tired."

"Well it's not much longer, right?"

"Yeah, it's not too much longer. By the time we do the

showcase, I would be between 36 - 40 weeks so I could deliver at any moment around there."

"Wow, okay. You sure you want to be at the showcase?"

"I'm going to be at the showcase. There is no doubt, no one is stopping me from being able to see Marcus and Franklin's hard work come to fruition. I will be there." Siedah quipped.

"Yes Ma'am." I saluted her, she shook her head and smiled. "I'm outta here. Is someone coming to be with you?"

"Yeah, Monica should be here shortly so we can finish up the last few details."

"You don't need me to stay?"

"Nah, we'll be good. We'll text you if we need you." Siedah gave me the thumbs up, I nodded and left.

Alicia

I got a text from Shaunice telling me that there was a double booking again with Roberto and I. Roberto got a little irritated, however he wasn't mad at anyone in particular only because of the situation dealing with Maurice. If Maurice was stalking me, he was well aware that I was going to be at a different station then Roberto *again*. This time we were ready this time, just in case he decided to show his face.

When the show was over, Shaunice was already there waiting for me, along with about 30 fans and followers in the parking lot. I actually had a fan base! It was a group of young women who supported me because I promoted a positive image for plus size women and girls. The group called themselves the - *'P.H.A.T. Girls'* - which stood for *'Pretty Hot And Tempting'*.

We stood outside greeting the fans, taking pictures and selfies and with the help of Shaunice, being the great manager she is, I went live for the first time online and my followers grew instantly. It felt good to have someone who appreciated what I was doing; It all felt surreal signing autographs and taking pictures with total strangers. It wasn't until I heard the roar of the motorcycle in the distance that I remembered I was supposed to be looking out for Maurice.

Shaunice was still recording as Roberto roared into the parking lot, his music blasting from his bike and him looking delicious as fuck. He wore his black outfit, the one I loved to see him in so much. He wore a pair of baggy, black motorcycle pants, along with his black 6" double zipper biker boots topping off the look perfectly with his body armor shirt on looking like he just came from a race rally. Most likely he had on a nice t-shirt underneath but he looked like he was ready to battle.

Everyone turned around and watched as he got off his bike and walked his bow-legged ass across the parking lot to greet me. Shaunice kept recording while he approached me.

"Shaunie is recording, fyi." I said as he walked up.

"I know." He instantly cupped the back of my head and pressed his lips against mine, holding me close.

Butterflies instantly filled my stomach as he planted such a luscious kiss upon my lips. A soft moan slipped from my mouth, mid-kiss. His tongue danced with mine as he slid his hand around my waist pulling me closer; Shaunice walked closer towards us still recording as we slowly parted, his forehead still pressing against mine. He held me close, rubbing his nose against mine; I felt his breath against my lips as he gazed at me. He turned his head towards Shaunice, smiled and then held his hand up and covered the camera. Shaunice finally ended the recording.

"Y'all just too cute." She said smiling. The fans were screaming at our interaction. I blushed and buried my face in his chest.

"¡Hola Ladies!" Roberto screamed at the fans which made them scream more as they stood patiently waiting for his autograph as well. He wrapped his arms around me and gave me a tight hug.

"I missed you Mami, you okay?"

I smiled, "Yes, I'm good. Are you ready to go to the clinic?" I asked.

"Yes and no." He said, looking differently. I hadn't seen that part of Roberto before, so I wondered where it was coming from.

"Why? What's wrong?"

"Promise you won't laugh, Mami." Roberto demanded.

"I won't laugh, Papi. What is it?"

"I don't like needles." He replied. I looked at him and smiled. He looked at me and rolled his eyes. "See, I knew you would laugh."

"I'm not laughing. Just smiling." I wanted to laugh so bad. It amazed me that Roberto was ready to beat the living shit out of Maurice yet he was afraid of needles.

"Ah, te ríes por dentro. *(You're laughing on the inside.)*" Roberto uttered and frowned. I laughed out loud when he spoke. I knew he'd said something smart ass, even though I hadn't a clue what it was; I just had an inkling.

"Uh-uh, what you say?" I asked. He smiled.

The fans were still there, begging him to come and sign some autographs. Shaunice was good at crowd control along with the help of two security guards that stood outside the radio station entrance.

"Let me go over and greet the fans real quick." He snickered and walked over to the small group of people.

Shaunice helped Roberto with taking pictures with the group of young ladies. I jumped in for a few group photos and then finally the crowd thinned out.

"A'ight Shaunice. We'll meet you over at the studio, we gotta make a stop before we head that way."

"Oh ok, y'all be safe."

"Thanks again, Shaunice. I appreciate you helping us out like that." Roberto told Shaunice.

"I'm her manager therefore I need to make sure she's taken care of, *until you show up*." She tilted her head and smiled.

"My dawg." Roberto held out his fist and Shaunice bumped it.

"I'm outta here, see ya at the studio." She turned, waved and walked off weaving through the cars in the parking lot heading for her ride.

"You ready to go?" I turned to Roberto. He looked at me and touched my cheek.

"You are something else."

"I know."

Roberto helped me with the helmet and I assumed my position behind him. I wrapped my arms tightly around his chest and leaned against his back. He started the bike, the roar of the motor vibrated between my legs. I closed them against him as he revved the bike. He strapped on his helmet, patted my hands signaling our take off and off we went.

As we turned out of the parking lot, I caught a glimpse of Maurice's car parked along the wall in the last row of cars.

He was seriously stalking me.

Chapter 23 - Best Thing For Me

Suave Rob

Alicia and I walked out of the clinic bandaged up and ready to head to the studio. Alicia helped me a lot when the nurse came to draw the blood as she held my hand and kept me distracted. I don't think I would have made it through without her to be honest. I had only gotten a test one time before and that didn't go too well. Alicia and I made it back to the studio with time to spare. Marcus was working with Analia and Taye when we arrived so we chilled out in the lounge area.

"Hey y'all, I sent both of you the song with the lyrics we want you to sing for the showcase." Marcus said as we sat down.

"A'ight we'll take a look at it." I pulled out my phone to pull up the message.

"Roberto," Alicia called my name. I love when she says my name. Her soft voice delighted my ears.

"Huh?" I responded still looking at my phone. I held her hand, rubbing the back of it with my thumb.

"Papi?" Alicia called me again, this time I turned towards her. She looked like she needed to tell me something as she looked worried.

"Wassup Mami?" I leaned in closer to her, giving her my undivided attention.

"I saw him today. He was at the station."

"Who? Maurice?"

"Yes. I saw him parked in the last row of the parking lot. I saw his car." She said, her eyes filling with tears. "Why won't he leave me alone?"

I wrapped my arms around her as she cried. "It's okay Mami. I won't let him hurt you." I held her tight and rocked her back and forth.

"I'm just tired of him." She whimpered into my chest. I consoled her until she composed herself and wiped away her tears. "I just want him to go away and leave me alone!" She was afraid of him and she had every right to be, he was relentless in showing up in places unexpectedly.

I looked at Alicia; she looked so tired. Tired of dealing with him.

I wanted to snap his neck but that would take me away from Alicia altogether which defeated the purpose.

She sniffed as she covered her face with her hands as tears began flowing again. Alicia looked at me with her big, beautiful brown eyes full of tears, cascading down her cheeks hoping I could save her. The way she gazed at me, angered me; Not because she needed me to take her away from her misery, she shouldn't have been put in that position in the first place. And then to continue to attack and mentally fuck with her because she's trying to move on and live her life is fucking ridiculous.

"I know Mami," I wiped away the last of her tears from her cheeks. "I'm sorry, but it will be over soon."

"How can you be so sure?" She looked at me needing reassurance; I caressed her face and she looked away. Alicia was afraid to believe me, every guy she's been with gave her empty promises and just told her what *she* wanted to hear.

"Mami, I know for a fact that he *will* get what is coming to him. *I promise.*" I held her face as she looked at me. "I promise, Mami. Lo juro, I swear." Her eyes searched my face for the smallest inkling of hope.

"You promise?" Alicia asked.

"Si, lo prometo." I nodded. I leaned forward and planted a small kiss on her lips. "We gotta tell them though."

"I know. I just don't want Marcus and Franklin to get tired of having to deal with Maurice to the point they drop me from the label."

"They won't drop you, Mami." I smiled, kissed her forehead and gave her another hug. "They will drop Maurice, though." I leaned back to look Alicia in the eyes.

"Somebody should."

"Somebody will, Mami." I kissed her forehead again and got up off the couch and walked over to Marcus and Franklin. I needed to let them know how serious shit had gotten.

"Hey, can I holla at y'all for sec?" Franklin turned around while Marcus removed one side of the headset from his ear.

"Wassup?"

"Yo, Alicia told me that dude was at the station today. She said she saw his car parked in the parking lot."

"This fucker just won't give up will he?" Franklin snapped.

"Does she know where he lives?" Marcus asked, standing up and picking up his phone.

"I don't know, I'm sure she does. I'll ask."

"Do that. Looks like we're gonna have to pay him a little

visit." Franklin quipped.

"Do y'all need some help?" I wanted to get in on this motherfucker.

"Yes and no. We don't need *you* out there doing some dumb shit. We got people for that." Franklin was scrolling through his contacts on his phone.

"Naw, you stay with Alicia. She's safer with you until we get this nigga under control." Marcus said.

Franklin nodded. "Get the address and we'll handle the rest."

"No hay problema." I said and walked back to Alicia. She was listening to the song we needed to learn.

Alicia and I shared similar qualities. When I got upset, I needed to change my mindset in order to change my attitude. I would do things to direct my energy elsewhere and music was my go-to in order to make it happen.

I watched her as she bounced to the music in her earbuds. I smiled as she closed her eyes and began singing the chorus of the song. She sounded amazing singing softly. She hadn't noticed me watching her until she turned around and jumped a bit. I had startled her, which made me chuckle. I smiled and walked over to her and gazed at her; she was so precious to me, I didn't think I would have feelings for someone so soon after Marisol.

"How's it going?" I asked.

"This song is hot! I can't wait to sing it with you." She smiled and placed her hand on my chest. I held her hand against my chest, tilting my head and smirked. I didn't want her mood to change so I felt it would be best if I asked her later for the asshole's address.

"I can't wait either, Mami." I sat down and grabbed my earbuds to listen to the song. Alicia was right, it was hot! I love the Latin flavor the song had. It was a perfect song for us. It gave us a chance to sing to each other as well as dance together. "Mami, we need to dance to this."

I listened to the song and started to move my hips. This song was a nice pick for us, it would allow us to be sexy and sensual while we sang together. *It was our song.*

Alicia

Roberto and I were waiting in the studio waiting to go in the booth; Analia and Taye were finishing up their song so I decided to get a start on ours. I was happy to be at the CFE studio, I knew Maurice's stupid ass wouldn't dare come here - *he made me exhausted.* So much so, I broke down in front of Roberto. I feel as though I'm have so much fucking baggage in this relationship, I didn't want him to second guess his decision of being with me.

We were listening to the song together and dancing, feeling the vibe of the song, which was really good. It was a Latin song with a really nice beat; it featured lyrics of the song to be sung in both English and Spanish which fit us perfectly. We had learned the song by the time Analia and Taye finally finished their song.

They were a cute couple that had gotten together shortly after they joined CFE just like Roberto and I. They matched perfectly, I thought as I watched them talking to each other. I could tell they loved each other.

"Hey Alicia," Analia walked over to the couch, leaving the guys chatting together on the other side of the room.

"Hey Analia, how's it going?"

"It's going well, they are keeping us busy, but I love it."

"I know right. I'm glad I gave my notice for work, because it was impossible to make all of the appointments and get work."

"Well, that's the thing about CFE, they take care of their artists, so don't worry about it. They really do have your back."

"Thanks for that, I appreciate it."

"You're welcome." She smiled at me. She was really down to earth. "Hey, are you ready for the showcase?"

"We're getting there. It's wild huh?" I asked. She sat down while we chatted as the guys were laughing and clapping hands as if we had nothing else to do.

"It is. We've done showcases before, but this will be about the largest scale we've done."

"I've never done any of this, so I'm nervous as hell." I hoped she had some kind of advice to give me.

"Don't worry about it. I still get nervous. But as soon as I step out on the stage, it melts away. The lights will be bright and there will be a bunch of people, but don't focus on them."

"How can I *not* focus on them? I'm panicking just thinking about it. My anxiety level just went through the roof." I started fanning myself thinking about all of those faces looking back at me.

Analia giggled a bit, but I could tell she was caring. She looked over at the guys; they were still talking going back and forth and laughing every once in a while.

"You and Suave Rob are dating right?" She asked with her eyes still on the guys.

"Yeah, we are." I said smiling. She turned and smiled at me.

"Focus on *him*," Analia said. "When you sing, focus on Suave Rob and sing to him. Do you have any songs together in the showcase?"

"Yeah, we have one song together but it's after I sing 2

songs first." I answered.

"It's okay. He'll be off to the side of the stage waiting to join you. You can also improvise too, if you feel nervous you can have him come out and be with you on the stage until y'all sing."

"Oh," Analia helped ease my anxiety a lot by filling me in on some tips to get me through the show. "Thanks for that. Having him where I could see him would help me a lot."

"Once you pop your cherry, you'll be fine."

"Pop my what?" My ears must have wiggled.

Analia laughed. "Pop your cherry. You're a virgin when it comes to doing this. You said you never did this before."

"OOOOoohhh, okay. I got you." She laughed again and joined in. It got the attention of the guys.

"What'chall laughing at over there?" Marcus said pretending to be interested.

"Nuh-thin." We both sang at the same time, which made us giggle even more. In doing so, Taye and Roberto walked over to the sitting area.

"What are y'all on over here?" Taye said massaging Analia's shoulders. He was so attentive to her. She held his hand as he gently rubbed her shoulders.

"Nothing much, I was just telling her what to expect when she does the showcase. She's never done one before."

"Oh ok." Taye responded.

"Alicia said she was nervous about singing in front of so many people." Analia added.

"Understandable. I was a bit nervous too. This is the largest stage we've done so far."

"And it only gets bigger from here." Robert chimed in.

"I know. I'm excited and scared at the same fucking time." I smiled. Roberto walked over, stood next to me, wrapped his arm around my waist and kissed me on the cheek. I loved his support.

"You know, we should hang out more. How about a double date one day?" Analia proposed.

"That sounds fun. Hit us up, Taye has my number." Roberto suggested.

"A'ight y'all, we're done for the day. We have dinner and a movie waiting for us." Analia said getting off the couch.

"Thanks for the tips, girl I appreciate you."

"No worries girl, we're all in this together." Analia said, giving me a hug. Taye gave Roberto a 'bro hug' and they left.

"You ready to sing with me?" Roberto caressed my cheek, tracing the outline of my jaw. He gazed at me and ran his finger across my lips. "Dulce.(Sweet)"

"Yeah Papi, I'm ready." He smiled, tipped my chin and kissed me softly.

"Let's go knock this out."

Roberto held my hand and led me over to the booth. I was happy I had Roberto to go through this with me. He makes me have a little hope that things will be alright - eventually.

Chapter 24 - Punch

Franklin

Things were flowing well and we were still on track with everything we had to get together. We had two weeks left before the showcase and the team was working at full steam. Everyone hit their marks and sang their songs and they were on point. I didn't want them to burn themselves out so I went to the studio to tell them we were giving them the day off. Marcus and I only had a few loose ends to tie up so they could use the time off to relax before the big showcase.

As I exited my car, I had an eerie feeling that I was being watched, aside from the cameras on the building. I checked out my surroundings, everything seemed familiar but I couldn't shake the feeling that I was being watched. I quickly walked inside; everyone was sitting down waiting for someone to arrive.

"Where's Marcus?" I said looking around.

"He had to leave to relieve Shaunice, so he let us in and told us you will be here shortly."

"Oh ok, well Monica is on the way over there so he'll be back anyway but I'm glad I got all of you here because I wanted to tell y'all something." I had everyone's undivided attention.

"Is everything okay? Is it Siedah?" Taye asked, looking concerned. Jacobi pulled out his earbuds and the others stopped scrolling through their phones.

"Everything is fine. Siedah is fine. I spoke with Marcus already and we just wanted to tell you guys that we are so proud of all of you and we truly appreciate all of the hard work you are putting into this showcase. We know you are doing it for us but we want you to do it for you as well. This is your showcase and your opportunity to show off your talent."

"Awww thank you Franklin!" The girls sang out.

"Yes thank you Brah, this wouldn't have happened if it weren't for y'all." The guys came over and fist bumped with me and I passed out 'bro hugs'.

"With that being said," Everyone stopped immediately. I smiled as they thought I was going to deliver bad news. "We are giving you the day off today. We don't want y'all to burnout before the event so, nothing will be done today. So go out and enjoy yourselves and we will see you tomorrow."

"Hey!!" Everyone cheered. They were happy to have time away from the studio and time to spend with others.

"So y'all get on out of here. Marcus is on his way back because we have a few things to finish up on." I said holding the door open as they filed out. I figured since I was going to be there, I would lock the door - Marcus has a key to get in.

I watched at the door for all of them to get in their respective vehicles; Suave Rob and Alicia were standing next to Taye and Analia talking, probably trying to figure out what everyone was about to do since they had the day off. Jacobi and Darius left leaving the four standing outside. I watched from the door as I assumed they agreed upon something.

Taye and Analia jumped in their car as Suave Rob and Alicia jumped on his bike. Suddenly, lights from a car parked down the street turned on as the car started. I wasn't sure who it was; I didn't pay attention to anyone else who may have been outside at the time. I assumed it may have been someone leaving the area as there were other businesses located on the same street. I watched Taye and Analia pull out of the parking spot with Suave Rob and Alicia following behind them. Shortly after the car, located down the street, pulled out of the parking spot. I watched it as it passed the studio, dark tinted windows obstructed my view of the driver as they rolled past. I closed and locked the door and waited for Marcus.

I didn't want to assume the worst, I just felt I needed to be cautious, especially with what Alicia was dealing with. I had enough with Marcus and Siedah, I didn't need it happening again.

Suave Rob

It seemed like it was the perfect time for us to hang with Taye and Alicia since we all had the day off. After Franklin let us go, we decided to hit up a place called @Scene75 Entertainment Center in Romeoville. It was practically a huge place to play video games, roller coasters, batting cages, bowling, laser tag, mini golf along with food and drinks; it was the perfect place for us to go on a double date.

Alicia and I walked around hand in hand enjoying each other's company as we played games and rode the roller coasters with Taye and Analia. After about an hour and a half, we decided to sit down for a bite to eat.

"I am starving, I haven't eaten all day." Analia said, looking at the menu.

Alicia scanned the menu checking out everything while I checked out the burgers. "They got a lot of stuff."

"I see."

"I want a BBQ pizza but I don't want to eat the entire thing. Will you eat some if I get it?" Alicia asked.

"Mami, get whatever you want. What you don't eat, we can take with us." I answered by kissing her cheek. She sat next to me in the booth smiling and finally enjoying herself.

"Ok, well I'll get that. Y'all can have some if you want." She looked at Taye and Analia, closing the menu.

"What do you want to drink?"

"I'll drink water. You can't drink so I won't either." She

smiled looking at me. I leaned in and gave her a quick peck on the lips.

"Thank you Mami." I turned to see Analia and Taye looking at us. "What?"

"Y'all make a cute couple. Taye and I were talking about y'all from the last time we spoke." Analia said.

"Aww, Thank you for saying that." Alicia responded.

"Yeah, y'all don't look like y'all just got together. Y'all look way comfortable with each other."

"We are." We said in unison. We chuckled and they smiled.

"That's how it was with us. We were just comfortable with each other."

"Now, how did you two get together?" Alicia asked as I put my arm around her as we waited for our waiter to come.

"Well," Analia started and looked at Taye.

"You want me to tell them how we met?"

"You can." She nodded.

"Ok, well she was stuck on Darius when I met her." Analia's eyes grew huge as she looked at Taye who was smiling from ear to ear. He leaned away from her in the booth, making us both chuckle.

"I just know you didn't just start off like that?!" She looked at Taye and he smiled. He leaned in and kissed her quickly on the lips but she didn't move.

"I'm sorry, I had to because you were," He said, raising his hands. "But Darius was just too stupid to notice you." He said smoothing it over with her as he scooted closer and wrapped his arm around her shoulders. She softened and smiled as he kissed her cheek. They made a great couple as well.

"Oh wow, so did he ever find out about you liking him?" I asked.

"He did, but he was busy fucking Isis." Analia quipped.

Alicia and I froze. I instantly had so many questions.

"Wait, Isis? As in Isis Bradley? As in Isis, who is married to Tavion Sanders of TSE?"

"The exact same one." she replied.

The waiter came over to our table and took our order while I tried to process the information that I had received. After we placed our order, I had to go back to the conversation.

"I tell you, every time Tavion, Isis or anyone else from TSE is mentioned, I am so grateful that I left."

"I'm glad you did." Alicia chimed in. I smiled and nuzzled my nose to the side of her face. She was so cute when she smiled with her dimples showing in her adorable cheeks.

"Yes, be glad you did. They were trying to get Taye and Darius." Analia said.

"For real?"

"Yup," Taye responded. "I was looking around when I came back to Chicago and Tavion reached out to me to come for an interview, and so did Isis."

"I'm sure she wanted to test the merchandise." I quipped.

"Yes she did." Taye responded.

"Yup, figures. She did the same to me."

"Both of them are very good at hooking up with other people." Analia said as the waiter brought our drinks to the table.

"Oh trust me, I know that oh too well." I said.

"It's amazing how nonchalant they are about it."

"That's because they are swingers. They don't care. They want to share the intimacy with others."

"Well they took one from me. I won't let it happen again, I promise you that." I removed the paper from Alicia's straw and placed it in her drink and did the same for mine.

"Who did they take?" Analia sipped on her drink.

"Marisol. I caught her and Tavion fucking in his office."

"Damn!" Taye and Analia said in unison.

"Yeah, that's what I'm saying."

"But if it didn't happen, you wouldn't have left and been with me." Alicia added. I smiled and turned towards her.

"And it was the best thing that had ever happened to me." I kissed her quickly on the lips, making her blush.

"Ok, so, you know I gotta ask." Taye sang, hinting around a question that I already knew would be asked inevitably.

"What?"

"The baby. Who's the father?"

"Honestly, I don't know. But I do know, it ain't mine. That's my story and I'm sticking to it." I quipped and the group laughed.

"Wow, I couldn't live such a messy life like theirs."

"Messy ain't even the word for it." Alicia shook her head back and forth.

"And Darius was with Isis?" I asked again trying to find understanding.

"Yup, all the way up until she got married."

"Damn!"

"I heard a rumor that she sent him out of town on a wild

goose chase so he would be gone when she got married."

"What'd you mean by a wild goose chase?" Alicia asked.

"Girl, she had his ass thinking they were going away for the weekend and booked a cabin in Wisconsin Dells, telling him to meet her there and this fool goes."

"Oh shit!"

"Yes! While she had no intention of meeting up with him, she just wanted to get him out of the vicinity of Chicago so he wouldn't ruin her marriage."

"Wow!"

"Right, and he found out she had gotten married from the news." Analia uttered. My mouth dropped open and I heard Alicia gasp; Taye was smiling, shaking his head while he took a sip of his drink.

I shook my head trying to understand how people could live their lives that way, with so much drama. I was a one-woman man and proud of it. Alicia completed me fully, therefore I didn't have the need for someone else; I thirsted for her only.

Our food finally came and we all devoured every bit of grub that was placed on the table. We sat and laughed the entire time. It felt nice to have another couple to hang with. I had never experienced it with anyone I had dated. Alicia was special to me, she gave me new experiences and she had no clue what she was doing to me. Alicia had her head laying on my shoulder, I knew she was ready to go home and we had a nice ride back to the city.

"Are you ready to go, Mami?" I raised my shoulder lifting

her head. She smiled and looked at me.

"Yeah, we can go. Let me go to the bathroom first."

"Let me go with you, girl." Analia raised up off the seat and out the booth. I moved out of the way for Alicia to slide out of the booth on our end.

"Dude, this was nice. I'm glad we did this." I said to Taye. He nodded and held out his fist and bumped mine with his.

"Franklin giving us the day off was perfect timing."

"Yeah it was." I said.

Taye and I decided to meet the girls by the bathrooms located nearest the entrance of the facility.

"We gotta do this again, girl." Alicia told Analia as they walked out of the bathroom together.

"Yes we do, but we gotta find a place closer to the city, I'm gonna fall asleep on the way back."

"Well at least you're in a car. I'm going to be awake the entire ride back home." They both laughed.

I wrapped my arms around Alicia and Taye did the same to Analia.

"Vámonos a casa, Mami *(Let's go home)*. After you." I said.

"Si, Papi." She replied. Alicia knew how to make me smile. I opened the door and gave her ass a smack as she walked out; I heard her giggle afterwards.

We walked out of the entertainment center and ran directly into Maurice. He had to have followed us here, there was no way this motherfucker just popped up at this place, I thought.

"Alicia!" Maurice yelled.

"I just know you fucking lying to me, right now. Did you

follow us?" I asked this motherfucker as I walked in front of Alicia pushing her behind me. Alicia held me from behind as I made sure I was between and him.

"Who the fuck is that?" Taye asked.

"My ex boyfriend."

"Oh shit. Is this motherfucker stalking you?" Analia asked.

"Yes." Alicia and I said in unison.

"Damn."

"Alicia! I know you hear me!" Maurice screamed.

"Stay behind me, Mami." I ordered Alicia. "I know I done told you what's gone' happen if you try to contact her, now didn't I?" I directed towards him.

"You ain't gonna do shit, you stupid ass bitch!" He yelled back.

I chuckled and shook my head. "You just ain't gone' learn until I beat dat ass, I see."

"Whatever bitch! Motherfucking pussy! Alicia, c'mere and let me talk to you!"

"Don't answer him, Mami. Please let me handle this."

"Handle yo' shit, Papi." She said stepping back from me and over to Analia.

"I got your back Brah," Taye said from the side.

"Cool, Brah. 'preciate it." I started stepping closer to this motherfucker and he got a wild look in his eyes and decided to charge me.

I stepped back twice and swung. I clocked him on the right side of his jaw with my left hand, spinning that motherfucker in mid air, and knocking him the fuck out. He landed right in front of Taye, eyes closed and everything. Taye checked to see if he was okay.

"Oh my goodness!" Alicia and Analia screamed as he landed.

"You got knocked the fuck out!" Taye snapped. He was on point with the famous line from the movie *'Friday'*. "He's good, he's breathing."

I was determined to defend her, I didn't want her to live in fear of this asshole. I had to step up and be the man that I knew I could be for her.

"All those years of boxing have paid off, I guess."

"In more ways than one." Alicia said as she held my hand. I was in pain, I gave him everything I had and connected directly with his jawbone. To be honest, I could have broken his jaw. "Are you good?"

She looked at my hand, it was flushed red from the impact of bone on bone.

"I'm good, Mami. Are you good?"

"Si, Papi."

"Let's bounce before people see us here."

We all agreed and headed back to the city leaving Maurice's ass, asleep on the ground.

Chapter 25 - Mine

I couldn't believe what happened, Maurice had gotten knocked the fuck out by Roberto and we were heading back to the city after leaving him asleep on the ground. We were all the way in Romeoville so we figured he must've followed us and thought he was gonna do whatever, but my Papi handled his shit. That shit turned me the fuck on so much, I wanted to jump his bones right there!

It was exhilarating! He handled his business and I was so grateful. I held him tightly around his chest as we rode home; the bike felt as if we were gliding down the expressway. Seeing him take control of the situation, pushing me behind him to protect and defend me made me so damn horny. I slid my hand down between his legs and resting on his member, he slowed the bike down and sat up a bit. He tried to turn around and look at me while we were still riding.

I patted him between his legs and moved my hand back into place on his chest. He patted my hands and revved the bike, he understood the assignment - *get us home faster*. We pulled up into the parking lot and drove slowly to his spot. I love that he had a designated spot otherwise I would hate to have to drive around trying to find a place to park.

I removed my helmet and scarf, stuffing it inside the helmet. Roberto grabbed my hand and pulled me close to him. I held his face and kissed him quickly, growing butterflies in my stomach instantly. I just needed to feel his lips against mine. He defended me, he protected me and it turned me on in more ways than one. Aside from having to lay eyes on Maurice, it was a perfect day.

"Mami," he said, looking at me.

"I want you." I whispered between us looking directly into his eyes.

He quickly grabbed my hand and pulled me to the elevators. He knew exactly what I wanted and he was ready to give it to me. He kissed me gently as we waited for the elevators. I was getting hot and I needed to feel him. He gazed at me wantonly; those hazel brown eyes saw a side of me nobody knew about but him.

As soon as we hit his apartment and locked the door, we headed directly to the bedroom. Clothes flew off instantly and the music was on. It really didn't matter what played, I just wanted to feel him. *Mine*, by Alex Isley played from the soundbar as each kiss we shared was magical. I stood in front of Roberto butt ass naked as his dick poked directly at my stomach.

He held the side of my face while I closed my eyes feeling his lips move over mine. I inhaled taking him in, his tongue exploring my mouth. I took a hold of his dick and slowly began to stroke him.. He moaned softly in between kisses, yet the more I jerked him off, the more intense his kisses got. He moved down my neck, across my collarbone as he pinched my nipple sending a jolt down to my core awaking my secret garden.

I kissed him all over his chest and pinched his nipple, sending a jolt directly to his dick as it moved in my hand.

"Me vuelves loco *(you drive me crazy)*, Mami." He panted as I continued to stroke his meat at a steady pace.

"I want to ride you, Papi," I confessed. "Can I ride, Papi?" I begged.

Roberto picked me up and carried me to bed. He held onto my legs wrapped around his waist as he fell backwards onto the bed, with me landing directly on top of him. I leaned down and kissed him, pressing my lips against his and sucking his bottom lip. I inhaled his exhale as he gave my ass cheek a smack.

"Oh Dios mio, Mami. Quiero sentirte ahora. I wanna feel you Mami." He professed.

He had already left a box of condoms on the nightstand next to the bed, which provided easy access on such an occasion. I leaned over and grabbed one, opening it and rolling it down his shaft.

I straddled him again as he held my hands, his fingers laced with mine; I felt the tip of his member at my entrance. I leaned down and kissed him while I slowly took him inside.

"Mmmmmm," We moaned together. He was so thick, I loved the way he felt deep inside me.

As I adjusted, he pumped his member deep inside me from underneath, hitting my spot and started my honey pot boiling. I wiggled my ass and started bouncing up and down on dick. I was determined to give my knees a workout.

"Ooooo....aaaaa...aaaah.." I moaned as we found our rhythmic stride. I loved the way Roberto felt deep inside of me. He held his mouth open as I bounced up and down on his member.

"Mami," He moaned. "Hmph...mmmm...you feel so good..." he moaned. Roberto sat up and held me as I bucked my hips back and forth on top of him and picked up speed.

"I can't wait to feel you without the condom. I wanna feel you cum deep inside me." I whispered between us.

"Si, Mami, I want to feel you so bad!" He said breathlessly.

I rocked back and forth, working my hips and my thighs at the same time. Sweat covered our bodies as Roberto held me so close to him that our silhouettes combined. He kissed my breasts as he held my ass while I rode his soldier with pleasure.

"Aaaaaa.....aaaa.....aaaa....aaaa." I mewed softly as I rotated my hips in circles.

"Si,   si....aaahhhh...si   Mami....aaaaah....shit...hmpf...hmpf." Roberto moaned.

He wrapped his arms around my waist and flipped me over, onto the bed while still deep inside me. The man had skills and he wanted to take control. I loved a man who could take charge!

He raised my legs, held onto my ankles and spread them wide. Releasing one leg, he licked his thumb and rubbed my bean as he glided in and out of me effortlessly.

"Yes Papi!" I said as he thrusted in and out of me at a steady pace. I grabbed my tits and pinched my nipples sending pleasuristic pain down to my southern region. I could hear the wetness and stickiness of my nectar connecting us.

"Ahhh...ahhh....mmmmm...Si Mami...this is all mine Mami, Si?" Roberto asked. He wanted to make sure his *good stuff* wasn't being shared with anyone else. No one was getting anything that he had already claimed.

"Si Papi, all yours...aaaa....aaaa...all....aaah..yours Papi." I moaned as he pumped his dick deep inside me. I closed my eyes as my body moved with his.

"Good Mami, Papi likes that. You belong to me, Mami...mmmmm...Yes?"

"Si....yes....yes....uh...uh...mmmm...yes."

"Bueno Mami. Mmmm...you're so wet...Mami....and you feel so good....mmmm." Roberto had me going. I was getting close to bursting.

"Si... Papi...Fuck me Papi!... please...fuck me!" I begged as I lived my ass to meet him.

"Si, Mami." He granted my wish adamantly.

Roberto leaned down on top of me and wrapped his arms underneath mine and grabbed my shoulders pulling and holding me towards him. Robert buried his face near my neck and went to town fucking the shit out of me! He rammed me so fast I didn't even think it was possible for a person to fuck that fast.

"Ooooohhh.....yess....yes....yes....si....si...Papi...si   fuck me...aaaah...aahhhh..." I moaned loudly with delight. His balls made a smacking sound as hit against my ass as he pounded my mound.

"Si Mami...Quiero follarte hasta la mañana, Mami *(I want to fuck you until the morning)*...uhh...uhhh..uhhh...mmmmm..." Roberto moaned in Spanish. I didn't understand a word and I didn't care.

"Si Papi, si!" I moaned.

"Te he estado esperando toda mi vida ya no voy a dejarte ir, nunca Mami," he moaned loudly. *(I've been waiting all my life for you and I'm not letting you go ever)*

"Si Papi....aaaaahhh yes!"

I could hear our bodies connecting while we fucked; the entire bed started squeaking due to our motion, we were really rocking the bed. With each thrust inside me, Roberto filled my body with pleasure that flowed across my entire being. The heaviness of his body, laying upon me made me feel comforted and protected. He was my man and he wanted to make sure I was pleased well.

Wave upon wave of ecstasy filled my body as he pounded within me, hitting my g-spot easily. Chills ran across my skin as Roberto kissed and nibbled my neck as his hardened soldier thrusted deep inside me. I raked my nails across his back and he pumped harder, banging me deep into euphoria. I could feel my nectar running hot as he banged his dick deep inside me.

I could hear the slickness of my juices and the suction we made as we fucked like animals. The pillows had fallen off the bed and we were drenched in sweat. The room had the musty odor of sex that was still in play.

"Aaah....aaahhh....aaahhh...Mami...I'm...uhh...uhhh.."

"Uhhh...mmmmm...aaahhh...aaaahhh...Papi...come with me....Papi...let me feel you come Papi....." I moaned. I was ready to climax as he had been knocking at my door ever since he entered the first time.

"Si Mami...Uhh...uhh...uhhh...come with me Mami...come....Mami..."

"Si Papi...si....si...AAAAAAAAAAAHHHhhhhhhhhhh!" I released my juices and reached climax as did Roberto. My toes curled and my body convulsed as I felt my juices run. My skin ran hot as pleasure rolled over my body as he rammed me continuously.

"Fuck...Mami...Si...uh...uh.....uhh....UUUUUUUUU-UUUHhhhhhhhhhh!" I felt him shoot his load inside the condom, as he continued pounding my pussy.

Roberto kissed me deeply; he slowly grinded inside, releasing every drop. He smoothed my hair back as he looked at me, smiling. His eyes danced when he looked at me.

"You are so beautiful." He said caressing my face.

"Thank you Papi. You are very handsome. I'm a lucky girl." I said smiling and tracing his lips with my finger. He kissed my fingertips and smiled.

"I'm the lucky one, here." He winked. "Nah, we're both lucky."

"I agree."

I gazed into his eyes wanting to tell him that my feelings had grown stronger for him. He pretty much sealed the deal for me by protecting me from Maurice. He planted another kiss on my lips, this time lingering longer than normal. He looked like he had something to say. He slowly touched my face, slightly smiling and gazed into my eyes.

"Creo que me estoy enamorando de ti, Mami. *(I think I'm falling for you)*" he spoke softly, touching my lips.

"What is it, Papi?"

"I think I'm falling for you." He said. Instantly my heart pounded loudly in my chest. He had just blown me away confessing his deep feelings for me. I saw reason to hesitate to express mine.

"I am too." I confessed. He smiled a big grin from ear to ear, getting excited that the feeling was mutual.

Roberto closed his eyes and rubbed his nose against mine and I did the same in return. Our breath became intertwined between us; I felt him slowly release himself from me and remove the half-way filled condom from his semi-erect penis. He rolled off of me and the bed, walking quickly to the bathroom to discard the condom.

I pulled the comforter up to my chest as I waited for him to return. I watched Roberto, and all of his nakedness, exit the bathroom with two towels in hand - one wet, one dry. He was so thoughtful. After we cleaned ourselves, we decided to cuddle. I never would have thought that Roberto was a cuddler, but he was and a big one. He was like a baby who needed to feel someone holding on to him or him holding on to someone.

Well I was the one he was holding on to and by the way it seemed, he was going to be holding on for quite some time and honestly, I had no problem with that.

Chapter 26 - Forever

Suave Rob

Alicia and I were cuddled together when I woke early in the morning. The sun had just started changing the night into day as I looked out at the blue ombre sky through the window. It was still dark in the room, Alicia was snoring softly and drooling a bit on my chest. I must say she went directly to sleep. I knew she would go ballistic on me when we fucked. She was a beast; she brought out my carnal desires.

"Mmmmm," She stirred, tilting her head underneath my chin, nuzzling my neck. "What time is it?"

"Shhhh, go back to sleep Mami." I caressed her face, she wrapped her arm around my waist and scooted closer. Her breast laid softly against my chest. I embraced her, bringing her closer and kissed her cheek.

"Why are you up?" She mumbled into my neck. I smiled, feeling the vibration of her voice and the warmth of her breath against my neck.

"I'm not up, I just opened my eyes." I threw my leg over her ass and scooted her closer to me.

"You just woke up?"

"Yup, just before you."

"Mmmmm, I wish I could stay here forever."

"You can." I was being serious. Alicia could give up her apartment when her lease was over and move in with me. I had already thought it out.

"You're funny." Alicia replied. I moved back and tipped up her chin to look in her eyes.

She opened them wide, going back and forth to each eye. "I'm serious. You can move with me when your lease is up."

She searched my face and realized I was being totally honest, I wanted her with me always - especially now. "Really?" she asked.

"Yes Mami. I want you with me always." I gazed in her eyes emanating confidence.

"I would love that." She gazed back; I felt like she was saying more than just she would love to move in with me, *I heard she loved me.*

"Te amaría para siempre, Mami *(I would love you forever).* I would love that too." I kissed the top of her forehead nearest her bonnet. I inhaled, closed my eyes and thanked God for bringing this woman into my life.

"What time is it for real though?" she asked.

"It is about 5:45, almost 6. The sun is about to show its face soon." I said pulling the comforter over our heads.

"You're silly." Alicia giggled as she pulled it down. I couldn't help but to put my finger in the dimple on her right cheek. "I've been thinking about getting them pierced." She pointed to her cheek.

"Really?" I think that would look hot, but that was her decision, not mine to make.

"Yeah, I think it would be cute. Whatchu' think?"

"I think it would just add to your cuteness." I kissed her on the nose and again on her forehead. "Are you hungry?" My stomach growled softly.

"I know you are." She smiled.

"I am, you took a lot out of me last night!"

"I did?! You took a lot out of me! I know I crashed as soon as you got back in bed."

"Yeah, you did." I agreed. "We had a nice workout last night."

"Si, we did Papi." I smiled. She was just adorable and I saw she cared for me even though she hadn't admitted it. "I have a confession to make though."

I raised my eyebrows and looked at her. "Una confesión? ¿Qué has hecho? Whatchu do?" I asked. She smiled at me hesitantly wanting to reveal her secrets.

"I got kinda turned on when you fought Maurice." She confessed. I smiled, closed my eyes and buried my face in her neck; only she knew how to make me blush.

I composed myself and looked at her smiling. "Oh really? Was that why.."

"I initiated it?" she interrupted.

"Yeah?" I answered.

"Si, Papi." I chuckled, she amazed me each and every time.

"You are something else."

"No, you are. It was my first time seeing you in such a defensive and protective manner, it thrilled me and turned me on so much. I got it bad for you." She was so vulnerable as she opened up to me letting me know that my protection of her stimulates her. I see that as a win-win.

"Well you don't have to worry, Mami. I will always be that way when it comes to you. I got it bad for you too."

Alicia smiled and snuggled her face against my chest as I

held her close to me.

"One thing though, sorry to change the subject," I yawned and rubbed my eye as I remembered. "Do you know where that asshole lives? Marcus and Franklin need it so they can handle him."

"Oh yeah, of course. What are they gonna do to him?"

"I don't know, but from what I've been told the less I know, the better."

"Oh shit."

"Yeah."

Marcus

Franklin told me about a feeling he had when I came back to the studio. At first I was thinking he was crazy and overreacting , but then I had to remember that was the same mentality I had when it came to Gerald. Gerald was the psycho asshole that almost erased Siedah and myself from the earth. We failed to take his actions and comments seriously and he showed us how serious he was.

Franklin and I had received the address for the nigga that's been stalking Alicia. Suave Rob filled us in about what he did, showing up at a damn place in Romeoville. This motherfucker, tracked her down and had the audacity to try and speak to her. After he beat the shit out of her! I was tired of his ass fucking with my people and he deserved to get his ass beat for laying a hand on a woman - *period*.

Franklin and I made arrangements to have Maurice followed and basically given the same treatment he gave Alicia. Hopefully he got the hint, I didn't want to involve the cops because a stupid ass niggas don't give a fuck about a piece of paper telling them they can't go somewhere. I received a text message when the deed was done. From what I understood, he was left with no car and no shoes, no other details were provided to me. When it came to matters such as those, it was best not to know all of the details.

Siedah was getting down to the wire with the pregnancy, I wasn't sure she would make it to the showcase. She told me she would be there and she would be the best person to know. I just knew Franklin and I had been so busy tying up the last details as we kept everyone busy with radio spots to promote the showcase.

We had the team out every day, saturating the radio waves, morning news shows and social media broadcasts with reminders to catch the talent at our showcase stage at the Taste of Chicago. We knew the event would attract a huge crowd of people as it did every year, we just wanted our talent to be seen by everyone possible.

I walked into the bedroom looking at my beautiful fiance; her feet were resting on pillows, Monica had painted Siedah's toenails since she wasn't able to reach them. She was resting comfortably surrounded by her laptop, paperwork spread out in various places, her task notebook along with empty yogurt and fruit cups. I gently touched her protruding belly, hoping not to disturb her. I held my hand on her belly and leaned over giving her a kiss on her forehead. MJ kicked my hand hard enough from the inside to stir her awake. She moved and opened her eyes, smiling when she saw I was there.

"Hey Babe, how long have you been standing there?" She held my hand on her belly, lil man was still kicking.

"Hey Babygirl. Not long, I just came in."

"Looks like someone knows when his daddy is in the house." She smiled. I leaned down and kissed her lips.

Siedah was having my baby, I owe her everything. She came into my life when I thought I all hope was lost. She loved me unconditionally when the both of us were going through our own issues. I looked at her holding and growing my seed, willingly and wholeheartedly. I caressed her face and sat down next to her, still holding her face.

"I love you Babygirl," I held onto her pregnant belly and got emotional. "I love you so much."

"Aww babe, I love you too," Siedah touched my face as tears dropped. "Now you can't be coming in here crying, I'm already emotional enough for the both of us." She said as tears swelled in her eyes.

"I'm just so happy to have you in my life." I managed to utter.

"I am too. I'm not going anywhere." I leaned over and planted a kiss on her lips and another on her belly.

"Babygirl?"

"Huh?" She said taking a sip of water from her water bottle.

"Do you know when you want to get married?" Siedah looked at me and tilted her head.

"I hadn't thought about it. I figured you would tell me when you were ready." She said, running her fingers over my dreadlocks. I took her hands into mine and gazed into her eyes.

"I'm ready." Siedah looked at me and tears swelled up again in her eyes. She smiled the brightest smile I had ever seen. She was so happy, and so was I. She truly completed me.

"Oh Babe!" Tears streamed down her face as I planted another kiss on her lips. "Are you serious?"

"As a heart attack." I held her hands.

"But I'm huge right now, and we don't have time to plan a wedding."

"I know, don't panic. We can have the big wedding after

you have MJ, but we can go to the courthouse tomorrow afternoon and have a small reception with dinner someplace."

"Marcus, are you serious?" Siedah's eyes lit up. She was ecstatic.

"Siedah, will you marry me tomorrow?" I asked again, holding her hand.

"Yes, Marcus. Let's get married." She smiled. I leaned over and kissed her deeply. I wanted her so badly, but I had to slow things down because I knew I wouldn't be able to hold back and Siedah would be having Lil' Man early.

"I love you babygirl."

"I love you too babe."

Siedah and I called everyone the night before to make last minute arrangements for our nuptials. Monica worked her magic and got in contact with one of her friends who was able to cater the food for a small group of people as Franklin opened their home up to us for the reception dinner. It would be easy for Siedah to chill out on the couch while still partaking in the festivities instead of being stuck in the bed at home.

We all filed into the small judge's chambers; Siedah was dressed in a white maxi dress and sandals while I wore a pair of white cotton shorts, a pair of white Jordans and a white, cotton button up, matching her color scheme. Franklin was my Best Man and Monica was Siedah's Maid of Honor. Everyone showed up, looking nice and comfy. We knew it was last minute and hot as hell outside, therefore we didn't expect much but got so much more.

Alicia and Analia brought flowers while Taye, Darius, and Shaunice snapped photos. Shaunice was on top of it, posting them to the internet and going live on social media as we took our vows.

"Do you Marcus Anthony Harper take Siedah Renee Jackson to be your lawfully wedded wife? To have and to hold, through sickness and in health; to love, honor and to cherish, all the days of your life?" The officiant spoke.

"I do." I gazed at Siedah, her eyes filled with happy tears as she smiled at me.

"You may place the ring on her finger." I slid the ring we had already purchased when we got engaged.

"Do you, Siedah Renee Jackson, take Marcus Anthony Harper to be your lawfully wedded husband? To have and to hold, through sickness and in health; to love, honor and to cherish, all the days of your life?"

"I do."

"You may place the ring on his finger." Siedah slid the ring on my finger, I smiled as I was hers forever.

"By the authority vested in me by the State of Illinois and before God, I now pronounce you husband and wife. You may salute your bride." The judge's chambers echoed with the cheers from the CFE group as we solidified our marriage with a kiss.

I picked Siedah up and carried her to our decorated SUV, sporting a *Just Married* sign painted on the back window. I placed her gently in the passenger seat and headed to Monica and Franklin's place for the reception dinner.

I was so happy I thought I would burst. I was truly blessed to be able to call Siedah my wife.

Chapter 27 - Thunderstruck

Alicia

I believe so much went on in the past two weeks than I had ever experienced so far in my lifetime. Aside from Roberto knocking the shit out of Maurice, which unexpectedly turned me on so much that we fucked like rabbits ending in Roberto and I confessing our feelings for each other, Siedah and Marcus got married. It was last minute but it was perfect and I was so happy that I was a part of it.

Everything after that was a blur and before I knew it, it was time for the showcase. Nerves and anxiety raced through me as I sat backstage waiting to go on. The crowd was lively and loud while I tried to focus and get outside my head. I had my earbuds in trying to go over the song that Roberto and I had together when he came up behind me.

"Hey Mami, how are you feeling?" He said, sliding his hands around my waist as he held me from behind.

"I'm good now, but honestly a little nervous." I said pulling out my earbuds.

'Aww Mami," he said, turning me around to face him. "Focus on me, once you get out there on the stage, I will be right off to the side. I won't leave you." He said gazing at me.

He kissed my forehead as heard Taye was being announced to hit the stage.

I looked at him, our eyes met and I melted. We held a gaze that seemed like forever, he caressed my cheek and kissed me softly upon my lips. He held me and we swayed to Taye singing in the background. I was ecstatic being with Roberto, he made me smile. I didn't pay attention to anyone around us, it was as if we were in our own little world, it was just the two of us.

Things started getting hectic backstage while the crowd grew a bit larger and got louder. Just as Taye was on his last song, I made my way to the side of the stage. Roberto was right there with me as he said he would. The night sky was clear and the weather was humid. I wore a cute and sexy multicolored cami mini dress and strappy heels. Roberto looked good in a tan, vintage cotton-linen blend short sleeve shirt and a pair of washed, ripped black jeans with straps and zippered pockets.

I watched Taye from the side of the stage, captivating the audience. They were singing along with him as he worked the stage making sure he involved as many fans as possible. Suddenly I wanted to throw up as Taye was ending his song. My nerves were getting the better of me as I looked at Roberto. I felt like a panic attack was going to happen. Roberto held my face in my hands and smiled. He kissed me deeply, taking me away from everything that was going on in my head. He took my cares away quickly with one kiss.

"You got this, Mami. I believe in you." He said as my name was announced. The crowd went wild as I walked out on the stage, I was extremely flattered.

"Thank you everyone for coming out tonight!" The crowd cheered and applauded as the music started. "A'ight y'all, let's do this!" As soon as the beat hit, I was transported into another realm and I sang my heart out.

I looked over to the side of the stage, and just like he promised, Roberto was there. He smiled and swayed to the music off to the side as I performed for the crowd. Then just as quick I took the stage, it was time for me to pass the torch to Roberto. My last song was our duet and we killed it. We were so in tune with each other as we danced and sang on stage together. We sang our duet to each other; it felt as if we were the only ones there. As we finished our song, we gave the crowd a bit of something special, as Roberto kissed me just before I left the stage. The crowd went wild, screaming and chanting our names. I hesitantly left the stage, wanting to absorb all of the energy the audience was supplying.

Roberto started his set and the ladies went crazy. I knew the ladies would love him, but I was happy he was going home with me. I had to use the bathroom so I decided to run quickly to the ladies' room so I could be waiting for Roberto when he finished. There was so many people scattered around backstage working on lights, sound, audio and everything, I kept getting bumped as I made my way to the bathroom

On my way back, I heard Roberto was on his second song which made me quicken my steps. As I turned the corner to head back towards the stage, a door opened not far from our dressing room and someone snatched me inside. Instant fear filled my soul in the dark room. I couldn't see anything or anyone in the room. I turned and tried to get to the door, I held my arms out in front of me trying to find the door.

Whoever pulled me in, spun me around and I didn't know which way I needed to go in order to exit.

"Who's there?" I screamed. The music was too loud, no one heard me outside the room. There was silence. "Who's there? Hello?! Hello!" Suddenly I felt instant pain as I was hit on the side of my face. I was hit so hard, I fell to the ground, my phone slid out of my bra and across the room. The lights flicked on and I raised my head to see - Maurice!

"Yeah Bitch!" He said as he kicked me in my stomach, knocking the wind out of me. He looked like shit. His face was busted up and his arm was bandaged up. He had been beaten up, but apparently not enough because this mother-fucker was about to kick my ass.

"Maurice, what the fuck?! Why?"

"Why?! Bitch are you serious? You know why?!" He said, slapping me across the face, busting my lip.

"I didn't do anything to you Maurice!"

"Shut up! Yes you did!" He said, slapping me again as I tried to get up. He punched me in my back, leaving an intense pain as if I was in a boxing match.

He paced back and forth, looking wild and crazy. "You know I got you started! You know I was out there hittin' the streets for you!"

"Yeah, while you was fucking bitches behind my back!" I yelled. I knew I shouldn't have antagonized him, but I was determined not to go down without a fight.

I got up off the ground and stumbled as he walked over to me and punched me in my face, knocking back across the room, hitting the wall. I slid down the wall right next to my phone that had slid under what looked like a huge pipe. I looked around the room to see where Maurice was, he was pacing back and forth again while my face was in pain. He had hit me right below my eye thank goodness, but still - he hit me.

I kept my eye on him and tried to dial Roberto. I knew he would be looking for me because I didn't come back to the stage as I promised. I watched Maurice as I tapped my phone and secretly dialed Roberto. I didn't put it on speaker because I didn't want Maurice to hear, so I just hoped Roberto would pay attention. I needed him more than anything.

Suave Rob

I finished the set and Alicia wasn't at the side of the stage, which got me worried. I figured she might have gone to the bathroom but she should have returned before I finished. I walked backstage to see if I could see her among the crowd. I ran into Marcus coming from the dressing room and stopped him in the hallway.

"Hey Marcus, Have you seen Alicia?" I frantically looked around glancing at everyone that passed us.

"Naw, to be honest, I haven't seen her since she left the stage." Worry instantly filled my stomach. It wasn't like her to be away from me, especially when she said she would stay by the side of the stage until I was finished.

"Shit! She left the side of the stage by the time I was on the next song. She didn't come back!"

"She wasn't in the dressing room, I just left from there." I pulled my phone out to dial her and she was calling me.

"It's her, she's calling me." I quickly answered. "Hello Mami!" I said speaking into the phone. She didn't respond. It was loud as hell in the hallway, I closed my other ear to hear her, but I couldn't

"Is she okay?" Marcus said, looking at me. I shook my head.

"She ain't answering. Either she can't hear me or she can't speak." I said, trying to listen to see if I could hear anything. "It's too loud in this hallway."

"Go to the dressing room, two doors down." He said pushing me down the hallway to the room.

Inside, all of CFE was in the room and it was a bit quieter but it was still frantically trying to find Alicia.

"Hey, anyone of y'all seen Alicia?" Marcus yelled as he got in the room.

"I saw her go to the bathroom after her set, but not after that. What happened?"

"She's missing. Rob can't find her. She ain't answering her phone."

Suddenly I heard something over the phone. "Ain't nobody gonna find you bitch! Not when I'm done witchu!" I heard Maurice yelling at Alicia, then I heard a thud as if he hit her.

"THAT MOTHERFUCKER GOT ALICIA!" I screamed! Marcus turned around and came back towards me.

"What?!"

"I can hear him! Alicia must have called me and she couldn't get to her phone! He got her! He's beating the fuck outta her!"

Marcus listened to the phone and heard Maurice screaming at her. "A'ight, we need to contact security and we need to search all these rooms back here, every last one of them! Leave the fucking doors open so we know it's been searched!"

Everybody piled out and went separate ways, I didn't know what the fuck to do, my blood was BOILING! As soon as I catch that motherfucker, I may just kill him. I didn't want to hang up but I wanted to find her before anyone else did, I needed to get her safe.

I checked her location on the phone while still on the

phone. Alicia and I agreed that it would be best if we shared our location after the first time Maurice showed up at the radio station when I wasn't with her. I never wanted to use it, but for times like this, I was happy we decided to do so.

Her phone pinged not far from the dressing room!!! I checked the doors nearest the dressing room and came upon a locked door. I saw a light underneath the bottom of the door. I banged on the door and I thought I heard Alicia screams get cut short as she had been hit.

"Alicia!! Mami! Are you in there?!" I banged on the door as hard as possible and then the light went out.

Panic set in as I tried to break down the fucking door! I threw my body against the door, rattling the door jam. It was solid and it was not giving. I kept ramming the door, as I heard Marcus screaming, coming down the hallway. As I ran to ram the door one last time, it opened and I fell directly into the dark room while the door slammed behind me.

Someone flipped on the light and I saw Alicia on the floor, her face swollen and bloody. I turned around to see Maurice holding a gun to my head!

Chapter 28 - For The Last Time

Suave Rob

"You Bitch ass nigga!" I said facing Maurice with the gun on my forehead.

"Really nigga?!" He engaged the gun, loading a bullet into the chamber.. "Who the bitch ass nigga now!" He yelled holding the gun at my temple. I looked at Alicia and she was crying, I got so angry at myself that I couldn't protect her.

"Don't Roberto, please!" She said, holding up her hands trying to calm me down from trying to beat the shit out of him.

"Yeah Roberto, you betta listen to dat bitch!" He said and he swung at me, connecting his fist with my jaw. I stumbled and walked to charge him. He laughed and pulled the gun up towards my head again, this time he switched off the safety.

"NO! MAURICE!, PLEASE DON'T! Please, I'll do anything!" Alicia pleaded for my life.

"You hit like a bitch!" I said antagonizing him.

"Really motherfucker?! Well I got your bitch, now what?" He said walking backwards over to Alicia and grabbing a handful of her hair pulling her over in front of me.

I winced seeing him treat her like that and I couldn't do anything. This motherfucker was so unstable, he would shoot me, then Alicia and then himself and what purpose would that give?

"You hear her? She said she'll do anything. Anything to save your life. I bet she would."

"Fuck you Maurice!" Alicia screamed trying to swing and claw at his face but he still had a tight grip on her hair.

"Oh you will, and he's gonna watch!" Maurice said, pointing the gun back at me. I looked at Alicia and tears started to fall from my eyes. I couldn't bear to watch him rape her. Anger started building up in my core and I had to do something before this nigga killed both of us.

"Fuck you Maurice!" Alicia said again and started kicking, screaming and clawing, distracting Maurice.

I took the opportunity to charge him just as he smacked her across the face. Alicia fell on the ground and I pounced on this nigga like a lion on prey. I grabbed him from behind and held his arms trying to get the gun away as he tried to point it at Alicia. He quickly elbowed me in the nose, making me stumble back away from him. He pointed the gun at me as I tried to focus from the excruciating pain racing through my face - *that bitch ass nigga had broken my nose!*

"Now who's the bitch, you pussy ass bitch!" Maurice said as he pointed the gun at me and grabbed Alicia by her hair again. "Get on your knees, Bitch!" he yelled at her.

Alicia got on her knees, crying and blood dripping down her face. Maurice looked at her and smiled. By his facial expression, he was determined to rape her - *in front of me.*

"I know y'all together. That's all good. I know how you feel Brah, she's a good fuck, ain't she?"

"Fuck you Maurice!" Alicia screamed. I was hoping Marcus would come to the door. He had everyone checking all of the rooms but this one hadn't been checked yet.

"Oh you will. And Rob over there is gonna watch you enjoy it." Maurice said and I couldn't hold it, I charged him again. I had to at least save Alicia if no one else.

POW!

A shot rang out in the room.

"NOOOOOOO!!!" Alicia screamed.

This motherfucker shot me! I felt instant pain as I was blown back against the wall. He literally shot me, thank goodness he had bad aim. He looked surprised that he actually pulled the trigger, I could only assume he had never done so before. I had gotten shot in my left shoulder as he kept the gun on me.

"Now as I was saying," Maurice said, pulling Alicia towards him. "I know she's a good fuck. And she gives some *hellafied* head. So, as a warm up. Alicia here is gonna suck me off real good, like she used to," he said, jerking her head back and forth in front of his groin. "And YOU are going to watch!" He pointed at me with the gun.

Anger immediately filled my soul. I felt helpless. This bitch had Alicia and he was going to force her to suck his dick. She should bite that shit off! I wasn't going to be able to watch her do that to him, and I wasn't going to allow it to happen, even if it meant I would get shot again, I would do it for her.

He forced Alicia to unbutton his pants as he held onto her hair while still pointing the gun at me. He threatened to shoot me if she didn't, so she did unwillingly. She pulled his pants down, thank goodness this nigga didn't go commando.

Suddenly, someone jiggled the door handle and finds

out it was locked. They bang on the door and Alicia and I scream as loud as we could.

"IN HERE!! WE'RE IN HERE!!!" We screamed in unison. I didn't hear anything. The person didn't respond because they couldn't hear us - it was too loud.

Maurice hit Alicia across the face and dared me to move.

"Pull it out bitch! Pull my dick out!" He demanded Alicia. Alicia looked at me, crying and secretly begging me to help. I needed to find a way to get that motherfucker off of her.

"No Maurice, don't do this! Please, please! Maurice. I'll give you credit, just don't do this." Alicia begged him. She held onto his knees crying and begging for her life and I couldn't do a damn thing.

I felt useless.

Marcus

I couldn't believe this stupid ass nigga came to the showcase, it seemed like we were gonna have to just end him all together. I didn't want it to come to that but he'd left us no choice. We all raced around the venue, checking all doors until we came up on one last one, which was locked.

"Get this motherfucker open right now!" I demanded looking at security.

"I don't have the key. Maintenance would have it. It's a utility closet."

"Ain't y'all supposed to have a master key or something like that?" Franklin asked.

"Yeah, but the Supervisor has it." He answered. I looked at Franklin trying to figure out something. The security guard was looking at his tablet with a floor layout and noticed something. "Wait!"

"What?!" Both Franklin and I said in unison.

"There's another way into that room. It's not used and probably blocked, but there is a door through the dressing room that leads directly into all of these rooms." He said pointing from the dressing room to the utility room.

"Let's do this." Franklin said and we walked to the dressing room.

Inside, backup had arrived. All the people Franklin had got in contact with the first time, were getting paid again. We pushed everybody out of the room who didn't need to be in there, leaving Monica having to sit outside the room - like we said the less anyone knows the better. We located a door behind a bookcase that had been placed in the room, they were using it for storage therefore there were a lot of unused items placed in front of and stacked up against the door.

We moved all the shit and opened the door. We walked through the door which led us directly into the next room. No one was in there so we kept going. As we got closer, we heard Maurice yelling at Alicia, trying to make her suck his dick.

I hope she bites that shit off if we don't get to him fast enough.

"I SAID SUCK MY DICK BITCH!" I heard Maurice yell and then a smack followed. She must have hit her again.

"YOU FUCKING BITCH!" I hear Suave Rob yelling back at Maurice. I cracked open the door and he's holding a gun at Suave Rob and this nigga got Alicia on the floor with his pants down.

"A'ight," I whispered. "We gonna have to sneak in and come up on this nigga. We're gonna have to do it fast and quick 'cause he got a gun." I said.

"It's all good, we got ours too." The back up stated.

"Let me see if I can get Suave or Alicia to look my way to get him to focus on them while we come in."

I went back to the door and eased it open a bit wider to get a better look. Maurice had walked over to Suave Rob and was holding the gun at his forehead. Alicia looked and saw me coming, I put my finger over my mouth so as to not alert Maurice. She understood the assignment and nodded slightly and then crawled on her knees in front of Suave, making sure Maurice turned his back fully towards us.

"Don't do this Maurice! I'll tell Marcus it was you. You deserved all the credit, I swear!" She cried, keeping his attention. "Please don't do this!"

He kept his back turned as we quietly piled in through the door. As soon as everyone was in place, the back-up went to work. They swooped in on Maurice so fast he didn't even know what happened. One of them cocked their gun right next to his head and laid the tip of the gun on the back of his head behind his ear. "Don't move nigga." Maurice instantly froze.

I came around and looked this nigga in the face. He looked scared than a motherfucker, he thought he was gonna fuck up my talent and get away with it all because his name wasn't attached to someone.

Another member of the back up crew, walked around and grabbed the gun from Maurice's hand while the first still had the gun pointed at his head.

"You 'done fucked up now, Brah." Suave Rob said standing up, looking at him in his damn face. It wasn't until I got a good look at Suave Rob, when I realized he had been shot!

"He shot you?!" I yelled.

"Yeah, and he beat the shit out of Alicia." I looked at Alicia and she was hit pretty badly. What he did was unforgiving.

"Nigga, you know you got some nerve coming up in here fucking with my people!" Franklin yelled. He was hot, just like I was and we needed to get our point across.

"Apparently you didn't learn from the last ass whopping you got!" I said smacking directly across the face.

"I'm sorry!" He started crying. This bitch ass nigga.

"Sorry!" Suave Rob yelled. He was trying to console Alicia when he broke loose. "Did you just say you were sorry?!"

"I wasn't gonna, I swear.." Suave Rob swung on that motherfucker with his good arm. Maurice stumbled back trying to keep from falling.

"Sorry ain't gonna cut it!" Suave Rob threw another punch right to the face and broke his nose. "YOU BITCH ASS NIGGA!" And Suave Rob swung one last time, it was an uppercut; he hit that motherfucker so hard, he knocked him the fuck out. I caught Suave as he stumbled afterwards, he had lost a lot of blood.

"You good, Brah?" I said holding onto him.

"Yeah, I'm good. Thanks Man."

"No problem dude, we family. This is how we do." I gave him a bro hug and he walked over to Alicia.

He wiped her tears away but the bruises were still there, however they will face in time. He held her as she cried in his arms. I'm sure Suave would have killed him if he had too. I'm sure by the look of it. He probably would have taken a bullet for her.

"Let's get y'all asses outta here and let the clean-up crew handle that motherfucker." Franklin said as he waved Alicia and Suave out of the room through the door we entered. We left Maurice's ass with the clean-up crew.

We didn't care what happened to him.

We didn't need to know.

Chapter 29 - New Beginnings

Suave Rob

Marcus and Franklin were able to get us to the hospital without the news outlets and social media getting wind of what went down at the venue. They split Alicia and I up, taking us to two different triages. Unfortunately, with me being shot, I had to go through surgery to remove the bullet that was lodged in my arm. Alicia's face was bruised badly, but she was alive. She refused to leave my hospital bed when I arrived back after surgery. It was a short two day stay but she was happy I was okay, so was I.

Marcus and Franklin had my bike towed over to my condo after the showcase and had a driver pick us up from the hospital. Marcus was there when I was finally released.. He made sure we had everything we needed and asked us to call him if we needed anything. Marcus really looked out for us which made us really feel like family.

Alicia and I had finally made it back to my place; I could tell she was happy to be back home. She refused to leave my side, even after *she* was released from the hospital a day earlier. I sat on the chaise, with my arm in a sling. I was out of commission for a minute but I was happy she didn't have to endure the turmoil Maurice was trying to put her through.

"Hey Mami," Alicia came and sat by me laying her head on my shoulder while holding my free and available hand. "How are you doing?"

"I'm good Papi, now that you're home." She traced the back of my hand with her finger.

"I'm sorry you had to go through all of that shit, Mami." I said, looking at her. Tears started flowing down her face. "Awww, ven aqui Mami." I waved her over and she laid her head on my chest and slid her arms around my waist as I wrapped my arm around her, pulling her closer to me.

"I thought I was going to lose you. I thought he was going to shoot you." She cried. She was worried about me and I was worried about her. I got emotional hearing her cry, she was terrified and I felt helpless.

"I'm sorry Mami, I should have..."

"It wasn't your fault, Papi." she interrupted. "You did everything you could, I know you did." She sat up looking at me, her eyes full of tears.

"I know but I'm your man, Mami."

"And you're human, Roberto. Not superhuman." She looked at me, and I wiped away a few tears and kissed her lips. She was right, I wasn't superhuman. However, I would have taken a bullet for her.

"I'm sorry, you're right. I'm not superhuman, but no one is going to take you away from me."

"But he could have killed you?" She said, looking at me. I caressed her face, I could see she loved me. She didn't want anything to happen to me and she didn't want me to leave her.

"I know," I had to let her know of my plans for that night. "Just before Marcus came in, I was going to try and rush him again."

"Why? He could have shot you, *again*."

"That was a risk I was willing to take, Mami." I voiced. She tilted her head and frowned trying to understand why I would do such a thing.

"Why?" She asked, her eyes filling with tears again. I held her hands and kissed them, and gazed back at her. I wiped her tears away as fast as I could but she made me emotional just by looking at her.

"Porque te quiero, Mami." I confessed. "Because, I love you Mami." I couldn't hold it back anymore. I needed to express my feelings to her. Alicia looked at me, and tears fell harder.

"I love you too, Papi!" Alicia straddled and embraced me while we cried together. .

Alicia was my person. She was the one that I would wait for forever. She was the one I had been searching for a long time. She absolutely completed me.

"Te amo Mami con todo mi corazón Nunca te dejaré. Soy tuyo, para siempre. *(I love you Mami with all my heart. I will never leave you. I am yours, forever.)*" I softly spoke as she sat up on my lap, facing me.

"Tell me what you said." Alicia demanded wiping away my tears.

"I love you Mami, with all my heart. I will never leave you. I am yours, forever."

"I love you too, always and forever." Alicia made my heart sing as she smiled and held my face in her hands; She leaned forward and planted a nice, deep kiss upon my lips.

I held her close to me the entire night, not wanting her to leave my side. After that ordeal, I had planned to have her by my side - *permanently*.

Marcus

The showcase itself was outstanding. Everyone did exactly what I knew they could do. It brought attention to our label and put CFE on the map as a force to be reckoned with. As for the incident that happened at the event, *it never happened.* That's the story everyone is sticking to as well, even the security guard that helped us. I had him sign a NDA and paid him well; he was so happy he asked if he could work with the CFE Group. Franklin and I agreed it would be nice to have someone on the payroll who could do security when needed, so we hired him on a temp to perm basis, as needed for now.

We didn't expect to have another incident like that one to happen again, but we could never be so sure. Shit, we didn't expect the first incident with Gerald so I guess we needed to be prepared should certain situations arise. I believed we were at least two steps ahead when it came to the stalking shit, I could guarantee we will be looking for the warning signs going forward.

Siedah had left the showcase early, due to her being uncomfortable. Monica was able to stay but she left shortly after we sent Alicia and Roberto to the hospital. I didn't want either one of them to stress as they were the most important people in the world to Franklin and I.

Suave Rob and Alicia were released after he had surgery to remove the bullet. He told me privately that he was going to rush Maurice before we arrived. He loved Alicia so much, he was willing to take a bullet for her. Suave Rob was willing to protect his woman at all costs, even if it meant making the ultimate sacrifice. I was proud to have someone like him on my team but I also didn't want him to have to make such a decision ever again.

I sat down on the bed next to Siedah who wasn't feeling the best. For two days after the event, she had been having contractions. I didn't expect her to last this long and neither did the doctor. She looked like she was ready to pop at any moment and I was ready to have our lil man in my arms, so was she. As I watched her walk around the room, I massaged her back trying to relieve the pain she was having. My phone rang on the dresser and I grabbed it as she continued back walking.

"Hey Franklin, wassup?"

"We're on the way to the hospital, Monica's water broke!"

"Oh Shit, a'ight. You good?" I asked while checking on Siedah. She had stopped and held her swollen belly and started her breathing techniques.

"Yeah, we good. I'll call you once we get situated."

"A'ight dawg, keep me posted." Siedah looked at me waiting to hear the details.

"Monica's water broke, they're on their way to the hospital."

"Awwwww," she said as she walked around to me, putting her arms around my neck. "Lucky bitch." she laughed.

"Awww babygirl, it'll be your turn before you know it."

"Will it though? It seems as though I've been pregnant forever, Marcus." She whined. She was tired and ready to deliver.

"He's gonna come when you least expect it. He's just like his daddy," I smiled at her. She rolled her eyes. "MJ wants to wait until the right time to make an entrance."

"Well, he's been served an eviction notice - 3 days." She snapped. I chuckled and massaged her back as she lowered her head to my chest.

She was uncomfortable and miserable from the annoying pain she was in. I wished I could take the pain from her but I don't think men could ever deal with the pain women go through. Of course, we men want to be there for our significant others but God knew exactly what He was doing. He made us the providers of the household whereas He made women the caregivers. He knew women could endure so much more than most men, especially when it came to bringing a life into the world.

I looked at Siedah and she amazed me; no matter what pain she was in, when she looked at me she always gave me a smile. She was so strong beyond compare, I couldn't even match her in that department, she was *Top Dawg* in that category. I loved her so much and I was proud to call her my wife and mother of my child.

"You hear that MJ, she's kicking you out, dude. Mama said you gotta come and sleep in your own bed." I said talking directly to her belly. Siedah smiled as I kissed her belly. Apparently he had heard about the eviction notice and kicked Siedah hard enough to make her sit down.

"Shit! Okay," she sat down on the side of the bed. "He didn't like what I said." she smiled.

"Oh I bet. He was like, why kick him out of his warm and secure place?" I laughed and Siedah hit my arm.

"Well, I'm gonna lay down a little bit." She said grabbing her body pillow and putting it into position. She laid on her side with her leg over the pillow with her protruding belly laying on top of the pillow as well.

"A'ight, Let me know if you need anything okay?"

"Where are you going?" She asked with panic in her voice.

"To the kitchen to grab a snack. I'm not leaving until you tell me it's ready to go."

"Oh ok, cool." She relaxed and flipped through the channels while I left to grab a quick bite to eat.

We were sleeping comfortably in the bed until I felt as if Siedah forgot to go to the bathroom. I flicked on the light on the side table nearest me and pulled back the comforter. It was as if the bed was saturated with liquid but it wasn't urine. And then it clicked, Siedah's water had broken!

"Babygirl," I nudged her gently. "Babygirl, wake up." I whispered. She slowly opened her eyes and turned towards me; She looked at me and then her expression changed as she felt the bed and between her legs.

"Oh Shit!" She looked at me, her eyes wide as ever.

"It's okay, let's get you to the hospital." I grabbed the bag out of the closet she had prepped for going to the hospital.

"I need to take a shower first."

"Do we have time?" I asked, starting to panic.

"Yes, from all of the baby books I have read and with this being our first child, it usually takes a while. And I'm not going to the hospital without having washed up."

"Ok, you're in charge." I wasn't about to argue with her, she was calm and in control whereas I was panicking.

Siedah jumped into the shower as I grabbed a few things and checked my phone. Franklin had texted me, Monica had delivered their baby an hour prior. He sent a picture of him holding Franklin Jr. I smiled looking at them, I was so proud and happy for him. Emotions came over me as I scrolled the collection of pictures he had sent. In just a few hours I would be holding MJ, I thought.

I was excited and ready to see my son.

Epilogue

Alicia

After the incident, I didn't want to stay at my apartment anymore. I didn't know what happened to Maurice and I didn't want to give him any way to find me, so I decided to sublease my apartment and moved in with Roberto. He was happy I moved in and so was I. I felt it was the next step for us as we had gotten so close after everything that happened.

We opened up tremendously and confessed our feelings towards each other. I was floored when he told me that he loved me. That was the first time that I was told and I believed it. I finally had a chance to feel real love and I was going to hold onto it as long as possible. I truly loved Roberto, in more ways than one. He still holds himself partly responsible for what happened, but I told him it was out of his control and he had done the best he could do given the circumstances.

He still feels as though he could have done more, yet I tell him had he done more, he probably wouldn't be with me. I told him everything happened for a reason and he had done everything right. I'm glad he didn't do more because I don't think I could live with myself if he had died trying to save my life.

We are forever indebted to Marcus and Franklin. If it weren't for them doing what they do, we probably would have been killed. But they took care of us just like they said they would. We never heard from Maurice again, not even a lone text message. Marcus and Franklin told us that we didn't have to worry about him anymore - *ever*. I had so many questions, but I've learned after joining CFE - there are some things I just didn't need to know.

Everyone was ecstatic with the news of Monica and Franklin having Franklin Jr. a day before Siedah and Marcus welcomed MJ into the world. Shaunice was on it when it came to being their PR person because she handled her shit well. She was in her element and I was happy for her. She released the announcement of the babies to all the media channels and satisfied the fans with a vague photo of the parents holding the hand of their newborn children.

The entire CFE Group was at the hospital after Siedah delivered MJ. The hospital made arrangements to have both Monica and Siedah in the same room, which helped a lot giving their visitors a two-for-one stop. Flowers, balloons, baby gifts started arriving at the hospital, filling their room to the brim. As we all sat in the room, a huge basket was delivered for both Monica and Siedah.

"This shit is huge!" Monica looked at it as Taye put it on the table.

"Who is it from?" Siedah asked, sitting in the bed as Marcus sat in the recliner holding MJ.

"There's a card in there, pull it out." Monica instructed

Taye. Taye carefully opened the cellophane wrapping that surrounded the basket full of newborn outfits, bottles, bibs - just a plethora of items they would be needing. He grabbed the card and passed it to Monica.

Monica opened the envelope and read the card.

"Oh Shit!" She yelped. Everyone turned to her, her face was filled with astonishment.

"What?!" Siedah asked.

"Give this to Siedah." Monica held out the card to Taye, who passed to Siedah. Siedah opened it and read the card as well.

"Oh Shit!" she exclaimed.

"Exactly!" Monica replied.

"Ok y'all gotta give us more information 'cause y'all leaving us hanging." Franklin said, bouncing Franklin Jr.

"Who is it from?" Marcus and Franklin asked in unison. Siedah and Monica looked at each other and replied simultaneously.

"Justine."